T0405820

INTO
THE
DEEP
BLUE

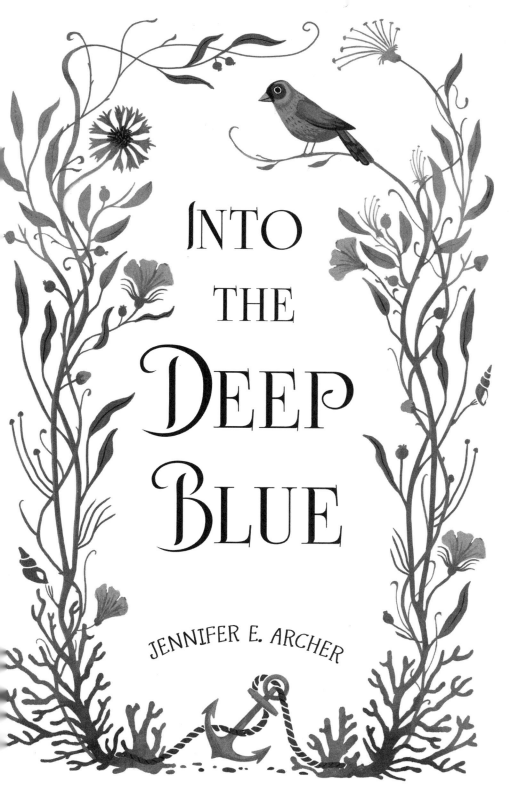

INTO
THE
DEEP
BLUE

JENNIFER E. ARCHER

ISBN: 978-1-958325-37-7 (hardcover)
ISBN: 978-1-958325-38-4 (ebook)

Library of Congress Control Number: 2025935463

Any references to historical events, real people, or real places are used fictiously. Names, characters, and places are products of the author's imagination.

Cover art and design by Susan Szecsi.
Edited by Jodi Keller.

Printed in China through Asia Pacific Offset.

First printing 2025.

Marble Press LLC
2260 Hanover Street
Palo Alto, CA 94306
www.MarblePress.com

MARBLE  P R E S S

For Cole

Nick

They say if you stand on the peak of Mt. Pissis and shout into the void, your echo will ring out for one minute. It's not recordbreaking—to do that, you have to go to Burma—but it's top five, I think.

Sometimes, I imagine myself standing there, thinking maybe if the words echo long enough, she'll hear them. That I'll cast some kind of spell over the valley and bring her back in a swirl of stardust. I mean, it happens in the movies, right? Like magic.

I like to think she survived the crash. That her eyes were open, and as she sat strapped in her seat with the roof of the plane ripped off, she looked up and locked eyes with some majestic creature like a monkey or a parrot. I don't really know what they have in South America, but I hope her last moments were filled with a divine connection to something greater—that my mom died with a smile.

But let's be real; I'm not on a mountain. I'm in my room, staring into the soulless pit of YouTube, and what I'm about to do feels so dirty that I get up and close my door.

In the search bar, I type South American Airlines flight 501. The page fills with videos. It doesn't matter which one I choose—they're all the same. I know because I've watched them all.

I randomly click on one in the middle and slide on my headphones. My finger hovers over the volume key, and I tap, tap, tap until it's all the way up because I need to *hear* every gut-wrenching second of this. The image on my screen shakes. Brown hiking boots come into the frame, sliding down a dirt trail. A breathless voice says "Oh my god" more times than I can count, and the camera pans up.

Plumes of smoke rise from a pocket of newly demolished trees in a dense jade-green jungle. The smoke grows thicker, blacker, as it gushes from the shell of a plane engulfed in a giant ball of fire. The plane explodes and the fire rages against a soundtrack of the hiker's helpless breaths.

There's nothing magical about it.

The clip stops, and so does my breath for so long that my lungs ache for air like I'm the one in the fire.

It's dramatic shit. Prime time news special kind of stuff, except plane crashes are no longer considered important enough for a full hour of coverage unless they contain presidents, athletes, or A- through C-list celebrities. Moms are nowhere near that list even though they should be, because mine was really important to me.

The top comments under the video are news stations asking for permission to air the footage so the entire world can consume the spectacle. Cue the popcorn emojis. It hurts every time I watch, but I can't help myself. I'm afraid if I stop, I'll forget her.

It used to take about an hour before it would hit me—the reality behind the YouTube drama. Then, I'd close my laptop and cry. A few months ago, the crying stopped, and I'm not sure what that means.

"Nick?" Dad's muffled voice calls out from behind my door.

At least he knocked.

"Uh, yeah, just a sec." I close YouTube and maximize the ever-present Spotify window so it fills the screen. My Dead Mom playlist is already cued up and with my headphones on this looks totally normal. "Come in," I say, swiveling my chair around.

He pushes open the door, but he doesn't come in. He just leans against the frame and scans my room. This is always the extent of his commitment to our conversations—on the periphery looking in.

I slide my headphones down. "What's up?"

He draws in a breath like he's an actor about to break into the defining monologue of his stage career. "What the hell, Nick?"

What the hell could encompass any number of things concerning me, so I wait for more details. Why didn't I show up for work last week? Did I drink the rest of his bourbon? Did I swipe twenty bucks from his wallet? I leave a decent trail of what the hell behind me, so I have no idea what he's talking about.

"What's up with the plane crashes?"

Oh. That. This is getting off easy. I play dumb. "What do you mean?"

"They fill the search history for weeks on end! Brooklyn grilled me about it for an hour."

So, it was his girlfriend who found them. Not Dad. That makes more sense. She must have been trying to bust him on porn and found my searches instead. All because I was too lazy to go upstairs for my laptop. But there couldn't be weeks' worth. I didn't watch *that* many. I don't think. And Brooklyn should stay the hell off our computer if she can't handle the dark burning embers that fuel this family.

"I dunno. Wanted to see how it works, I guess."

I mean, what the hell, Dad. Mom died in a plane crash. What's up with the plane crashes, seems pretty obvious, but I'm not about to spell it out for him. It's like we speak different languages.

Dad looks away. Now he's thinking about plane crashes. "It's a little morbid. Maybe, give it a rest. Why don't you search some . . . you know . . . God stuff or something?"

That's it? This is all he has in the Dad-advice arsenal? I lean back in my chair and interlock my fingers behind my head the way he does. It's his trademark I'm-not-listening pose.

"God stuff?"

"Or yoga or whatever the hell people search for to find peace. No more plane crashes."

This is the part where I'm supposed to have a revelation about the error of my ways. "Okay."

He nods, satisfied like he's done some solid parenting—way to draw that line in the sand, Dad. "Okay," he says, then taps the door frame twice as if to say we're done.

And while it might seem like he's trying, what he's really done is add another tally mark under the column labeled:

Things that are Nick's fault.

The time on my screensaver reads seven, and holy shit I'm so late. I promised Fiona I wouldn't be, and now she'll give me that squinty-eyed you're late stare the second I walk in.

I close my laptop. He'll find the password screen if he opens it, not that he will. "Good talk, Dad. No more plane crashes." I say it with a grin, so he can tell how effective this chat was and clap him on the shoulder on my way out. "Gotta run."

"Remember, I'm in Sacramento for a few days," he calls out after me.

As I fly out the door, I try to recall the reason he gave me for this, but I wasn't listening when he told me last week. It's hard to feel anything but pure rage when he talks to me.

It's kind of cold outside for June, so I pull on my hoodie before wheeling my bike from the side of the house and pedal down our never-ending driveway. It takes longer to bike out of this yard than it does to get into town. Okay, that's not true, but I hate it—the interlocking brick, the bushes trimmed into perfect globes—nothing but the best for the home of Salem's number one landscaper. Dad landscaped the shit out of our yard, which brings me to my theory that the more landscaped the yard, the worse the lives are inside. I'm ninety-nine percent positive about this.

Now that I'm outside, any urgency evaporates. It's tough to be in a rush when you count on a bike to get you any-where. It's like being in slo-mo no matter how fast you go, but I actually like the ride into town. It feels good biking hands-free down our deserted side road, to pedal until my lungs burn. It helps to show up to a meeting exhausted.

Somehow, it's easier when you're empty going in.

When I finally turn into the community center, the parking lot is quiet, which means I'm later than usual. I shove my bike into a rack out front, but don't have a lock and wonder if tonight's the night someone will steal it. It hasn't happened yet. The universe is on my side with this one. Fi's car is parked where it always is, under a streetlight one row back from the entrance, because "it's the safest spot."

Inside, the halls are empty. It's the upside of coming late— no annoying people. I turn down the first hall and walk until I reach an army-green door with a tiny rectangular slot for a window. Places like these must have the same architects as prisons. Maybe there's a one-stop shop: *Architects available for prisons, community centers, and schools. Drop by today for our classic floor plans.* Then they hire people like my dad to landscape the shit out of them.

A tattered paper that says Sharing After Death is taped to the window. It used to read S. A. D. Support Group, but random strangers kept interrupting in the winter, thinking it was for the seasonal affective disorder thing. *Sorry folks, we are full-time fucked up here, so move along.* Some kid drew a sad face on the sign with a tear falling from the tiny dots penciled in for eyes. I kind of love it, and I'm surprised that our counselor, Grace, hasn't taken it down or at least tried to erase it.

My hand hovers over the handle. Before every meeting, I hope I'll walk into an empty room and the world will feel a little lighter, but it never happens.

I open the door and instantly regret it. Someone inside is crying.

Fiona

Everyone looks at the door as it opens. Everyone except Maddie, the new girl, because she's crying. No, not crying. Sobbing. Thick, choking sobs that have no end. I mean, I feel bad for her, but my sadness well is running a little dry. Maybe we all come with a sadness saturation point, and I reached mine a long time ago.

Nick freezes in the doorway and bows his head, which I guess is what you do when you interrupt someone crying. He moves to the empty chair across from me and pulls it back, the legs squealing against the linoleum. He glances at Grace like he's about to be busted in some covert operation, but she's still focused on Maddie, so he sits.

His cheeks are flushed, and he runs a hand through his sweaty brown hair, making it stick up in tiny spikes. He won't look at me even though I know he senses me staring.

He steals a glance at the clock instead, not for the time but to figure out how much time is left. Then, he tries to dislodge a leaf stuck to the sole of his not-so-white sneaker by wiping it against the floor. He crosses his arms, forms his shield, and only then does he eye the gray squares of tile between us until his gaze lands at my feet and moves upward, his eyes finally locking with mine.

We're the only two people in the room not staring at the floor. I give him the slightest scolding shake of my head because he's late. Again. At least he came in. Crying in group is his kryptonite. He drops his head forward and fights a smile, because he knows every thought racing through my head right now. *Where the hell were you? Why didn't you text me? I'm going to kill you.* But when our eyes reconnect, my irritation melts away. It's like we're the only two people here. The room feels brighter, the ceiling enchanted, and everyone disappears but us.

Maddie's sobs drift through my fantasy and shatter the moment. Reality soaks in and it's cold, gray, and bottomless.

We've been coming to group for six months, and neither of us has had this kind of breakdown. Sometimes I wonder if it's the only reason we're friends—our numb hearts.

As if he's reading my mind, he raises an eyebrow.

Nick's eyebrows can talk. A whole language happens in the upper third of his face, and I know it by heart. I know him by heart. This is his kill-me-now look. The crying is too much for him. He bounces his leg and bites at the skin around his thumb. I glance at Grace, to see if she notices that Mt. Nick is about to erupt, but she's still talking to Maddie.

Nick bolts from his chair and heads for the door.

He lasted six minutes. Not bad.

Grace claps her hands against her jeans. "Let's take a break."

A few people get up and head for the snack table. Grace can't go after Nick since she has her hands full with Maddie, so she passes the baton to me with a glance. I don't remember when going after Nick became my thing, but I get up. Honestly, I would have followed him anyway.

A rush of cool night air hits me the second I open the door. It was warm when I got here. Nick is like Oregon's own personal Elsa, leaving an icy trail in his wake wherever he goes.

He's standing at the bottom of the steps, leaning against a pillar with his heel kicked up against it. He doesn't turn to see who followed him out. He doesn't have to.

"Why do we still come here?" he says to the sky.

I head down the stairs and sit next to where he stands. We both know why he comes here. Therapy was a court requirement for him, but he's served his time, so I'm not sure why he hasn't stopped. "What do you mean?"

He pushes away from the pillar and faces me. "I mean, it's depressing."

The parking lot is quiet except for some kids practicing skateboarding tricks. Their boards scrape against the curb with every attempted jump. They can't be much younger than us, but grief adds a difference of a million years.

"Maybe that's the point. Like exposure therapy: the more depressing stuff you subject yourself to, the less it bothers you."

He considers this. "Listening to someone cry for an hour every week is an excellent way to test that theory."

"You got here ten minutes ago."

His lips quirk up in a smile. "You're timing me now?"

"Where were you?"

He leans back to watch the skateboarders. "Nowhere. Just got sidetracked." He's clearly in a mood and when he faces me again there's a glimmer of something else brewing behind his eyes. "So? Did you book Monterey?"

Monterey? Why is he bringing this up now? The word *book* sends my brain into meltdown mode.

And it shows. My mouth hangs open.

Nick doesn't miss a beat, raising a suspicious eyebrow. "Last week, you said you were booking it, so did you? Because I need to take that weekend off."

I say this every week. We've had countless conversations about Monterey on the drive back to his house after group, and they all meet the same fate: crumpled up and forgotten like the fast-food wrappers in the back of my car. Tonight, there's a hint of desperation in his voice like he might need this more than I do, so instead of grilling him over the obvious topic change, I do something different. I go with it. "I did."

He eyes me, doubtful. "For real?"

"For real."

Then he pulls out his phone and opens an actual calendar with a smug expression on his face like he knows how full of it I am.

"The twentieth, right?"

He points to August 20th on the calendar as if I don't remember the day my mom died. I melt a little, knowing that he does.

"Uh-huh."

He adds a new event right in front of me and types MON-TEREY TRIP. "What time are we leaving?"

"Are you kidding me?"

"I don't want to forget."

We both know what he's doing. He's making a point of watching the date come and go. My butt is numb from the cold concrete, so I get up and dust off the tiny pebbles. Even on the bottom stair, he's still got a few inches on me. I meet the challenge in his eyes. "You don't think we're going."

His head tilts to the side. "Ninety-nine percent sure we're *not* going."

"Six." I answer too quickly, because I want to prove him wrong, show him he doesn't know me as well as he thinks he does. But he knows me so damn well.

He seems impressed. "In the morning?"

"It's a long drive. We should leave early."

"So logical," he says, adding a six A.M. start time to the event. "There we go, it's set in stone."

"As it should be." I smile—a badly plastered-on smile.

The door at the top of the stairs swings open, and Grace steps out. "Everything okay out here?"

Nick ruffles his hair. "Yeah. The waterworks stop?"

"Maddie has stopped crying, yes. Come on in, we're ready," she says, holding the door for us.

Nick puts his hands on my shoulders, pushing me up the stairs.

We're the last to rejoin the circle. Maddie cradles a paper cup of herbal tea in her hands, her blotchy face hovering over the steam.

Grace's curly auburn hair is pulled into a loose topknot tonight, long tendrils framing her face. She's a grad student, not that much older than the rest of us. "You all know there is no wrong way to express yourself here. There is no shame in crying. Ever. Nick, do you want to talk about why crying makes you so uncomfortable?"

Nick crosses his arms and leans back in his chair. "Crying makes everyone uncomfortable."

"I wouldn't say *everyone.*"

He eyes her. "Come on. Have you ever been to a funeral, Grace?"

"I've been to a few. *Uncomfortable* isn't how I'd describe the people in mourning."

"Maybe you're not looking close enough." Nick's bravado starts to crumble under her watchful gaze. He bounces his leg again. "Look, she's new. We've seen this a hundred times. Everybody cries in the beginning."

"In the beginning, and then what?"

He focuses on a spot in the middle of the floor. The room falls quiet as everyone waits for some magical prophecy to spring from his lips. "And then what?" He repeats. He digs his hands into the pocket of his hoodie. "That's just it, isn't it? Endless days of and then what?"

Grace's gaze is fixed on him, but she lets it go, addressing the group instead. "Why don't we leave with that thought? Let's think about what we can do to find purpose, to make sense of our lives after a loss. See you all next week."

The circle disassembles, and before I can pull my tote bag off the floor, the door closes, and Nick is gone.

Maddie and I walk out together. I wait with her on the sidewalk for her mom to show up. "You did great today," I tell her. "I know it's not easy to share."

"Thanks," she says, wiping her nose on her sleeve. "Who did you lose?"

"My mom."

"I'm so sorry. What happened?"

I've answered this a million times. "She was a photographer on assignment overseas with the military and yeah . . . " That's usually where I leave it.

Maddie nods like the rest is understood. A car pulls up, and she quickly hugs me before running into it. She's sweet but seems breakable like she's hollow inside.

The parking lot is dark and peppered with the golden glow of streetlights. I weave through the cars and find Nick leaning against the passenger door of mine, Mom's old gecko green VW, his bike beside him. This is our weekly tradition.

He rattles the handle. "You do that on purpose. You stay longer every time."

"Maybe," I say, biting into one of Grace's post-meeting smiley face cookies.

"One of these days I won't wait." He serves up his empty threat with a smile.

"And save me the hour round-trip back to my place? Why would you be so kind?"

"You know you'd miss me."

The second I unlock the doors he starts his routine of cramming his bike in the back. He still hasn't figured out a way to do it without practically ripping my car in two.

He catches me staring. "What?"

"If you'd let me pick you up, you wouldn't have this problem."

"It's not a problem," he says through strained grunts. "Besides, I like biking here. You just need a bigger car."

"I don't need a bigger car. You need to get your license back."

He pretends not to hear me, slamming the trunk at light speed to keep his bike from spilling out. Losing his license was another part of his DUI sentence. He could re-take the test now, but he hasn't.

We get inside, and the car comes to life with a faint rumble. He points at the other cookie in my hand. "Is that one for me?"

"Uh-huh." He reaches for it, but I hold it back. "But only if you promise to stay next time and talk to some people." I pull out of the parking lot and head toward his house.

He plucks the cookie from my hand. "That's not fair. I tried. There was that one guy, what was his name?" I know where he's going with this, so I don't want to tell him. He snaps his fingers. "You know who I'm talking about. I know you know."

"Roger," I concede.

"Yes! Roger. I bet that wasn't his real name. I mean, have you ever met a Roger in your life?"

It takes me a second to scan through the list of names in my almost-empty social circles. "No."

"Exactly. And how long did he last? Like two weeks?"

"At least four," I say.

"No way. That long? I wonder what happened to him?"

"He drove his car into a Starbucks."

Nick looks at me, mouth full of cookie. "What?"

"Yeah, he was on something. I sent you a link to the article."

"Damn. I didn't open it. I thought it was something random about Starbucks. Wow!" He shakes his head, but he doesn't judge. How can he when he has a meltdown history of his own. "That's the thing with this group, Fi, we're tran-sients. I don't need more people disappearing from my life.

It's like the whole reason we're here."

"Wait a minute." I hold up a finger. "Are you saying our entire friendship is basically a process of elimination, because I haven't dropped out of group?"

He thinks for a minute, trying to figure out how to play this. "Yes?" Even though he's joking, it hurts. "I don't want to get to know them. I know you. I'm maxed out." He quickly backtracks, and not a minute too soon, because I'm legit driving him home.

"You're maxed out at one?"

"I'm maxed out at one," he says.

It's a good save. Enough to stop me from pulling over and kicking him out, and I kind of like knowing I'm the one he's maxed out at.

"Did you defer NYU to January?" I ask.

We both got in but couldn't wrap our heads around starting in the fall. I don't even know what I want to take. I may as well close my eyes and click courses at random.

He doesn't look up from his phone. "Not yet."

"Ugh. Nick!" I shove his arm and his phone falls to the floor.

He glares at me.

"How can you be all over me about Monterey, which I booked by the way," a hint of a smirk plays on his lips, "when you haven't even deferred!"

"Chill. I'll do it this week. I guess that means you did?" he asks, rooting around the floor for his phone.

"Yes. And did you book the appointment for your driving test?"

"No, Mom."

"Oh, don't do that."

"Why are you all over me tonight, Fi?"

"You started it." I glance over, and he's back to scrolling on his phone. "And I can't drive you forever." I say this every week.

"Why not?"

Tonight he responds, and I don't have an answer. It's not like I'm going anywhere.

He turns up the volume on the stereo, and Kendrick blasts through the speakers.

Back when I started driving Nick home, I read into all of his music choices. Every song he played was obviously a secret message about his feelings, because six months ago, I thought he might be into me. Then one night, he played Smashing Pumpkins, A$AP Rocky, and Marshmello all in a row, and my brain short-circuited. That was the end of reading into his song choices. Besides, I don't think there's room in Nick's head for serious relationships.

I turn down the pitch-black side road leading to his house. As it comes into view, he blurts out, "Wanna stay over?"

It's a tip of the iceberg kind of question. I eye him, suspicious. "Where's your dad?"

"Where's Zombie Bob?" he fires back.

Nick's been calling my dad that since day one, because "he never does anything." Not to his face, but I'm waiting for the day it slips out.

"Out saving the world. Night shift again," I answer.

"Shocker. Well, mine's out making it more beautiful. Someone needs to drop some rocks across the lawns of America." He bites at his thumb. "He's in Sacramento or some bullshit. Who knows, he could be anywhere."

"Is he still with Kate?"

"No. That was like three girls ago. It's Brooklyn now." He looks out the window and doesn't last a minute before he spills the rest. "Alex is coming over tomorrow."

There it is. His older sister, the rest of the Titanic-sized iceberg. "Ohhh."

"She's picking up some of Mom's stuff."

There are times it's like our brains connect. It's easy to fill in the blanks. "So . . . you need an extra hand."

His eyes flicker up to mine. We both know it's bullshit. We could do this blindfolded.

"Yeah."

Nick

When Fi turns into my driveway, it's an agonizing crawl the whole way down, because she "can't see anything." It's my fault. I didn't turn on the lights—the pot lights lining the driveway, the house lights, any of the ten thousand lights that Dad installed and can be turned on with a tap of a button by an app. The problem is the driveway lights up like a runway, and it triggers me every time, so I usually leave them off.

Fi cuts the engine and texts her dad. He won't text her back, and it kills me that she still bothers.

It's not that the guy doesn't care. I know he does.

The first night she stayed over, he showed up at midnight in an ambulance just to see "what we were up to." He hovered in the foyer for a solid ten minutes, waiting for a pack of partying teenagers to crash out of a closet.

"Don't do anything stupid," he threatened in a dad tone-of-death while swirls of cherry light strobed across my living room. He said it to both of us, but we all knew it was meant for me. I think it was supposed to be intimidating, but come on, it was just an ambulance, not a police cruiser.

The next day, at their house, I had to play twenty questions over dinner. I guess he could tell there wasn't a single romantic vibe between us because he was okay with the sleepovers after that. Listening to each other rehash the worst day of our lives in group wasn't exactly a springboard for romance.

As I wrestle my bike from the back, Fiona gives me a dirty look over her shoulder. I sail it onto the lawn and watch it unceremoniously topple over.

Fi scrambles out of the car and catches up to me. She'd have a heart attack out here alone in the dark. To be fair, this place gives off some serious haunted vibes. Our porch swing creaks in the breeze, and the sound is straight out of a Halloween playlist.

The second I unlock the door, I tell Alexa to turn on the lights.

The house illuminates.

There's something weird about talking to Alexa since my sister Alex moved out. It's like Alex 2.0 except Alexa has her shit together, and Alexa doesn't tell me what to do. Whenever Alex comes home, it feels like an instant downgrade. Thankfully, that isn't often.

Fiona drops her bag on our blue floral sofa. Mom was big into flowers, so the house is covered in them. She even painted a floral scroll around the mailbox, and hung a fake blue hydrangea wreath over the front door. The thing about flowers is once you stick them on stuff like furniture, they just look dead. It's wrong when the outside of your house looks more alive than the inside. The same can be said for me.

"Movie?" I suggest, heading into the kitchen.

"Sure." Fi scans the room, still not entirely settled, as if the ghosts followed us inside.

I pull two Cokes from the fridge and a bag of Cheetos from the cupboard. I toss Fi the bag. She digs through her tote for her glasses, and we head upstairs.

My room is the only one not covered in flowers. The walls are a deep steel blue. I painted the whole damn thing myself, and I don't think either of my parents noticed.

It's a well-organized disaster. I drop my hoodie on the floor, on top of all the other hoodies. Fi tosses the Cheetos, and they land on my pillow. I swipe my laptop from the desk and flop onto the bed, beginning an endless scroll through Netflix, expecting Fi to join me, but she doesn't.

She's standing by my desk, her fingers twitching to pry. She can't help herself. Fiona goes through my things every chance she gets. Honestly, I don't mind being the puzzle she wants to solve.

She opens the cover of a book about Jane Goodall and her work with chimpanzees. It came in the mail yesterday, so this would be new to her. I'm sure it seems like an odd choice of reading material, but grief has a way of turning you into a junkie for details. She flips through the pages, but doesn't ask why I have it. Then she moves to my messy stack of notebooks, her finger trailing down until it stops and like a magician performing a card trick, she pulls out Mom's bucket list that I buried in the middle. No matter where I stash it, she always finds it.

LIZ'S BUCKET LIST
1. ~~Keith Urban concert~~
2. ~~Grand Canyon~~
3. ~~Swim with dolphins~~
4. ~~Fly first class~~
5. ~~Jane Goodall Experience~~
6. Watch E.T.
7. Hot-air balloon ride
8. Bathe in milk
9. Shelling in Bermuda
10. Rent a convertible

"You should frame this." She flips the list over to face me. "I'm buying you a frame."

I turn back to my screen, half expecting the paper to ignite. It hurts to see Mom's loopy handwriting on the page. Her unfinished life laid out that way. "Or I could burn it."

Fiona drops the list to her side. "Way to lean into the dark side."

"It's not dark, it's cathartic." The bucket list is an impossible problem. I don't want to acknowledge it like ever, but I can't let it go, either. Fi's still watching me. "You know what it's like. You have those random things you're tied to."

She slides the list gently back under the other papers. "Serial killers call them tokens."

Sometimes Fiona comes up with the weirdest stuff. "That's amazing. Zero degrees between serial killers and the grief-stricken. And you keep, like, everything, so how afraid of you should I be right now?"

"You should be very afraid. Tonight's the night, Nick," she whispers, moving closer to the bed. "F-f-f-f—"

I think she's doing an impression of Hannibal Lecter. It's terrible and fascinating. "What are you doing? Are you channeling an angry beaver?"

She laughs and tries again. "F-f-f-f-fava beans. What was his line?"

It's so bad, it's good. "Don't. Don't do that."

"How does he do it without looking ridiculous? It's impossible."

She scams a pair of Simpsons pajama pants from my drawer and carries them to the bathroom down the hall.

I've never really had a girlfriend. I hooked up with a few girls over the years, but it was nothing like whatever the hell this is. Those "relationships" had all the depth of an Instagram post. They were having fun, I was having fun, and that was the end of it. With Fiona, it's different. I know everything about her, and maybe I have Mom's death to thank for that—for pushing me to be real with someone. The way Fiona slid into my life felt so easy, like it was a place she always belonged.

It's not like I never think about us being an *us*. Sometimes I suspect she's looking at me with something more in her eyes, but then the next time I see her, those vibes are long gone. It's like the whole passing ships in the night thing, except how many times can the ships keep passing before they move on for good?

When she comes back in my pajamas, she bends over, shakes her messy chestnut waves over her head and ropes a scrunchie around them, forming a topknot. Then she slides on her glasses. And I can't explain why this transformation makes me smile. Every. Time.

She tramples over me, to get to the side by the wall and tears open the Cheetos while I scroll through the same comedies we scroll through every weekend. The second I hit play, she lets out a sigh, and I may as well close the laptop. Something's on her mind.

She's staring out into the hall. "Do you ever feel like jumping over the railing?"

This seems like a good time to press pause. "The hall railing?"

"Yeah."

"No, can't say that I do." I wait for some kind of explanation, but it doesn't come. She eats a Cheeto. "Do *you* think about it?"

Her head falls to the side. "Sometimes. It's not a big deal. Like we'll be sitting here, and I imagine I step out of my body, walk over, and jump off."

Alarm bells ring in my head—five-alarm—so I turn back to the screen, because people can always see that kind of worry on your face.

"It's not weird," she says, "I googled it. It's normal. It's the call of the void."

"The what?"

"The call of the void. Wow. Do I really know something you don't?" She pushes the bag away and licks her fingers. "This is incredibly satisfying. You're going to google ten articles about this as soon as I leave, aren't you?"

I make a face. "No." But, yes. I absolutely will.

"It doesn't mean you're going to do it. It's just a thing like when you imagine driving your car into another . . . "

I shoot her a look. "Hold up. You do that too?"

"Not as much as the railing."

It's time to close the laptop. "Okay," I say, holding out my pinky finger. "Promise me right now, that you won't pull any Rogers or jump off any railings without at least texting me first."

"Pinky swear? Really?"

I mean, it's all I can think of. I don't know what the hell people do these days. "You want to do the blood thing?"

She swats my hand away. "Eww, no."

I wiggle my pinkie closer to her face until she hooks it with hers, and I look straight into her hazel eyes. It's not fair that she's wearing glasses, it's like the barrier shaves twenty percent of the promise away. "Swear it."

"Nick, I swear I will not drive through a Starbucks or any other fast-food establishment or jump off so much as a trampoline without letting you know." She's phoning it in, but that's okay. She needs this more than I do.

It seems safe to open my laptop again. "The Wedding Singer" is still frozen on the screen. I hit play and push the screen farther back so it's resting on the bed between us, but I'm not watching, because I'm looking into the hall, at the railing, with a level of anxiety I haven't felt in a while. I get up and close the door as if this is a normal thing and has nothing to do with what Fiona just said.

I flop back onto the bed and grab a handful of Cheetos, pretending not to notice she's watching me. Pretending she doesn't know how freaked out I am, because losing her would be losing everything.

"Next time we should stay at your house," I say.

Nick

At some unholy hour of the morning, a car horn blares from the driveway. Max must be behind it. There's no way my sister would ever announce her arrival. Her preferred way to get into this house has always been in secret—under the cover of night, through the basement window, or after everyone had left for work.

Fiona crawls over me on her way out of bed, purposely kneeing me in the side to wake me up, because she thinks I'm sleeping.

I'm not, but I don't want to move either. She leans over my desk and looks out the window. "They're here," she mumbles, now checking her texts. Probably to see if Zombie Bob ever texted her back.

I bury my face in my pillow. Asking Fi to stay over suddenly seems like a huge mistake. Now she'll have a front-row seat to whatever craziness comes out of Alex's mouth. I throw off the covers and get up, hating my sister more by the second for a) making me freeze my balls off at the crack of dawn, b) making me deal with Mom's shit in the basement, and c) making me feel like a shitty uncle for not seeing Max more often—which comes with the bonus title of shitty brother.

Fiona's at the window, and I lean over her to bang my fist against it. Alex darts her head around, not knowing where the sound came from, which irritates me even more. The only upside is every second it takes for them to look up, is another I get to stand pressed against Fiona this way. Max finally spots me. He points at us, and I wave.

"This is going to be such a shit show," I say, heading for the door.

"It'll be fine," Fiona says, but she sounds unsure.

She picks up one of my black hoodies from the floor, shrugs into it and grabs her jeans, heading for the bathroom. She catches up to me downstairs, and we head outside to meet them.

Alex is wearing a tank top covered in fringe and isn't the least bit affected by the morning chill. She's one of those eternally warm people. She even wears shorts in the winter.

The sight of Max instantly melts all of my bitterness away. "Yo! Little dude! Holy shit, look at you!"

"Uncle Nick!"

He runs into my arms, and I swoop him into the air. It looks like the happiest family reunion ever. Except my heart is heavy with the weight of everything wrong with this. The guilt for not seeing him in two months, plus flashes of Alex moving out when he was two. There's so much more to coming home than hugs and hellos.

So. Much. More.

"You're so big! What are you, like twenty now?"

Max giggles. He lost another tooth, and it crushes me a little. "No! I'm eight!"

Alex was seventeen when she had him. People always think she's his sister.

"Max, bring your stuff inside please," Alex calls out in a tone straight out of Mom's playbook.

I put him down, rustling his hair. He peeks out from behind me and gives Fi a shy wave. "Hi, Fiona."

Fi waves back. "Hey, Max."

"Go up to my room, you might find something in my closet." I wink at him, and his face brightens. It's kind of our tradition. Every time he comes over, I hide a small Lego set in my room for him. He runs past us and dashes up the porch stairs.

"Max!" Alex calls after him in defeat. "You didn't take your stuff."

But who cares? He's a kid. Let him be a kid. "I got it," I say.

Alex narrows her eyes at me like I've seriously undermined her. I don't know if it's me, or being home, but it's like the sunshine she reserves for everyone else evaporates right in front of me.

"You don't have to buy him something every time," she says.

I pull Max's backpack from the backseat. "I want to. I barely see him."

"And whose fault is that? You could come up anytime, Nick."

There it is. Guilt trip number one. "With what?"

She leans in for a quick hug. "You get around when you want."

"So do you, and you didn't even come to my grad." Two can play that game. I sling the pack over my shoulder and head for the house.

"Come on! We FaceTimed with you." She doubles back to the car to grab her phone. "It's a three-hour round trip. Max had soccer, and you know I can't stay here. And you said it was okay."

What else was I supposed to say? It sucked being stuck with Dad, but that's clearly the theme of the year, and besides, I know how Max gets carsick. I just want this conversation to end, so I don't reply.

Alex gives Fi a tired smile. "Hey, Fiona. Thought we might see you here."

Fiona's hands are buried in the sleeves of my hoodie. She's met Alex twice before, and I think she's a little afraid of her. She smiles in that uncomfortably big kind of way. "Thought you might need a hand."

Everyone knows it's bullshit. She's a buffer, but we're all really good at pretending.

"That's so nice of you. I'm surprised Nick hasn't scared you away yet."

"Shut up," I say, climbing the porch stairs.

Alex ignores me, walking beside Fi. "We moved in with my partner, Casey, last week, and the place is pretty empty. I'm hoping to find a few things here."

I turn back. "Nice of him to come and help."

"Actually, *she* is working today," Alex says matter-of-factly. "Casey's an English TA at PSU," she explains to Fi in a much nicer tone.

"Oh, that's so cool," Fiona says.

There's a bottomless rabbit hole of a conversation here, and I should walk away, but I can't help myself. "She?"

Alex scrunches up her face. "Grow up." She pushes past me, making her way inside.

It's a ballsy thing to say from someone who doesn't understand the concept. "This is classic Alex." I follow her in, dropping Max's backpack on the living room floor.

Alex squints at me. "Classic Alex?"

"Running away in high school, the affair with that one married guy after you moved out—"

"Moved out?" She interrupts. "Is that how you remember it?"

I face her, instantly feeling guilty. "No."

I don't know why I always phrase it that way. Maybe because that's how it was always phrased to me by Mom and Dad: *Alex and Max are moving out, Nick. It's for the best.* But no, Dad spearheaded the movement to kick her out, and the reality of that is so awful, I try not to think about it.

"But, come on. You always do these impulsive things. What about Max?"

She steps closer to me, and I can practically feel her hands around my neck. "What about Max?"

Fiona slides to my side and claps a hand on my shoulder. "I think it's great. I mean, it sounds like you're happy." She shakes me a little like my bad attitude will slide from my bones and clatter to the floor.

"Thank you, Fiona. See?" Alex says, opening the kitchen window. "That's all you had to say."

My eyes grow wide, because I can't believe she's not getting it. "I don't care who you date, but you don't think things through. And don't you think it's irresponsible to be dragging Max through this revolving door of people?"

"Are you seriously lecturing *me* on responsibility right now?"

I'll admit, my track record isn't great, but hers is off the charts.

She hauls Max's backpack onto the table and pulls out a mini box of Cheerios and a graphic novel. "Casey's amazing and the best thing that's ever happened to us, and if you bothered to come up, you would see that. I finally have some support. Be happy for me. You have no idea how hard it is raising a kid. You play the hero for an hour. You're not cleaning up vomit at two in the morning."

"Hey, I didn't make those choices. You did."

Crickets. Mission accomplished. That hurt her. She shoots bullets of disappointment my way, and I absorb every hit. Why is it so important to me to hurt her this way? Why do I have to win? I just can't crush this hostility inside of me every time I see her. *You had it all,* it screams. *Two parents. The best of them.*

Their journey through the sea was getting rocky by the time I climbed aboard, and Alex just made it worse. She was a live wire on our soggy ship, and she singlehandedly fried it.

Fiona tugs at my arm. "Let's make some coffee. It's early, everyone's still tired." She's trying to fill the silence, but nobody moves.

"Does Dad know about Casey?"

"No. It's not like it's a secret, we just don't . . . "

"Yeah."

"And could you not mention we were here today?"

She didn't even have to ask. I'm not team Alex by any

means, but team Dad doesn't even exist. "I'll be sure not to bring it up during our nightly heart-to-heart."

She goes quiet, which is never a good sign. "We need to talk about the lawsuit."

My chest tightens, and it feels like the room plunges into darkness. I knew it was coming, and *this* is why I didn't want to be alone with her. "You've been here seven minutes, Alex. You're killing me."

"Did you write a victim's statement?"

"No."

"Nick . . . "

Fiona bails—like, completely. She's off in the corner making coffee, and when I try to get her attention, she fully turns the other way.

"I told you, I don't give a shit about your lawsuit."

"Our lawsuit. The lawyer thinks an emotional letter will carry so much weight in court. We're talking about a life-changing settlement. And this is what you do. This is your thing." She shakes her fists as if she's giving me some epic motivational speech before I go off to battle.

"No, this is *your* thing."

The lawsuit was Alex's idea. Dad wanted no part of it. He thought it would be a bad look for his business and didn't think it was worth the time, but she went ahead with it, putting it in both of our names.

"Come on, Nick. You're the writer. You're good at this. Think about Max."

It's the lowest of blows, using my feelings for Max this way. Before I can say another word, he flies down the stairs, shaking a box of Lego. "Mom, look!"

"Wow!" Alex tries her best to sound excited. We all act like we were talking about happy little clouds down here. "That's so cool! Let me see!" She helps him crack open the box.

Fiona comes up beside me and touches my arm. "Do I need to take away any metaphorical car keys?"

I puff out my cheeks and let the air escape with a quiet sigh. "Honestly?"

Her eyes meet mine. "Always."

It's funny how you do something a few times, and it turns into a whole thing. I try to remember which one of us first said "honestly," and who replied with the "always," but it's a blurry history.

I dig into my pocket, turn her hand over in mine and drop a set of imaginary keys into her palm.

Max tears open a Lego bag and pieces spray across the floor. "Mom!" he wails, his eyes filling with oversized animé tears. Alex rubs her eyes. She looks so tired.

"Maybe Uncle Nick can help you with that," she says, rinsing her hands of this.

"Of course, I will. I mean, if you want."

"Yeah!" Max cheers.

We crawl under the harvest kitchen table together, gathering all three hundred and forty-four pieces.

I should have bought a smaller set.

Alex watches us, with her arms crossed, in a zoned-out way as if our conversation is still going on in her head. Part of me wants to hug her. Tell her I'm sad too, tell her I don't want things to be this way, but I just can't do it.

"So, where is everything?" she asks.

"It's downstairs." Fiona answers for me. "We packed up

33

most of it a few months ago. I can go down with you." It comes out as more of a question.

The next thing I know, they're heading for the basement door.

I close my eyes. She's only been here for a few minutes, and I'm already so relieved she's gone. With my hands full of Lego bricks, I crawl out from under the table and dump the pieces on top.

"Were you hiding under the table, Uncle Nick?" Max asks with a giggle.

"No," I say, but the kid's smiling like he sees right through me.

After I help sort the pieces by shape, Max shoos me away. He wants to do the rest himself, so I ruffle his hair and head for the basement.

The rec room is a wasteland with our sagging green velour couch, stains on the carpet, and cobwebs in every corner. The culmination of a million parties left to fossilize on the floor. After Mom died, the parties stopped, my so-called-friends disappeared, and the room started to decay. The upside was that my grades improved—dramatically.

"So, what's the deal with you two?" Alex's foggy voice carries from the storage room.

Instead of bursting through the door and interrupting like I should, I lean against the wall and listen.

"No deal," Fiona answers.

"Fiona, you're wearing his clothes, sleeping over—there's obviously something going on."

It's so skeezy to be eavesdropping like this, but I want to hear her answer. Except, she doesn't give one, and Alex doesn't wait.

"Can you talk to him about writing a victim's statement?"

That's when I pop around the corner and kill the conversation dead. "You decide what you want?" I ask Alex. Fiona gives me a desperate *don't-leave-me* stare.

"Yeah, let's start with a few of these bigger pieces, and I'll take whatever boxes I have room for."

"Great. Let's do this," I say, clapping my hands together.

Alex plucks a lamp from the shelf and carries it out of the room. I grab two curved antique plant stands and pause in front of Fi. "You okay?"

She looks a little rattled. A few minutes with my sister can do that to a person. "Yeah."

But when I reach the stairs, I glance back and see her head fall against the wall.

We fill Alex's car to the brim. The only free spots are Max's seat and hers, yet she's trying to figure out how to squeeze in even more.

"It's not going to happen, Alex. You'll have to make another trip." Max tosses me his new Lego Batman, and I toss it back to him.

We both know it won't happen any time soon.

She closes the trunk. "You sure you don't want any of this stuff?"

"What am I going to do with it?"

"Well, if you ever change your mind, you know where it is."

"At Casey's," I say with a grin.

"At *our* place," she corrects. "Where you're always welcome.

I don't want you to think I'm taking your share or anything. Nana's shitty dishes are every bit yours as they are mine."

Our eyes meet. We both know how much Mom loved those dishes.

"Promise you'll save me the crusty ones."

That gets a laugh out of her. "Gross. And deal."

We actually shake on it.

Alex treats us to pizza for lunch. Max runs around the front yard, flying his new Lego Batmobile, and I chase after him while Alex and Fiona sit on the stoop. Alex can't stop talking about how much she loves Portland and how nice it is to be in the city. It's deliberately loud enough for me to hear. Everything she says sounds like a suggestion for me.

They leave at four. Max squeezes me so hard, he refuses to let go, and I have to pry his fingers from around my waist. All I can think is *Don't cry. Don't fucking cry.* I bend down on a knee to face him. "We'll hang out soon, okay?"

"When?" He blinks his bright green eyes at me, and my heart liquifies.

Soon isn't enough for him, he needs something concrete, but how can I give him concrete when my life is mostly quicksand?

"Soon," I say.

He raises his pinky finger toward me. "Pinky swear?"

Fi's probably figuring out this is where my inspiration for last night came from. I lock my finger around Max's. This seems to satisfy him. He scrambles into the back seat.

"You dropping by Bryce's?" I ask Alex now that Max is out of earshot.

Bryce and Alex were the *it* couple in high school until they had Max. His support has been spotty at best, but she still takes Max to visit him a few times a year.

"No. Not this time. He might come to Portland next week."

"Right."

She gives me a hug and pats my back. "Later, loser. Bye, Fiona."

Fi waves. "Good luck with the new place!"

"Drive safe!" I call out as she gets in the car.

"No, *you* drive safe!" She shouts back before slamming the door.

I pretend to scratch my face with my middle finger, and she honks at me. Fiona jumps, and I shake my head feigning ignorance. We wave as they reverse out of the driveway, my smile falling the second they're out of sight.

Home feels so empty without them.

Fi's already got her keys in her hand. She's dying to get out of here. "So? Did Alex give you the hard sell?"

"Yup."

"What'd she say?"

It's a shitty question, because I already know what was said. *What's the deal with you two?* It's just never been said between us and part of me wants that conversation to happen. What is our deal?

Fi shrugs. "The usual. That the suit is in your best interest, and she asked me to talk to you about the letter."

I guess she doesn't want to have that conversation. She tucks a strand of hair behind her ear. "You should apologize. You were pretty brutal."

"Yeah. I'll text her." That's when I spot something in the grass. "Shit." Max's Lego Batman. I pick it up and show Fi. He'll freak out. I call Alex, but she doesn't answer. Probably on purpose.

"It's okay. You'll see him soon."

I shoot her a look. We both know I won't.

"Or we can go to Portland," she offers, before correcting herself, "I mean, *you* can go to Portland."

She's getting all flustered, and I don't blame her. My head is spinning with we and you and whose life is whose anymore.

She takes tiny steps backwards heading for her car. "I'm going to head out."

"You must be so sick of my bullshit."

"It's still better than my bullshit."

She climbs in, and I lean on the car by the open window. "So, what's the name of the hotel you booked?"

"I don't remember, it was something really forgettable," she says, smiling wide. "The ocean . . . side . . . inn or something."

She is such a liar. "It should be in your emails."

"I used my dad's email, so it's not."

A good one though, I'll give her that. "Mmm, well, text me the link when you get in. I'm dying to see it."

"Wouldn't you rather be surprised?"

I consider this. "No. I'd rather have something to look forward to."

"Okay, but have low expectations. I'm on a budget."

"I have faith in you, Fi." I hold a hand up in a wave as she backs out of the endless driveway.

She didn't book anything. Not a chance.

But now, I hope she will.

Fiona

The Monterey trip is supposed to happen on the first anniversary of Mom's death—like a pilgrimage except, I haven't been able to pull the trigger and book anything. Now Nick's waiting for a hotel link, so I have to deal with this ASAP, and I want to, but . . .

What if the weather is bad?

What if it's a total waste of money?

What if my car breaks down? What if Dad gets lonely? What if the hotel has bedbugs?

And then there's Nick. It's one thing to crash at his house. We have a routine. It's familiar. But going away for an entire weekend together and staying in a hotel? It's kind of freaking me out, and I don't know why.

When I get home, Dad's asleep on the couch in an undershirt and his work pants. His navy paramedic's shirt is crumpled in a heap on the floor, and there's a hardcover of *Eat*

Pray Love open across his chest. Dad usually reads the news, never books, especially not Mom's books, so I'm not sure what to make of it.

Three giant portraits are on the wall behind him. Mom's work, black and white and double-exposed. They're supposed to be "artsy," but all I see are ghosts watching us.

He stirs awake and lets out a yawn, eyeing me over the top of his reading glasses. Dark inky bags hang under his eyes. "How's Nick?"

"Same," I say, kicking off my shoes by the door. "Angry with a strong breeze of bitterness."

"I feel like I should do something. Should I talk to his dad?"

"Why would you? You don't even know his dad."

"Know he's an asshole. Leaving his kid all the time."

I wait for the irony to sink in, but it doesn't. My dad, the paramedic, recognizing and treating others' distress, yet blind to it happening right in front of him. I could light myself on fire, and he still wouldn't notice. But Nick, he's concerned about.

Dad thinks Nick is one of those people who will "do something crazy." I told him that's just how Nick is, he's not the "do something crazy" type. He just internalizes until he fizzles out. Then Dad reminded me that things need to explode before they fizzle out.

I point to the book on his chest. "I don't think Mom liked that."

"That's why I'm reading it." He picks it up, shielding his face.

I still don't get it. Everything he does these days is backwards, a winding of an empty spool, instead of the slow discovery of where it went in the first place.

"There's veggie lasagna in the fridge. I ate already," he calls out as I head into the kitchen.

A single slice of cold lasagna on a plate is the embodiment of sadness. I slide the plate into the microwave and watch it go around in a slow circle. Everything in our house is sad now. It lingers like greasy film, impossible to scrub away, the four chairs around the table, the fruit bowl, now filled with clutter, the *Mom's Kitchen* magnet on the fridge. She's everywhere, but nowhere, and the realization hits just as hard every time.

Every. Time.

The microwave beeps. The plate is a million degrees when I take it out, but the lasagna is still cold in the middle. It doesn't matter. I eat it anyway, standing over the kitchen counter. Standing seems to hurt less.

"May stopped by," Dad says. He puts the book on the coffee table and heaves himself off the couch, lumbering into the kitchen with a hand on his lower back. He fishes a container of strawberry ice cream from the freezer.

"Really? Why?"

"Looking for you. Said you had plans. Said she would text."

I dig my phone from my pocket. I forgot I had it on do not disturb. "Nooo! She's going to kill me. We were supposed to grab lunch."

I fire off a text.

So sorry

Was at Nick's

Long story

She texts back "It's OK, ILY" with a heart emoji a second later.

"She'll get over it. Want some?" He holds out the container, and I take a giant scoop with his spoon.

I notice a small, open shipping box on the kitchen counter. "What's in the box?"

"What's in the booox," he cries out like Brad Pitt in "Seven." This is our thing. He would have totally appreciated my Hannibal impression from last night.

I peek over the edge. A small, silver handheld camera sits inside.

"Your mother's camera," Dad says, like it's no big deal, as he digs out another scoop.

Except it's kind of a huge deal. He's staring at it in a daze, probably thinking the same things I am. Are there pictures of her last minutes alive, before her convoy rolled over the IED? Was she still taking pictures after? It may as well be a bomb. Leave it to a war to create an explosion strong enough for the debris to rain down a continent away.

"I thought everything was destroyed."

"Apparently not everything. It was being held in a processing facility in Poland, and now it's here."

"Are there pictures?" I ask, putting my plate in the dishwasher.

Dad eyes the box like something is alive inside of it. "I don't know."

"Are you going to look?"

He thinks about it for a second and puts the tub of ice cream back in the freezer. "No. It's yours if you want it."

But, I don't want to touch it, at least not now. "I'm going upstairs, I've got some stuff to do."

"Picking your courses?" he asks hopefully.

The absolute last thing on my mind.

"Monterey," I answer, and immediately regret it.

"You're serious about that?"

"I am."

"Don't you think . . . " I can tell he's choosing his next words carefully, "It's not the best use of your time?"

"Dad, you're reading *Eat Pray Love*."

He raises his hands in defense. "Okay, okay, but I don't know what you think you'll find out there."

"I could say the same to you."

He smiles. I think that means I win.

My phone buzzes from the counter.

Nick: You home?

Shit. The hotel link. I need to book this, like now.

"Everything okay?" Dad asks as I hurry out of the kitchen.

"Yeah. It's just Nick," I mumble, texting him back.

Me: Walking through the door now

Nick: Bullshit

I run upstairs, flop onto my bed with my laptop and google Monterey hotels.

Nick: I can't wait to find out how long it takes

to research and book a hotel in Monterey

Me: Just digging up the confirmation email

Six hundred results fill my screen. *Why are there so many?* I eliminate the chains, lower the price range, and the list shrinks considerably. I zero in on a small motel. It looks a little sketchy, with its white stucco exterior and grounds that are little more than a parking lot, but it's close to the ocean, and the rooms are renovated in shades of oceanic blues. The reviews are mostly positive, and the cancellation policy is generous. I book it—a lifetime record for me. When the confirmation email lands in my inbox, I text Nick the link.

> **Nick: I'm impressed**
>
> **Me: I don't know what you're talking about**
>
> **Nick: We don't have to go you know**
>
> **Me: I want to go**

I think. I think I want to go.

> **Me: What are you doing?**
>
> **Nick: Sitting at my desk in front of a blank screen**

Alex got to him with the victim's statement. I knew it. He talks a tough game, but he's really a giant marshmallow.

> **Me: Noooo stop**
>
> **Not tonight.**
>
> **Nick: Nothing to stop**
>
> **Me: Your self-torture**
>
> **Nick: That continues regardless**
>
> **Me: If it makes you feel any better, my version of a bucket list showed up today**
>
> **Nick: ?**
>
> **Me: Mom's camera from that day**

The day she died. I can't even type the words. There's a pause before he types back.

> **Nick: You okay?**
>
> **Me: Well, you know . . .**

How it feels to never be okay, but you have to be because you're alive and a level of function comes along with that.

> **Nick: Yeah, wish you were here**
>
> **Me: Yeah, but my room is way comfier than yours**
>
> **Nick: Goodnight, Fiona**

I miss him already. Sometimes, it feels like Nick lives on the flip side of my heart. That he's the upbeat, the oxygen that reinflates everything. He gets it—this lost-in-space feeling we're trapped in because no matter how many times we call out to ground control, nobody answers.

I slide my laptop onto the floor and pick up Mom's photo album from my nightstand. A narwhal is sketched on the cover in light blue ink, with two black dots for eyes and a horn bedazzled with seven carefully glued sequins. She even drew a simple blue line to make it smile. A giant red heart encircles the whole thing with *The Narwhal* written above in calligraphy. She was a photojournalist and only shot in black and white, so when I found this wedged in the back of her closet three months after she died, it seemed odd for three reasons:

1. The super happy rainbow-vomiting-unicorn equivalent of a cover.
2. The fact that it was hidden in the back of her closet.
3. The photos.

It's full of objects from this one bar, and they're . . . in color. Some are double-exposed, Mom's signature, but this album doesn't fit. Mom isn't a smiley narwhal drawing kind of person.

Was not. Still working on that.

Dad said the photos were part of a college project she did twenty years ago, but school projects aren't circled in giant red hearts. He gave me a location—Monterey. That was all he told me.

I flip through the pages for the millionth time. There's a red bar stool with silver studs around the seat, a worn wooden floor covered in black scuff marks, a jukebox lit up like a rainbow, and amber bottles of liquor lining the wall. Six pages of details.

When I close the album, Mom's narwhal grins like it's guarding a secret, dangling a key for me to find. I googled it. The Narwhal is still there. It exists—so I need to see it.

I put the album back on my nightstand and switch off the light. Doubt seeps in with the darkness.

We don't have to go, you know.

What if Nick doesn't want to go?

Maybe he just told me.

Fiona

There are only five minutes left of kinder gym, but when you're surrounded by a group of six-year-olds on a Friday afternoon, it feels like forever. On pointed toe, I take swift steps across the high beam with my shoulders pulled back, and my head held high. Balancing is easy for me. I could do this blindfolded.

When I pivot, a shrill "Hey!" echoes through the gym. I wobble, and there's a collective "Whoa," from my group when I nearly fall off.

I never fall off.

Once I'm steady, I search for the source of the yell. It's May, my best friend since sixth grade, in a standoff with a boy sitting in the middle of a wall-length trampoline.

"You can't sit there, dude. You have to go all the way down." She pushes the air with her hands as if he needs a visual.

May is the image of perfection. Her silky black hair is pulled into a polished bun, and she carries herself with poise, as if she's always on the world's stage. I, on the other hand, am practically invisible in my oversized Gym Rocks Coach T-shirt and track pants.

May glances over her shoulder and sees half the gym staring. "It's okay, jump around him. Keep going, everyone. When you get to the end, you can go," she calls out to her group in a much sweeter tone.

I dismount and tell my group to do a single pass on the beam before they leave.

Sarah, one of my private-lesson students, tugs at my arm. "Fiona, can we do walkovers?"

She's giving me her best puppy-dog eyes. "You know what? We don't have time, but how about on Wednesday when it's just you and me, okay?"

"Yay!" she shouts, racing out of the gym after the others.

A weekly private lesson pays twice as much as group, and they're the only real shot I have at making money with this job. I have four students, and May has eight. The kids seem to like me more, but the parents love her.

May walks up beside me. We wave with our super happy goodbye faces until the gym is nearly empty.

"Little assholes," she mutters under her breath with a smile.

I don't know why she works here. Her family is gross rich, so it's not like she needs this job, but she loves the constant adoration from the parents.

"They're not so bad." I say, pulling the scrunchie from my hair.

"You're too nice. It's the only reason they like you."

It's a classic May comment. The compliment dig. She's a real pro. Sometimes it takes days for me to unpack the insult from the compliment, they're so tightly entwined.

I pull myself onto the high beam to do one last pass before we leave. May strolls beside it.

"What's the plan for tonight? Wanna go out and grab a bite?" she asks.

"Raincheck? I'm tired. I just want to go home and veg."

May cranes her head up. "Why are you always tired for me and never for Nick?"

"Not even remotely true," I say as I take a small leap.

"It is true. When's the last time we went out?"

I glance down at her. "I don't do this to you when you're busy with Jaden or whoever."

"Yeah, because you're secretly grateful you don't have to go out."

She's right, and we both know it, so I don't say anything.

"At least tell me you're hooking up with him."

There's that wobble again. I dismount, pulling my shoulders back. May has a solid two inches on me, but her perfect ballerina's posture makes it seem like so much more. I feel like a tree stump next to her. "Nope. Not hooking up."

"And he doesn't have a girlfriend?"

Also, ninety-nine percent sure of this. "No. Unless he has a secret life I don't know about."

"I don't get it." May blinks at me as if it's a question I'm supposed to answer.

She never will get it. Nick doesn't need a relationship, he has something else—a loss—and it's as real as a body in the room, always imposing, always pulling your heart away, all-consuming.

"I told you, it's not like that. We're friends. It's like AA, and aren't there rules against that kind of thing?"

"Please. People in AA hook up all the time."

"Yeah, I don't think they're supposed to."

She twirls in front of me. "It's forbidden fruit, Fi. That's what makes it soooo hot."

"Nick is nothing like forbidden fruit. He's like . . . an apple. A good old Granny Smith. Or a banana. Run-of-the-mill fruit-bowl kind of fruit. No passionfruit, no kumquat, no prickly pear . . . " It's a revelation. My eyes widen. "I take it back. He *is* a prickly pear! That's Nick in fruit form!"

May side-eyes me like I've lost my mind. "Okay . . . because you're clearly bananas."

"Ohh, ba dum dum tsh. Nice one!"

May curtsies. "Thank you."

We pick up some stray cones and brightly colored floor mats and bring them to the storage room.

"We know each other too well. It's . . . different." It's hard to find words to describe our relationship. "He's familiar."

"Wait. Didn't you say he writes?"

I don't think I want to know where she's going with this. "Yeah."

"Why don't you snoop through his notes folder? That's where they put all the good stuff."

A few balls roll out of the storage room, and I toss them back inside, quickly closing the door before they can escape again. "Why would I do that?"

"To see what he's into. *Who* he's into." She gives me a mischievous grin. "To see if he writes about you."

"No! No way." It's crazy, and I hate that now, I'm thinking about it. We make our way back across the gym.

"Can you at least invite him to hang with us? I think it's the only way I'll ever see you in the wild again."

And there's no chance in hell of that happening. My life is perfectly compartmentalized. Nick, Dad, work, school. Everything works within the parameters of its box. Mixing boxes is a recipe for disaster. I've already mixed the Nick and Dad boxes, and that still feels like a work in progress.

May will never understand. Post-Mom Fiona is a different person. One who doesn't want to hang period, but it's easier to blame it on Nick. "Yeah, I don't think he'd be into it."

"Half a year, Fi! I've listened to you talk about this guy for half a year, and I've never met him. I'm not even sure he's real. It's weird that you're hiding him from me like this."

"I'm not . . . "

"Bring him out. He's probably lonely and desperate for some company like you! Invite him to Jaden's party. I'm not going if you don't."

"Okay, fine, I'll ask him," I say as if it isn't a big deal, but Nick and I don't hang out in the wild, so it's actually a huge deal.

"If he's as cool as you say, maybe I'll hook up with him." She shimmies her shoulders, and her tone is playful, but it feels like a threat. I add it to my stack of May comments to unpack later.

"I thought you and Jaden were together?"

Across the gym, Jaden swings back and forth on the parallel bars, giving a kid an after-class demonstration. Jaden is always happy to demonstrate. His muscles bulge through his fitted Gym Rocks Head Coach T-shirt. He's so built his muscles would bulge through twenty layers of winter wear. He's a total goofball, and the kids go crazy for him. He's nineteen, and this is it for him, his dream job. He sees us watching and ups his performance by two hundred percent. When he hits the mat and sticks a perfect landing, he turns to us and makes a ridiculous face like he's singing opera or something.

May squints at him. "Yeah, no, that's over."

This is something I should know. "Since when?"

"It was never serious and kind of a total disaster."

Jaden is trying to wrap up and come over, but May is eager for that not to happen. She tugs me toward the changing room. I give Jaden a wave before we crash through the door.

"Uhh, cliffhanger line if I've ever heard one."

Although not a surprising one. Disaster is a fitting label for all of May's relationships. We pull our gym bags down from our lockers.

May kicks off her sneakers and slides on her rhinestone-studded Flip-flops. She leans closer and whispers, "He wanted to eat meatloaf off my abs."

My mouth falls open, but no words come out. Sometimes, I'm not sure anything May says is real. All of her stories seem wildly unlikely. There was one about her parents' Airbnb being burglarized, and she had to hide in a closet in her underwear. And one where she was caught in a hotel fire with her older sister and had to flee wearing nothing but her underwear. And the time she was trapped in a car by a bear when she went camping (I want to say in her underwear). Every story goes the extra mile. It's hard to believe so much can happen to one person when nothing ever happens to me.

What am I supposed to say to this? We grab our bags and head into the gym atrium. It's almost empty now. A few kids huddle around the candy machines, carefully choosing where to spend their quarters.

A blast of warm, humid air hits us as we exit through the sliding doors.

"Why meatloaf?"

She shakes her head a little like she's annoyed, and I'm not sure if it's because I questioned the food choice or because she didn't get a bigger reaction from me. "Is there some other food that makes more sense?"

I think for a second. "Jell-O maybe?"

Her eyes grow wide. "Omigod, yes. Jell-O sounds like almost normal!"

We burst into laughter as we weave through the lot to our cars. "Anyway, it was with gravy and everything, but it wasn't that bad."

It takes a second for the words to catch up with my brain. I stop. "Wait. You did it?"

She grins. That's the reaction she was waiting for. "Technically, he did it. I kind of just laid there."

"Wow. I don't know what to do with that image."

"Yeah, it really embeds itself up in there."

"Is this what relationships are now? It's been a while, but I'm so confused."

"Oh, Fiona, you're such an innocent," she teases, and it chafes me again. The compliment dig.

Behind her, Jaden runs through the parking lot, waving wildly for our attention.

May turns. "Shit."

He doubles over, out of breath, when he reaches us. It's hard to look at him the same way now.

"Ladies, whoa. Where's the fire? Let's go out, get some dessert or something."

May shifts her gym bag in front of her like a shield. "I can't." She feigns disappointment. "My parents are doing a FaceTime thing with my cousins, and I'm already way late. You two totally should, though."

I look up at her. I can't believe she'd throw me under the bus this way, but yes, yes, I can. I try to think of a fruit for asshole.

Jaden looks at me, expectant. "Fi? You in?"

My mind goes blank as I search for an excuse. "Uh, yeah, I don't think I can either. My dad's home, and he's . . . really sad . . . on weekends."

Jaden's face softens. Grief is like a free pass. It gets you out of everything. He lowers his head and puts some solid effort into trying to act somber. "Oh, yeah, I totally get that."

He totally does not get that. I nod, trying to act as bummed as possible.

He brightens again after the obligatory five seconds of sad face. "At my party next Friday, we'll make up for lost time, yeah?"

May nudges my shoulder with hers. "Assuming Fi doesn't bail. Yes, definitely."

"Can't wait," I say, but my mind is already racing for a way out of this.

"Awesome. It'll be awesome," Jaden calls out as he bounds across the lot to his truck.

Stale, hot air oozes from inside my car when I open the door, so I lean against it, giving it a chance to escape.

May throws her bag into her back seat. She closes the door and faces me. "I know you don't want to go, but it'll be good for you."

Jaden drives past us, music spilling from his open windows, and honks. We wave.

She stares after him with a hint of a smirk. "Besides, it'll be fun."

I know that look. Whatever they're doing, it's definitely not over.

A long raven strand falls from her bun, and she smooths it back to re-secure it but then pulls off her elastic instead, shaking her newly formed waves free around her shoulders. "Don't overthink it, Fi. I mean, why is it always so hard for you to be happy?"

She says it like it's nothing, like it's so easy.

She flashes me a wave, gets in her car, and doesn't even wait for an answer, and I'm so relieved, because I don't have one.

Fiona

An imaginary cat sits on my chest. Its name is how do I get out of Jaden's party next weekend? It's sitting on top of another cat called what's on Mom's camera? And they're balancing on the bottom cat, named 101 problems with Monterey. The weight keeps growing. You know what they say, two cats are company, three are . . .

"A catastrophe," imaginary Nick says.

Sometimes I talk to him in my head. Imaginary Nick can be funny.

Why haven't I ever invited him out? There are a few worst-case scenarios:

1. He says no.
2. He stops hanging out with me to avoid future lame party invites.

3. May. In her thousand disastrous forms. I can already hear her next in-my-underwear story, this time, featuring Nick.

Inviting him out could ruin our perfect friendship bubble. Everything inside me is screaming bail! Abort! I need to kick a cat off my chest.

I shouldn't be thinking about this as I sit here in group, and when I look at Nick sitting across from me, I wonder if it shows. He was late as usual, but tonight so is Grace. The second he taps his watch, the door flies open, and Grace bustles through.

"Sorry everyone, but it's been one of those days." She collapses in her chair and rummages through her bag for another minute before she spots what she's looking for—her notebook, which is on the floor in front of her.

"You want to talk about it, Grace?" Nick smiles.

"I appreciate that, but it was just a bad traffic day," she says, refocusing. "Why don't we begin with the last day you remember spending with your loved ones. What was the energy like? What details do you remember? Fiona? Do you want to start us off?"

Everyone focuses on me. "Yeah, sure." I'm always the default first pick, even though I never raise my hand, but it's fine. It's not like I can talk about this at home. Dad made that pretty clear when he forwarded me the link to these meetings after a fellow paramedic sent it to him. I think he saw it as a one-and-done solution the way a doctor prescribes meds, and they kick in twenty-four hours later. Grace gives me an encouraging nod as if she's waiting for me to say something brilliant.

"Uhh, she was excited." Hardly brilliant.

Grace presses. "Why?"

"Touring with the military was like winning an Oscar for her." I cringe at my word choice. "We were in Portland. She wanted to show me around PSU last summer, but she got a call from her agent, and we had to leave early. So, you know . . . " I shrug. "It was okay."

The day sucked. It was a million sticky degrees. We were a half hour late for the tour, couldn't find anyone, and I spilled a jumbo-sized iced tea all over myself. All the while Mom kept checking her phone, so it was far from the memory-making day I had hoped it would be.

Grace's plan works. My warm-up inspires Maddie to speak. "My brother made the football team." Her voice is so faint I have to strain to hear. "He was jumping across the house screaming, "In your face!" It was so stupid. He worked out all summer so he would make it, and he did. Dad ordered pizza and wings to celebrate, but my brother wouldn't even eat because he was on this crazy diet." She smiles at the memory. "So yeah, he was really happy."

"And that's a nice feeling to hang on to," Grace says. "When you find your mind lingering on the sad, sometimes it helps to shift to a broader time frame to remember the good." After a few others share their stories, Grace turns to Nick. "How about you, Nick?"

Nick shifts in his chair. "How about me what?"

"What was your mom feeling? What's the last thing you remember?"

He thinks for all of two seconds. "She texted from the airport. She said, 'Don't fuck up the house.'"

There's some nervous laughter from the group, but Grace isn't fazed. "That's not really a feeling."

Nick smirks. "Okay. Then I guess she was suspicious that I'd fuck up the house."

"Do you think she was happy?"

Nick takes her question as a personal challenge. "I don't know. How can anyone assume to know something like that?"

Grace thinks. "It's not always an assumption. There are indicators. Some people say it outright, and sometimes it's intuition."

"Yeah, but isn't intuition just a form of projection? And asking rarely yields the truth. My intuition would say no, she wasn't happy, but what the hell do I know? It could have been the happiest day of her life."

"That's interesting, Nick—"

He cuts her off. "I mean, unless you're asking a kid. Kids will tell you straight up. You ask anyone else if they're happy, and you'll get a tailored response."

Grace absorbs this. "Are you saying kids are the only ones who can be happy?"

"The only ones who can be honest about being happy."

"Isn't that kind of a jaded view? If you ask me if I'm happy, the answer would be yes, I am."

Nick's lips curl in a half-smile. "Well, I call bullshit on that."

The room falls quiet. Everyone watches the conversation volley between them with rapt attention. It's like the rest of us aren't even here anymore.

"Why?" she asks.

"For one, you're stuck listening to these messed up—no offense—stories, which have got to leave some kind of residual weight, so I find it hard to believe you leave these meetings and walk out into the world feeling happy."

Grace is quiet for a minute. "But your logic is flawed. What about surgeons, firefighters, teachers, students? No one escapes . . . *life*. With that logic, you're saying people are incapable of happiness."

Nick sits back in his chair. "Unless you're under the age of ten."

"Kids are bullied in school every day, so why exclude them?"

Now, he's silent. He leans forward, resting his elbows on his knees. "I don't know. I think happiness is an illusion. It's something manufactured in books and movies, and everyone buys into this idea that it's an attainable life goal, but it's all pain management, isn't it?" He gestures to me. "Is happiness going to a war zone or is that escapism? Is it playing football or is that an affirmation of a need to belong? I mean, isn't happiness essentially those brief, fleeting moments when life isn't shit?"

"It doesn't last," Grace says.

"It doesn't last."

"So, happiness is not a sustainable emotion."

"Right. I don't think so," Nick says.

"What about love? Is it sustainable?"

"Hard pass."

"No, really," Grace addresses the group with a new fire behind her eyes. "Our emotions appear and fade like a rainbow after a storm. You can't force a rainbow to stay. It fades. A rainbow is not sustainable. Emotions are not sustainable. Sometimes, we might feel happy for a month, a week, or ten seconds, when one small thing makes us smile, but the emotion inevitably fades. The same is true for grief and anger. We exist in a revolving door of feelings, and while your grief will never truly disappear, it will give way to something else. Sadness is not sustainable."

"Unless you're literally on antidepressants," Maddie pipes up.

Nick flashes me a smile. The epic crescendo Grace proudly built deflates in a second, and she couldn't be more done with this session. "This week when you're out in the world, be mindful of the small things that impact your emotions. Your emotional triggers, okay?"

Everyone nods. I predict none of us will do this.

"See you all next time. Nick, can you hang back for a minute?" Grace catches him halfway out the door, and his shoulders slump as he steps back into the room. Then she joins the rest of the group at the snack table.

I make my way to his side. He's quiet, staring at the others, as if he can will them to leave.

"Want a coffee?" I ask.

"No."

"Cookie?"

He shoots me a look. "What do you think she wants?"

"To murder you?" That wins me a tiny smile.

Maddie comes over, cradling a cup of tea in her hands. "Hey, that was really smart, what you said."

Nick isn't even looking at her. He's impatiently watching Grace. "Thanks."

"Maybe we can all hang out sometime."

"Uh-huh, maybe."

It's a total brush-off. I'm so mortified, I blurt out, "That's a great idea! Text me, and I'll set something up."

Maddie hands me her phone, and I punch in my number, but deep down, I know she'll never use it. "Sure. Thanks," she says when a text pings on her phone. "That's my mom. See you later." She waves and leaves.

I whack Nick in the chest, and he turns to me, clueless. "What?"

"She reached out to you!"

"Yeah, and I talked to her. I thought that's what you wanted me to do?"

I shake my head, exasperated. The room empties, and Grace heads our way, carrying a bag of leftover snacks. "Come on, take a walk with me."

Nick casts a wary glance my way. Grace flicks off the lights, and we walk down the long corridor of the community center. The shrieks of children's voices fill the halls where swimming lessons are underway. She still hasn't said anything, and Nick can't take the silence a second longer. "Let me guess, you're kicking me out?" A thread of worry laces through his bravado. He needs this group even if he'd never admit it.

Grace side-eyes him. "Why would I do that? You're the only reason half these kids keep coming back."

He thinks about this. "Damn. I'm the reality show drama."

"Why don't we go with intellectual provocateur?"

It's a compliment, but Nick is so self-effacing, he's immune to it.

"So, what? You want to stage a fight for the next session?"

"Not exactly." She stops to face him. "I was selected to be a guest editor for a national psych magazine. It's a special edition that's published yearly, and it's always a big draw, as far as psych magazines go."

Nick glances at me as if I might know where this is headed. "Sounds fancy," I say.

"Congratulations," he adds.

"We've talked about your writing in sessions before, and I'd like you to consider submitting a piece for publication."

He furrows his brow. "A piece on what?"

"Whatever you want. Happiness, death, love. You seem to have strong feelings about . . . feelings."

Nick zones out, focusing on a distant spot on the floor. She's throwing him this incredible lifeline of opportunity, and he's just bobbing in the ocean.

I nudge his arm, snapping him out of it. "It would be good for your writing portfolio."

"In a psych magazine?"

"In a national psych magazine," Grace corrects. "Published is published, right?"

We trail behind Grace when Sarah, my private-lesson student, springs out from around a corner, swimming goggles around her neck. "Fiona! It's Fiona!" she shouts. Her mom is a few steps behind, talking to another parent. I wave as we pass by.

Grace pushes open the front door. A blanket of fog hangs over the parking lot, making the streetlights glow like hazy fireflies.

"I know you don't want to hear it, Nick, but this could work out nicely for you," she says as we walk down the stairs.

He eyes her, doubtful. "You mean like a happy ending?"

"A step toward one."

The fog is so dense I can't see my car. Once we're on the sidewalk, I press the lock button on the key fob to make the lights flash.

"Why are you being so nice to me?" Nick asks her.

Grace tilts her head. "You don't think I'm nice to you?"

"I thought you thought I was an asshole."

A curious smile spreads across her lips. "Why would you think that?"

"Ugh, don't go all psych on me, Grace."

"No, really," she says, eyeing him with interest. "You gave an intriguing speech on projection tonight, so maybe *you* think you're an asshole."

Nick rocks back on his feet.

"I'll email you the submission details. You don't have to decide right now, but soon. Have a great night," she calls out over her shoulder.

"Hey, Grace." She turns back. "Thanks."

She gives us a wave and heads down the sidewalk. "Drive safely!"

Nick grabs his bike, and we cross the parking lot toward my car. Out of the blue, he asks, "Do you think I'm an asshole?"

I smile. I could answer, but don't. I just walk ahead and let his question disappear in the fog behind me.

Nick

Grace blindsided the shit out of me. Yeah, I write, but she's talking about real writing for really smart people, and I don't know if I'm the guy for the job.

And let's be honest, happy endings are bullshit. Nothing makes me want to throw a book at a screen more than a couple that walks into the sunset together. I mean, come on. Equally as offensive are champagne glasses clinking, making rain romantic, running through airports—all the tropes. Happily ever after is boring. It's a complete waste of a movie except when it isn't. I'll make an exception for "Romancing the Stone." It was Mom's favorite comfort movie, and she watched it more weekends than I can count, which meant Alex and I watched it, too. When that sailboat rolls down Fifth Avenue, I mean, it doesn't get any cooler than that. Plus, Michael Douglas is kind of a legend. That ending alone made me rethink my position on happy endings. Maybe there could be this whole gray area . . . like they don't all have to be sunsets and sap by the sea, so that's what I try to lean into.

After Mom died, I tested that theory. I imagined happily ever afters for strangers. It was an experiment that turned into a habit. Fiona was the only one who knew, and she joined in and started pointing out people for me to give a happy ending to. There's no shortage of jokes in there.

My only rule is not to imagine an ending for the people closest to me. It isn't even a rule so much as a roadblock. When it comes to Alex, Fi, and myself, my mind goes blank when I think about our future. It's like we've been tossed into the air and are all floating around up there, and I don't know where or when we're going to land.

I did Zombie Bob, but I didn't tell Fi. He finds love again in my story. He finally has enough of this homebody bullshit and chooses life. He's on a charter yacht with his crew, deep-sea fishing in the Pacific. He's got on a bright floral shirt, a straw hat, and an endless sun shines down on him. A pretty lady smiles at him from across the deck, and a swordfish is about to bite his line. I'm not sure Fiona would want to hear it, but in my ending, Zombie Bob gets his shit together. He's a really good guy, so I hope he does.

Mom doesn't get one. Death is the ultimate spoiler. Sometimes, I try to turn her accident into something else, but it's a tough sell, even for me.

Fiona leans over the steering wheel, wiping the condensation from the windshield with her sleeve. We still haven't left the parking lot. I press the defrost button, and air blasts out of the vents into her face. She jolts her head back and eyes me. Maybe it wasn't the right thing to do. I'm ninety-nine percent sure Fiona *does* think I'm an asshole.

She turns on the wipers, which shockingly do nothing to lift the white blanket of fog outside, and finally backs out of the spot. I'm a little concerned for us.

"So? Are you going to write the piece?" she finally asks.

I'm definitely not going to write the piece, but her voice has a hitch of hope, and I don't want to disappoint her. "I dunno. Why am I always being asked to write about things I don't want to write about?"

"What *do* you want to write about?"

I don't know that either. My writing is mostly a hobby. I haven't even decided if this is it for me. "Robots and space wars and fish that electrocute people."

She smiles, but I'm pretty sure it's her you're-such-an-asshole smile. "Stealing from Max's playbook?"

"His ideas are way better than mine."

The fog isn't any better on the main road. The world is cloaked in a thick haze. Staring into it kind of freaks me out, because I'm expecting some crazy "Doctor Who" shit to pop out on the other side. We're moving, but I can barely see any proof. The car feels like it's floating.

Fi squints at the windshield, which is all kinds of ridiculous. It's not like that's going to clear things up. "Do you want me to drive?"

She doesn't take her eyes off the road. "You don't even have a license."

"I could drive this road blindfolded. In fact, I'm pretty sure I have."

"On a bicycle!"

"Semantics," I reply with a shrug.

Her grip on the wheel is so tight her knuckles are white, so I try to distract her from stressing over the fog. "What are you going to do with the camera?" Okay, that might have made things worse. Except she relaxes her death grip on the wheel.

"I don't know? Maybe take it to Monterey?"

"And look at the pictures there?"

She turns off the cool air blasting through the vents, and the car goes quiet. "We'll see. It's not like the bucket list." She slides her hand down the side of the steering wheel and turns on the high beams, which only amplifies the fog outside. I open my mouth to say something before shutting it just as quickly. The further we get from town, the darker the road becomes. This feels like a metaphor for my life somehow.

I turn on the radio because in my head emergency alerts are being broadcast, saying you definitely shouldn't drive on side road five tonight, but all that comes out on every saved station is static, and that ups the creep factor by five hundred percent.

Fi glances from the radio to me. The car steadily accelerates like it has its own heartbeat and is screaming *Get me the hell out of here.* I lean closer to the radio because there has to be a logical reason for the static. This car is so old, maybe a fuse blew. Coincidentally, tonight. There has to be a station on here that works.

WHOMP.

My face smashes into the dashboard, and my body snaps back, flinging my head into the seat. It's like a brick wall grew from the pavement. We're stopped on the road. Pain radiates from behind my eyes through my cheeks, and it's the law of the universe that a car will hit something the exact moment your face is positioned to receive the maximum damage.

"Holy shit!" Fiona pulls onto the gravel shoulder and puts on the hazards. "Oh my god, Nick!" She's staring at me as if I took an arrow to the chest or something. I feel my chest. No arrow or other protruding objects.

"You okay?" I groan.

She touches her face and pats herself down. "Yeah, yes, but your face."

I pull down the vanity mirror. Blood gushes from my nose. It ain't pretty, but I've had worse.

"I think we hit something," she says in a panic, scanning the road.

"Thank god. I thought it was a force field from the underworld." My sleeve is already saturated with blood. I dig around for tissues before the entire car looks like it's been through a horror-movie car wash. Fi reaches into the back and pulls McDonald's napkins from the floor. She starts piling them on my lap. I could literally bleed out, and we'd have enough McDonald's napkins to cover it. The bleeding slows to a trickle.

"Did you see anything?" she asks.

These questions, honestly. I smile. I can't help myself. "I did. I just didn't say anything. Thought this would be more fun."

Fiona does not smile. "What if it was a person?" She unbuckles her seatbelt and gets out of the car, which means I have to unbuckle mine and go after her.

"This isn't 'Silent Hill,' Fi. It wasn't a person."

She scans the roadside and walks deeper into the endless fog behind us. I go to the front to check out the car. The headlights shine bright in my eyes. There's a small dent in the fender. And blood. When I look up, I can't see Fiona, and what could possibly be more dangerous than *driving* in fog?

"Fiona!" I jog until she comes into view. "This," I call out. "*This* is how people get killed!"

She stops, and her whole body stiffens.

Something's wrong.

Soft, raspy breaths float through the darkness and grow louder the closer I get. The fog unfurls itself from a fur-covered mass in the middle of the road—definitely not a person.

"I think it's a dog. Or a wolf," she says.

"Right now, it's not much of anything."

She elbows me in the ribs. "Don't say that."

Against my better judgment, I take a few steps closer, wishing I had a bat or a pipe. What if it's faking it, waiting for us to get close enough for one last hurrah? When I'm about three feet away, it growls. "Definitely not a dog." I glance back at Fi. There's nothing we can do. Its stomach rises and falls with a stutter. Fi doesn't move, so I give her arm a soft tug. "This happens all the time. It's not your fault."

Like plane crashes and explosions.

"We're just going to leave it?"

There's sadness in her voice and a hint of anger. And I get it. The urge to do something. The need to make this better. The refusal to accept this helplessness. I get all of it. There are a thousand things I can say to her. *He's gone, Fi. This is dangerous. I would do anything for you except drag a wolf to the edge of the road. We can't even end its suffering and even if we could, neither of us would.*

But all I say is, "Yeah, we are."

She follows me back to the car, turning back one last time.

We drive in silence. The fog is finally lifting, and a soft rain rattles against the roof. The radio works now, but I flick it off. A few miles down the road, a recycling truck roars from behind us and passes in the oncoming lane. If the wolf wasn't dead when we left it, there's no doubt about its fate now. I don't look at Fi. Don't have to, I know what she's thinking. None of this feels real.

An endless blur of trees fills my view. "Maybe the pack leader came out of the forest and pulled it to safety. Maybe there's like a wolf shaman who will heal his wounds overnight."

She lets my words sink in and faces me. "Did you just happy ending the wolf?"

I meet her eyes for a fleeting second. "Yeah. I think I did."

Fiona

I killed a wolf. A living, breathing animal. There's no way it survived, but in my mind, I needed it to. Delusional Fiona is the only one who has a shot at being functional, so I'm holding on to Nick's pack-leader-dragging-it-off-the-road story. Sometimes, I think he only does the happy endings for me, but I know he needs them just as much.

When we pull into the driveway, his house is dark as usual. I turn off the car, and we sit in the silence. Rain softly patters against the roof.

"I should head back."

Nick's eyes meet mine. "You can't drive in this."

I actually could drive in this, but it sounds like enough of a reason, so I text Dad.

The second we step into his house, Nick makes a beeline for the kitchen and fishes through a cupboard. He pulls out a bottle of bourbon and raises it—a question. I vigorously nod, and he pours two shots, already throwing his back as he slides the other toward me. I don't like bourbon. I'm not a big drinker, but right now, this seems like an excellent idea, so I down the shot and contort my face in a hundred horrific ways. It's so gross.

Nick nods at my phone. "No reply?"

"Nights," I say. "It'll be a while."

"Right." He turns on the faucet and splashes his face with water, rinsing off the blood. "Fuck this hurts."

"Is it broken?"

"No." He pinches his nose. "Don't think so."

"Let me see."

He comes over, and I cup his chin in my hand, running my other thumb down the side of his nose.

"Ow." He winces. "Do you even know what you're looking for?"

Our eyes meet, and my heart flickers. For a second, I forget he's talking about his nose. I refocus on his bruise. "Nope."

He pulls his face from my grasp. "Come on! I thought you knew some kind of ambulance trick."

"Why would I know ambulance tricks? I have a direct line, though, if you want." I pour myself another shot, and Nick eyes me, knowing this is wildly out of character.

"I think I'm good." He wipes his hands on the kitchen towel and flings it over the sink. "Movie?"

"Too depressing."

"How is a movie depressing?"

"It's too quiet. I need noise. You know what we should do? Karaoke."

"I don't have karaoke."

"I do! On my phone. It's an app." I hoist my phone and shake it around, heading for the living room with my drink. "I can cast it. You have that thing."

"I don't know what you're talking about."

"You know, that thing! On the TV!"

He leans against the doorframe, still shaking his head as if he has a choice. "No, I don't ... no ... "

I turn on the TV and open my karaoke app. May and I used to do this all the time at her house before Mom's accident. "Oh yeah, this is happening."

He throws back his head in resignation. "Fine! But we're going to need a lot more alcohol."

When he comes out of the kitchen, he's carrying the bottle, a soup ladle, and a wooden spoon.

"What's this for?" I ask as he hands me the ladle.

He crinkles his eyes mischievously. "Microphones, obviously."

We burn through all the hits, Beyoncé, Harry Styles, and by the time we hit the Ramones, Nick starts to get into it. Maybe it's the irresistible beats of "I Wanna Be Sedated," or he's just that wasted. I stopped drinking after the second shot, but Nick kept going. He's got a great voice—deep and smooth, and it has this soothing quality. It's the sound of him that gets me every time. Like he could totally land a job as one of those bedtime podcast narrators if the whole writing thing doesn't work out.

We're sitting on the floor, leaning against the couch, legs stretched out in front of us. At some point, he put a sweatband around his head, and his hair sticks out in every direction. A Sabrina Carpenter song comes on, and he smacks his wooden spoon against the floor.

"You tapping out?" I laugh.

"This one's all you, Fi," he says, and I don't even need to read the lyrics, I know them by heart, so I sing them to Nick. He throws his head back in a burst of laughter at how hard I attack this song, but the laughter quickly fades, and his gaze intensifies, giving the lyrics new weight, where there was none before. I probably should have realized that singing about hooking up with a cute guy with wide blue eyes to an actual cute guy with wide blue eyes *might* be a little extra, but that's what two shots will do to me.

The song ends, and I keep my eyes focused on the screen, feeling heat singe my cheeks. I won't look at him. The next song will cancel out this awkwardness. Except the next song is "Love on the Brain," which is the music equivalent of dimming the lights and filling the room with a hundred candles, so the awkwardness intensifies.

I make a move for my phone to skip the song, but he beats me to it and slides it away. It ends up under the wooden coffee table. Neither of us is singing. I lean back, letting my head flop against the couch, and he does the same. The music reverberates through the room like a private concert meant for two. Our hands are inches apart on the floor.

He nudges my foot. I roll my head to face him, and his steady blue eyes lock with mine. My mind empties, and my heart beats faster. He leans in closer, so I do, too—our lips, a breath apart.

The front door swings open and voices flood the room. We jolt apart.

His dad walks in, with a woman behind him. They're dressed up, holding hands, and partly unbuttoned as if this is the end of a date.

When my brain starts to work again, and I know we're not about to be murdered, I scramble to the coffee table and dive my hand underneath, searching for my phone. It's embarrassing how long it takes, but the music finally stops. The room falls silent.

This must be Brooklyn. She's the first to break the silence with a sweet "Hi!" and a little wave. She seems nice enough but oblivious that she's standing in the midst of an active volcano, ready to blow.

Nick's dad is tall and fit, with salt-and-pepper streaks running through his long, sandy-brown hair. You can tell he's successful by the way he carries himself, with that rich guy arrogance. Nick is almost his carbon copy, minus the ugly qualities.

He assesses the room—alcohol, sweatbands, kitchen utensils, Nick's face. "Jesus. What happened to you?"

Nick surveys the mess, trying to figure out what he's talking about. I touch my nose until he gets it. "Ohhh," he says, fighting a smile. "I fell."

His dad picks up the bourbon cap from the floor and turns it in his hand. Maybe we will be murdered after all, but he seems to make a decision to not let this ruin his night and pulls Brooklyn forward. "Brook, you remember Nick, and this is his friend, Fiona." The way he says *friend* is thick with condescension. He's never been my biggest fan. I get the feeling he thinks I'm a bad influence because Nick and I met in group, and he considers everyone there to be messed up. And okay, fair, we have our issues, but to his dad, *I* am the issue.

I wave to Brooklyn and give her an awkward smile. Nick doesn't budge from the floor and pulls at the carpet fibers. "I thought you were away again this weekend."

"Change of plans," his dad answers. "I did text you." He pulls Brooklyn toward the stairs. "Why don't we get out of your way."

"Sorry, we interrupted. Nice to meet you, Fiona." Brooklyn's voice trails from the staircase.

It's like Hiroshima happened in the living room.

Nick jumps to his feet and bolts for the door. I follow him outside, and he throws up over the porch railing into the perfectly landscaped rosebush below. "And that's how you do a Saturday night." He wipes his mouth with the sleeve not covered in blood.

"I think you're going to have to burn that shirt," I say. "You should've aimed for his truck."

"Nooo." His face falls as if it's the world's biggest missed opportunity. "Any chance you have to barf?"

"Not yet . . . but give me a minute. There could be a sympathy-barf situation happening."

He gives me a sad smile. I know his heart is breaking. "I don't think I can go back in there."

"Maybe we don't have to. Don't move."

I head inside to get him a glass of water, and wonder if I imagined what almost happened between us in the living room. He probably won't even remember it by tomorrow.

Wish I could say the same. I take a drink from his glass then search through the freezer, fishing out a bag of frozen peas because he should put something on his nose. I pop out and hand both to him, trying to act casual. "But there's more," I tease, ducking inside again.

I pull off the couch cushions, and when he sees me coming, he opens the screen door and takes them from me, dragging them to the porch swing to use as a makeshift bed. He flops on the swing and closes his eyes.

"Back in a sec." I consider grabbing a fresh shirt from his room but don't want to go upstairs, so I open the hall closet and find a burgundy hoodie. Then I grab the floral crochet throw from the sofa, and I freeze.

Nick's phone is on the coffee table.

It's sitting right there. *May.* Damnit. She got into my head with all of her notes folder talk. I glance at the door. There's a solid chance he's passed out by now. Even if he isn't, there's no way he's coming back in. A mini-war wages in my head.

Do it. Don't do it.

I drop the hoodie and blanket and grab the phone. My heart races at the thought of getting caught. It's password-protected, but I've watched him do this a million times. I type 1216, Max's birthday, and the home screen opens.

I go for the texts first, noticing one unread message. It's from his dad; nothing exciting there. I'm next on the list, followed by Alex, Max, and a foreman from his dad's landscaping company. I scroll to the bottom and find some old texts from his mom. The last one she sent was exactly what he told everyone. "Don't fuck up the house." It's followed by "xoxoxoxoxo," which he conveniently left out.

My chest feels heavy again.

The time on my snooping clock is rapidly expiring, so I go back to his home screen and scroll through the icons until I spot it. The notes folder. There are a ton of files. Easily forty. I quickly scroll through the headings—story related, appointment-related, work addresses. There's a list of gift ideas for Max, one with random facts about Brazil . . . something about monkeys?

One stands out.

Mom. 12:42pm, Dec 12. Blue button-up with white stripes, jeans rolled at the cuff, black flats, gold watch.

Understanding soaks in. This was the last time he saw his mom. It's a total gut punch. My next thought is *Why didn't I do this?* And now I'm thinking about what Mom was wearing the last day I saw her, and I don't remember. I don't remember.

The swing creaks outside, and I close the folder.

Why did I do that? Did I really think he was going to use his notes folder as a journal? Okay, yes, I did. I just had to know if he wrote anything about me in this supposed sacred space where he writes all the important stuff.

Maybe I'm not the important stuff.

I regather everything and go outside. He's stretched out across the swing, and it sways gently under him. His eyes are closed. I drop everything beside him and squeeze onto the opposite end, covering us with the blanket. When I look up, his eyes are open, and he's watching me.

"You don't have to do this. You don't have to sleep out here."

"I love sleeping outside." It's a lie. The only outdoors I like is the beach. My room and I, we're real tight.

"Bullshit," he mumbles. He peels off his filthy shirt, tossing it on the porch, and all of a sudden, there's a half-naked Nick in front of me.

He's searching for the opening to the hoodie, so it gives me a second to study him. His shoulders are broad, his arms lean but toned with new definition from all the work he's been doing for his dad. A faint red line is streaked under his rib cage. It's hard to see in the porch light, but I think it's scar. He catches me staring, so I refocus on the blanket, smoothing it out as if it's urgent business, as he pulls the hoodie over his head.

"Was that a scar?" I ask casually as if I was nit-picking his body and not *appreciating* it.

"Oh. Yeah." He lifts the hoodie on the left side and proudly shows me. "Jellyfish sting. Florida trip with Mom and Alex."

I nod.

"I've been told scars are sexy," he says with a bit of swagger as he lowers the fabric.

"By who?" I snort as if the suggestion is lame and feel instantly guilty.

But seriously. By who?

He doesn't answer. He only lies back, pulling the blanket tighter.

"Hey." I gently nudge his leg. "Do you believe all that stuff you said to Grace tonight? Like not believing in happiness?"

"Honestly?" His voice is a deep, sleepy haze.

"Always."

"I don't know. What the hell do I know, Fi? All I know is there's an ache inside." He hits his chest with a closed fist. "And it doesn't ever leave. It's like, you laugh right, and something's funny for ten minutes, and then it's back again, and I don't even know if it's grief anymore or something else. I don't know how to make it go away."

"Yeah." Dad called Nick a black hole once, but it's mostly how I feel, like a giant void. "Put the peas on your nose."

He gives me a half smile, reaches for the bag beside him and drops it on his face.

"Are you doing anything next Friday?" I ask.

"Why?" He mumbles from under the bag.

"I was invited to a party."

"Congratulations."

"And I'm inviting you."

"Why?"

"Because I don't want to go by myself."

"Then why are you going at all?"

"It might be fun."

He moves the bag away from his nose and gives me his bullshit look.

"May's been all over me about going out. She thinks it's weird I stay home all the time."

He reaches for the glass of water on the porch and takes a sip. "Do you really care what May thinks?"

"Ugh. Stop therapizing me." I poke his waist with my foot, and he sputters a laugh, pushing it away. "It's an easy yes or no."

"Of course, I'll go. Friends help friends with bullshit."

"Always."

"Now that's quotable," he says, reaching for his phone. He unlocks it, opens his notes, and starts to type because we're friends and that's what's important.

Fiona

A coffee grinder whirrs from inside the house, and it's loud enough to wake the dead, but Nick is still fast asleep. His leg dangles from the porch swing, his head is horribly contorted, and his nose all black and blue.

My body is a fantastic cocktail of sleep deprivation combined with a slight hangover. The swing was beyond uncomfortable. The cushions fell off overnight and are scattered across the porch, and Nick's gross shirt is covered in ants. My back is throbbing as I peel myself from the swing. I watch him sleep for another minute before shaking his leg until his eyes flutter open.

"I'm going," I whisper.

He rubs his eyes. Cupboards slam from inside. I'm guessing Brooklyn is still learning her way around the kitchen.

"What? No . . . stay."

"No, I need a bed. I need *my* bed. I'm so tired."

"Come on. Don't make me small talk with Brooklyn," he moans.

"You'll be fine. You're good at small talk." I pat his shoulder as I make my way to the stairs.

Thankfully, I left my bag in my car, and the keys are inside, so I can escape without having to see his dad again.

Nick follows me down the driveway. In the morning light, I get a good look at my bumper. It's dented, all right. Great.

Nick takes it in and squeezes my shoulder. "Now it has character."

I eye him. "Kind of like your face."

The bruising is so much worse this morning, spreading under his eyes. Yesterday was an accident, but I still feel terrible. I cup his cheek in my hand, and he presses deeper into it. Even with the bruises, his blue eyes shine.

"I'll be fine," he says softly.

"Put some ice on it."

He keeps his eyes on mine. I swallow and slide my hand away.

"It's not that bad," he says, checking out the bumper again. "Think of it as a keepsake to remember last night."

When I open my door, I swear there's a gamey smell. "I don't want to remember the wolf." I quickly get in and hit the buttons to roll down the windows.

Nick reaches up in a stretch and yawns, which makes me yawn, too. "Don't fall asleep. Text me when you get home okay?"

"I will."

He stays in the driveway as I pull out, probably thinking of a way to get inside without being seen.

My car feels like the Ritz after last night. I turn up the radio, hoping it will be the fuel I need to keep me awake for the drive home.

The trees along the side road glisten with morning dew. Everything looks animé, all the colors supersaturated. Once I reach the stretch of road where I hit the wolf, I slow down, searching for any sign of it, but there is none—no fur on the road, no bloodstains, no trace of it anywhere. It's like it vanished. A town worker must have removed it. The rational part of me knows this, but maybe that wolf is running through these trees, bathed in the glow of morning light, healed and alive. The Nick part of me wants to believe—to cling to the hope that some kind of magic still exists in this world.

The house is empty. I throw my keys on the console by the door and find a plate of banana muffins on the kitchen table, with Mom's Martha Stewart cookbook beside them. She never used it. I guess Dad's moved from reading fiction to cookbooks now. My eyes are already closing on my way up the stairs. I need to steal a few hours of sleep just so I can function. When I'm in bed, I text Nick.

Home

So tired

Sleep now no wolf

Nick: ?? night

He answered. I thought for sure he'd be sleeping. I type out a quick reply:

Night

love you

I drop the phone on my nightstand, and my face hits the pillow.

My eyes spring open.

WHAT? Tell me that didn't just happen. I grab my phone and stare at the text. It's there, all right.

Night

love you

The text echoes a million times in my head. "Love you?!" I shout across the room. Oh. No. Nononono. What did I do? It was a reflex. Something I text to Dad or May but not to Nick. Never to Nick. *It doesn't mean anything,* I want to scream. The words magnify the longer I look at them. Unsend. Of course! I can unsend, but it's too late. The message shows as 'read.' I wait and wait . . . and nothing happens. No three dots dance across my screen. He isn't replying.

This isn't happening.

I text:

haha now you know I'm tired

And delete it. Then I press on an emoji laughing face and delete that, too. Texting anything will only make it worse. *Don't make it worse, Fiona.*

He must have clicked off his phone or fallen asleep *in the twenty seconds since his last reply.* I roll my eyes. There's no way he's sleeping, so I die a thousand deaths staring at this text, wishing I could suck it out of cyberspace.

But it's okay, it's just Nick. This isn't a big deal. I push my phone to the far end of my nightstand as if it's toxic. My head sinks into my pillow, but my eyes are still open wide.

Because this could be a huge deal. This could ruin everything.

Nick

I came in through the bathroom window—climbed the trellis, hopped over to the eavestrough, slid open the window, and squeezed all six feet of me through like some kind of human fro-yo machine. Those were the hoops I jumped through to avoid breakfast banter with Brooklyn.

But I can't sleep. Instead, I think about Brooklyn downstairs, replacing the last of Mom's fingerprints in the kitchen with her own. I think about the lawsuit. Fiona. My fucking driving test.

Mom.

All these thoughts race around my head, and it's like chasing a tireless white rabbit on a track. I thought about going to the crash site after grad. Not seriously, but it became a light switch in my mind that I couldn't stop flicking. Go. Don't go. Go. Don't go. Ultimately, it was easier to turn it off, to let the thought fade into the darkness, except I wasn't sure where that left me.

Her bucket list is in the same place Fi left it. I pull it free and read it—again. It's not even ambitious. Visit the Grand Canyon and go to a Keith Urban concert in San Diego? It's all so random. That's not a bucket list. That's get me the hell out of Oregon.

She started it after Alex left. She and Dad were constantly arguing about Alex taking off for sometimes weeks on end and leaving Max with them. Dad said Alex needed to take responsibility and that this was their time, but he was consumed by the business, so it's not like he was around. Still, he pressured Mom until she finally caved and agreed to kick Alex and Max out. Mom was different after they left. Then came the bucket list.

She was on her way to number five—the Jane Goodall experience in South America. Follow Jane's footsteps and let the wildlife touch your soul.

But the first half? I don't even think she did half that shit. I bet she crossed off one through three every weekend while driving to the nearest outlet mall and checking into the Westin for a few days. Anywhere was better than here.

Dad surprised her with the plane ticket—that's the kicker. First class no less. I guess he saw the list as an opportunity for freedom, too, except he needed more than a weekend. He needed a whole week, and wouldn't you know he went away on business the same week of her trip.

At the time, I paid no attention to any of this. It meant having the house to myself after school and a week of parties. I was the king of my castle. My parents were gone, and

I didn't care where they were. It wasn't until I had nothing but time on my hands that I started connecting the dots.

Jane Goodall didn't even work in South America, she worked in Africa, which makes me think Mom never had this great passion for her work. She typed her name into a search engine and wrote down the first tour option that popped up, probably choosing it because South America was closer.

This is what grief looks like. It's not sitting in a pile of clothes in her room. It's googling Jane Goodall and plane crashes for months on end as if there's an answer I can find in the search results.

Jane Goodall named one of her chimpanzees Frodo.

I imagine the view was spectacular, looking down at the jungle from thirty-five thousand feet.

I imagine the fall was not.

Or maybe she never got on that plane. Maybe she's tucked into a Westin heavenly bed somewhere watching "Dateline" with some chocolate-covered strawberries just happy to be rid of us.

I don't understand why she took that trip. Why she couldn't get divorced like a normal person? Dwelling on the whys only leads to a mountain of heartache. Was it me? Was I too difficult? It's easy to text XO, but how can you say you love someone and do this to them?

I'm glad she died—fuck her.

And I don't need to go to South America. I don't need to yell from a mountain to hear my echo. I can do it from my room, right here, like it's always been.

My phone buzzes. I know it's Fi without even looking, and since my eyes are already closed, I almost ignore it, but what if she was in an accident or something?

Home

So tired

Sleep now no wolf

I have no idea what she's talking about. The one we hit? But I'm glad she's home. I text back:

?? night

Fiona: Night

love you

I sit up. Wide awake.

I reread it three times to make sure I'm not missing an "I" in front. No, "I," just "love you." It feels casual, but still . . . it's there. The words exist where they haven't before.

I'm about to type it back, but stop because I'm not the kind of guy who does that. If I type it back, especially after last night, it means something, and she'll know. Texting it just feels wrong.

So, I put my phone down, close my eyes and try to pretend I didn't see it.

Fiona

Dad comes into the kitchen dressed for work and peeks at the frozen pizza bubbling inside the oven. I'm sitting on the counter, compulsively checking my phone like I've been doing all week.

I haven't heard from Nick in five days. The worst part is picking up my phone every two minutes and seeing my "love you" text staring back at me. I could delete it, but it will still be on his end, so what's the point?

It hasn't been *that* long. But post love-you text Fiona is paranoid, because we've never gone this long without texting. Is he being weird, or am I?

Jaden's party is tonight, and I don't even know if he's still coming. I can't take a second more of this torture, so I cave and text him.

Hey

"I think it's ready." Dad slides the pizza out and drops it on top of the stove, eyeing me. "You know phones make sounds when texts come in."

I force myself to drop my phone on the counter. "Good one."

"Cut me a slice for the road?"

I scoot down from the counter and scorch my fingers as I snip through the gooey mess. I doctored the pizza with extra cheese and olives: my special creation. A quarter of the pie breaks free.

Dad tears off a piece of paper towel, and I drop the slice on top. Then he steals some of the olives from another piece to put on his. He catches me checking my phone—again. "Everything okay?"

"Yeah. I'm going to a party tonight. Just waiting for the details."

"A party?" He takes a bite of the slice but can barely chew it because it must be a thousand degrees.

"With May. It's a work thing. It's nothing," I mumble, trying to sound like I don't care.

"It's never nothing if May's going to be there." Dad's all too familiar with May's drama. She'll share it with anyone who will listen. "Call if you need me to pick you up."

"Dad, you're working."

"So call 911, and they'll dispatch me."

I roll my eyes. "I'm not drinking."

He kisses me on the forehead and wipes the pizza grease on his pants. "Didn't ask."

Dad says this all the time, as if he's cool for not asking when the reality is he doesn't need to. My responsibility is always a safe bet.

He opens the freezer, pulls out one of the banana muffins he baked last week and heads for the door with the rest of his pizza.

"See ya," I call out.

The door closes. The empty kitchen is so quiet I can hear the clock ticking. Mom's camera is still in the box on the counter, and Nick hasn't answered me. My Jenga tower of a life grows taller by the day. Avoidance is all around me.

My phone vibrates.

Nick: Yo

Finally. It took him long enough. I text him back four times in a row.

You

still

coming

tonight?

Yes, it's lame, but the love-you text had to go.

Nick: Of course—if you still want me to

Why is this so awkward? I'm hyper-aware of my words.

Me: Yeah! Pick you up in an hour?

Nick: Text me the address

I'll Uber and save you the drive

Me: Cool

Since when does he turn down a ride? Usually, I'd say *Stop, I'll pick you up,* but post love you that might be coming on too strong. Post love-you texting sucks.

All of my hard work doctoring this pizza only made it taste ten percent less like cardboard. I eat it, leaning over the counter, and send him Jaden's address.

449 Chalmers Street

Meet you at 9?

He thumbs up my text box, and I hate that.

The party starts in an hour.

I swap my sweats for jeans and slip on one of my nicer black T-shirts. My hair is a mess of tangles, and brushing it only makes it hang lifeless around my face, so I rope it into a high ponytail, hoping it makes me seem pulled together.

It rained this afternoon, and the air still holds that thick kind of moisture that makes you feel sweaty just walking through it. It's that weird temperature where it's warm and cool at the same time, so I toss a sweater in my car, just in case. It's a bit early to leave, but I don't want Nick to get there before me.

Jaden shares a bungalow in an older part of town with two college juniors. They have parties most weekends, so this is hardly a special event. I don't ever go, and thankfully he stopped inviting me, but he was extra pushy about the invite for this one. He's definitely hoping for another shot with May.

The house is easy to spot. Cars line the street, and the front yard is scattered with people holding Solo cups. I find a place to park three blocks away and walk back.

On my way down the sidewalk, I see Nick.

He's standing at the base of the driveway, his hands buried in his jean pockets. He's wearing a navy T-shirt, and his hair's wet like he just showered. The last time I saw him, he was covered in blood and barf, so this is a one-eighty. He spots me and waves, walking over to meet me. Faint bruises still hang under his eyes from the accident.

"Hey! That's looking better." I instinctively raise my hand to touch him, but catch myself and lower it.

"Yeah. It's getting there." He tilts his head, studying my ponytail, which I'm now regretting.

It's strange being here with him, doing something apparently normal people do. I kick at the dirt on the sidewalk like a grade schooler. "You ready for the time of your life?"

"Yes." He smiles. "When does that occur?"

I shrug. "No idea. Definitely not here, though."

We weave through the crowd and head up the worn wooden stairs to the front door, opening nonstop from people going in and out. The house is dim inside and reeks of weed. The rooms are aglow in different colors—the living room, purple, while aqua blue shines from the hall. Music pulsates from every direction. At least I won't have to worry about talking.

"Fi!" May calls out from the middle of the living room.

Nick is following so closely behind me that he walks straight into me when I stop. He grips my shoulders and my whole body tenses. He leans close, his mouth next to my ear: "Sorry," he says.

My heart flip-flops. I'm so glad I'm not facing him.

May's the center of attention, wearing a cropped halter top and a long pink pleated skirt. Her curled hair falls in beachy waves around her shoulders. Who curls their hair for a house party? She hurries over excitedly with a wine spritzer in her hand, and by the time she crosses the room, she has two, effortlessly sliding one into Nick's hand.

"You must be Nick," she yells, leaning in close to his ear.

"Nick. May," I say as I wave my hand between them in a lazy introduction.

"Nice to meet you," Nick says as May rakes her eyes over him.

"You too! I can't believe it's taken this long. I've heard so much about you. So you guys met at that place—the grief thing, right?"

"Yeah, the grief thing." Nick's radio voice takes over, answering like this is a red-carpet interview, and he's used to answering stupid questions.

"Cool. So, what happened to your mom?" May yells.

She yells it.

Blood drains from my face. I open my mouth, but I'm speechless. Did she really ask that in a crowded room of people partying while Cardi B blares from the speakers? She's even dancing in blissful oblivion while she waits for an answer.

But Nick doesn't break a sweat, he's smirking. "I'm sorry, what?" he asks, as if she'll hear how awful it sounds if she has to repeat it.

Which is not happening. "May!" I try to convey my massive disappointment through my bulging eyes. "You met him ten seconds ago!"

She's instantly defensive. "What? I thought you guys talked about that stuff all the time?"

"We're at a party!"

Nick is still figuring out how to play this. Classic Nick would say *Fuck you,* and walk away. And the words are there, in his eyes, but he holds them back, his wheels turning. "It's okay. I'm surprised you don't know. I mean, you two are close, right?"

Now May sets her sights on me like I've been holding out on some scandalous secret. "Are you kidding? Fi's my best friend. It just never came up."

And it never will. I guard his loss like it's my own. Now he knows. He faces me, new solidarity in his eyes. "I don't like to talk about it, but she was eaten by a tiger."

May leans back, her mouth falling open. She's not buying it and gives him a squinty-eyed stare. "Oh, come on."

All I can do is buckle up for the ride because once he starts down this path, there's no stopping him.

"It's true. It was an albino tiger. They're almost extinct, which is why she went to see them. The tigers."

May darts her eyes between us. Considering she's the queen of crazy stories, this must be a huge turn-on for her. "Is he for real?" she asks me.

I nod, keeping a straight face.

"For real?" she repeats to Nick.

He nods solemnly.

Nick has several versions of his mom's death, always at the ready, depending on who asks. He uses them like armor. The tiger story gets the best reactions. In another version, it was a scuba diving accident, and when he really doesn't want to talk about it, he goes with a car accident. There's zero interest in car accidents. He sells them all like a pro.

"Shit! That's . . . that's crazy!" She gasps. "You know that actually happened to my grandma's brother."

Of course, it did. Nick catches my eye. He raises an eyebrow.

"They were camping overseas. They went for a hike and walked right into a Siberian. It like jumped out of the bushes and grabbed him. Then a ranger came by and shot it, but I mean fucking tigers, right?" Her hand lands on his shoulder. I zero in on it.

Body contact.

"Fucking tigers," Nick says with a smile.

They clink their bottles together in a toast.

"So, why don't you ever come out with us?" May asks, dodging a fresh wave of people spilling into the living room.

"Never been asked," Nick says, directing his answer to me.

"That's not true," I say.

"It's factually true. Anyway, I live kind of far out, and it's a pain in the ass coming into town."

"You don't drive?"

Here we go. He's about to lose some cool points.

"Not at the moment."

"How'd you get here then?" May genuinely doesn't understand how anyone can get by without a car.

"Uber'd."

"Oh, cool."

The conversation volleys between them, and I feel like a referee, trying to figure out where Nick's responses will land him in May's rankings.

May touches his arm when she laughs. She's flirting like her life depends on it. The gap in our circle is closing, and I'm becoming the odd one out, the third wheel. My brain short circuits. Who is he right now? This confident, composed, borderline flirtatious guy beside me. Is this the real Nick, or is May that irresistible to every guy alive?

Or maybe he's just being nice, and I'm completely paranoid.

"So, what do you do? You're done with high school, too, right?" she asks him.

"Yeah. I work for my dad's landscaping company."

"Can we maybe lay off the twenty questions?" I interrupt.

May flicks her hair away from her neck. Again. "How else am I supposed to get to know him? Hey, you should come to USC with us so we can all hang out next year."

Nick's smile fades. He turns to me. "I thought we were set on New York for school?"

Now May's looking at me. "New York? Since when? You didn't tell me that."

This. *This* is why I don't mix boxes. I haven't told May about New York, because I'll never hear the end of it. I shrug so hard my shoulders go up to my ears. "I don't know. I'm still deciding." I lie. I'm definitely going to New York.

"That should only take about a hundred years," May says, taking a drink from her bottle.

Nick narrows his eyes at her. "So, then it takes a hundred years."

I blink at him in surprise. May steps back and raises her hands as if to say chill, and I never thought I'd be so relieved to see Jaden bound across the room. He grabs May from behind and lifts her into the air. "Hey, May-fair lady."

"Put me down." She swings her arms, trying to break free from his death grip.

Jaden lets her go, raising his hand high to Nick, confidently bro-fiving him. "What's up?"

May loops her arm through Nick's before he can answer. "I'm stealing you. Give me a chance to apologize," she says, pulling him away. "And I want to show him the wading pool," she calls out to me over her shoulder.

It happens too fast to stop her, and now I'm stuck here with Jaden. He seems as thrilled about it as I am.

We watch them fade from our view. Jaden eyes Nick as if he's competition, which is ridiculous. "That a friend of yours?"

"Yeah, but you don't have anything to worry about." I dismissively wave toward their path. "Nothing's happening there."

He reaches for a beer from a bucket of ice on the console table behind me. "You sure about that?"

And suddenly, I'm not. My pulse quickens. "Pretty sure."

"I'm not trying to stir shit up. I was just hoping she might give me another shot tonight, and you know how she gets when she wants something," he says, cracking open the can.

It's true, May can be relentless, but I saw the way she was staring after Jaden last week. "I don't know. I think you two will work things out."

"Really?"

I nod, and he brightens, unable to keep the smile from his face. He gazes out at the crowd in a daze as if he's playing out the rest of their summer together in his mind. "Want something to eat?" he asks, as if suddenly remembering I'm still there. "Or a drink? There's Jell-O shots in the kitchen, best of both worlds."

I can't help myself. "Yeah. They're almost as good as meatloaf."

Jaden bobs his head absentmindedly until it hits him. He slowly turns toward me, realization in his eyes.

The front door bursts open, and two guys in letterman jackets bound through, calling out to him. I push back into the crowd, trying to cover my laugh with my hand and head for the nearly empty kitchen. The fridge is jam-packed with beer and wine coolers, so nothing for me. I pass on the picked over bowls of chips and decide to check the backyard for May and Nick.

A fire pit rages at the far end, and the air is rich with the strong scent of woodsmoke. It's almost peaceful out here. A small inflatable kiddie pool rests on the grass, but I don't think it's filled with water because people keep dunking their plastic cups into it. So that's the wading pool she was dying to show him.

A few girls I know from school are standing around it and spot me on the lawn. They wander over, surprised to see me, and it takes forever to cycle through the hugs. They act like nothing sad ever happened to me, and it's a role I'm so used to playing, I almost believe it, too. They catch me up on the latest gossip, and when I ask if they've seen May, they point toward the side gate with a warning to "Hurry before she disappears into a room with the hot guy."

They laugh, and I laugh with them.

I make my way to the front yard. The crowd is borderline out of control, but I still can't see Nick or May.

A sea of people are having fun here, and it feels like I'm in another dimension—this kind of fun so far out of reach. Some girls are laughing, running circles around me, holding sparklers. It's almost as if they're laughing at me.

Why is it so hard for you to be happy, Fiona?

When I turn around, Jaden's front window becomes its own kind of picture. Nick is standing in the middle of a group, May beside him, and they're laughing hysterically over whatever animated story he's telling. It's like he doesn't even notice I'm gone.

Like he doesn't even care.

I pull my phone from my pocket and text him.

I'm leaving

This was a huge mistake. My Jenga tower might have been growing taller, but at least it was stable. Why did I have to move the pieces?

I watch them for a minute. They make it seem so easy, which means I'm the anomaly. I'm the girl who doesn't know how to be happy.

Two minutes is all I'll give him. But when they pass, I give him one more.

Then I leave.

Fiona

I'm in my pajamas, lying in bed, four songs deep into my Spotify daylist. I've washed my face and brushed my teeth, but not before finishing the rest of the cold pizza and the strawberry ice cream.

That's when his text comes. That's how long it took.

Nick: Where did you go?

I read the words again, unsure if I want to reply because if I do, I'll unleash a firestorm of rage onto the keys. He doesn't even deserve a reply. He deserves the silent treatment, but I can't help myself. I engage.

Me: I texted you

See above

Nick: I did see above

But it's not an answer

Me: Home

Nick: Why didn't you come get me?

Me: I

texted

you

Nick: Right

Because I could hear my phone in a room

with ten thousand speakers

Me: Were they playing a really funny song?

It's so petty, I roll my eyes at myself the second I send it. What am I doing?

Nick: ?? I don't get it

Me: I was sleeping

Talk later

Nick: Honestly?

Always with the honestly. Why did we ever start this?

Honestly, you're a dick.

Honestly, I've complained a million times about May, and you abandoned me for her. And yeah, maybe I didn't spell it out in the pre-party checklist, but did I really have to?

Honestly, I don't know if we should be friends.

Honestly, I don't even know who you are right now.

But I don't want him to know any of this. So, I text:

Always

On Tuesday, I do a google deep dive for gymnastic clubs in New York to take my mind off the party nightmare.

I'm hoping to land a coaching job when I get there. Two years ago, I quit competing, and thought I was done for good, but I missed it—painting my hands in chalk, the smell of worn leather on the beam, the way the fluorescent lights would flick on, one by one at six A.M. practices. So, I went back as a coach on my own terms and fell in love with it all over again. The only downside is having to deal with the parents.

I email a few places to introduce myself. My latest coaching certificate came in last week, and I search my desktop to scan it, but can't find it anywhere. I ransack my drawers, and a ton of other things turn up instead—menus from random restaurants, bottle caps, newspaper clippings from competitions. My drawers overflow with history, memories that hurt too much to think about. It all has to go, like now, so I dump everything into an empty CVS bag. The certificate has to be at the gym.

I run downstairs carrying the bag tied tight like it's trash. Dad's on the floor in front of the coffee table, putting together a model car. I wish he was still doing the baking thing. He was pretty good at it.

"Hey, have you seen any of my papers around?" There's a stack of mail on the kitchen table, and I rifle through it. Nothing of mine.

Dad doesn't take his eyes off his project. "Kind of papers?"

"For school. Work, actually."

He puts down the tube of glue and lifts his glasses. "This is new."

"Not really. Just trying to get organized." I grab the car keys from the side table. "I'm going to the gym. I think I left something in my locker."

"Okay."

Outside, I dump the bag into the garbage bin, marveling at how easy it is to erase yourself.

The gym doors slide open, and the lobby is buzzing with students. Classes have ended, and now private lessons are underway. I have Tuesdays off, so this is the last place I want to be right now, especially since May is working. We haven't talked since the party on the weekend. I spot her walking alongside a girl on the balance beam, framed perfectly by the parent viewing window, and wave my hands over my head to get her attention so she doesn't think I'm avoiding her. It works, except she freezes when she sees me, wearing a busted expression that I don't understand until the girl pivots at the end of the beam. It's Sarah, my student, and it's not our night.

This kind of thing happens all the time. When parents have a schedule conflict, they switch days, so I don't think much of it as I head for the locker room. May was giving off a strange vibe, though.

The changing room is empty. I go to my cubby and start searching under some sweats I left behind for my certificate. That's when I spot an envelope sticking out on the top shelf. It takes a few jumps before I can grab it.

The door flies open, and May hurries inside.

"Hey. What are you doing here?" she asks, hands on her hips.

"Was looking for this." I wave the envelope around. "Is that Sarah out there?"

She swallows, taking a little too long to answer. "Yeah."

"Oh. Cool. Nobody called me about the change."

"Yeahhh. Jaden was supposed to tell you." She blinks at me, and there's pity in her eyes. I brace for whatever's coming next.

"Tell me what?"

"It's more than a night change. Look, Fi. I don't know, this shouldn't come from me . . . "

"You can't not tell me now, so just tell me."

May fiddles with her earring and keeps her gaze fixed on the floor. "Sarah's Mom saw you coming out of one of those meetings at the community center."

I remember the night. She was at swimming lessons. She sprang out from around the corner, and I waved.

"I guess her mom was weirded out by it and asked if she could switch to me."

"Oh. Weirded out by what?"

"I don't know. The whole therapy thing?"

My eyes grow wide. "The whole therapy thing? Jaden ate meatloaf and gravy off your abs!"

May's cheeks burn. She whips her head around. No one's here. Her secret is safe. "I know, I know." She's pressing the air down with her hands, meaning I should shut up now. "It's not fair. It's total bullshit." She's saying the words, but she doesn't sound all that upset.

"What happened to 'yay mental health'?"

"Yeah, I think that's more like for Insta . . . and it's not just Sarah. It's Tori, Becca, and Rose, too."

I take a step back. "What? They're all switching to you? Permanently?"

"I'm so sorry."

This, I believe. Her face falls, and her eyes are sincere. "So, what? Do they think I'm crazy or something?"

May shakes her head. "I don't know. You know how insane the rumor mill is. It's stupid."

It's still not sinking in because everyone knows about my mom. It's not exactly breaking news. "Why would they hold therapy against me? Jaden has house parties every weekend, and he's the head coach!"

She shrugs. "I don't get it either, but the parents are always right, you know how it is. If you want me to turn them down, I will."

"No. Whatever. At least one of us can make some money."

"I don't care about the money, I care about you," May says.

"You should have texted me when you found out."

"I wanted to, I swear. But Jaden said it was policy that this kind of news comes from senior staff, and I don't know why I listened to him because here we are."

"It's fine. You know, I don't even care." Except I do care. A lot. Teaching these kids is one of the few bright spots in my week, and now it's being taken from me, too.

May waves me over. "Come inside with me. Let's catch up."

I follow her into the gym. Sarah's still on the balance beam practicing small jumps. I stroll by the viewing area window and make eye contact with her mom, giving her the boldest glare I can muster now that I have nothing to lose. She turns away, pretending to search for something in her purse, and it takes everything I have not to slam my fist against the window. I can see the headlines: "Crazy gym coach terrorizes parents."

"Hi, Fiona!"

I spin around. Sarah smiles from the beam, waving with both hands.

"Hey! Looking good up there!"

"May said I'm not standing straight enough." I make a *boo* face, and May swats me. "And she won't let me do walkovers."

"Looks straight to me!" I say, and Sarah proudly pulls her shoulders back even more. May and I walk alongside the beam while she practices walking backwards.

"You disappeared last weekend," May says.

"Did I? I thought you were the one who disappeared."

May doesn't get it. "Back the other way," she instructs as Sarah reaches the end of the beam.

"I was tired and went home," I say with a sigh.

She rolls her eyes. "You could've said goodbye." Then a hint of a smile plays on her lips. "I still can't believe you didn't tell me."

"Tell you what?"

"That Nick is hot."

I've been trying not to think about Nick, but it hasn't been working. "Is he?"

She nudges my arm. "Oh, come on. You know he is. Now, I get why you've been hiding him."

"Haven't been hiding him. We're equally hermits."

"I don't know, Fi, he seemed pretty sociable."

He really did.

"I think I like him." She stops walking and smiles wide like this is a big announcement, and because I'm still staring daggers at Sarah's mom, it's not computing.

"Who?"

"Earth to Fiona! Nick."

"Oh."

"Do you think, like, it would be cool if I called him?"

The cats are back. They're back, and they're multiplying. I think one's morphed into a dog and my chest might cave in. *Why is it so hot in here?* I can't breathe.

"Sorry, what was the question?"

"Can I call him?" She speaks slowly, enunciating every syllable. Her eyes are wide as she waits for my answer.

I blink. "Yeah, totally."

"You sure? You swear there's nothing going on there?"

"With Nick? No." It's like my brain has taken me hostage and is answering on autopilot.

"Because I won't call if you're into him. You have to tell me."

I scrunch up my face. "Noooo. Not into him."

"I mean, he's funny. He's got this dry sense of humor." She's actually gushing over him.

And I so don't need to hear May's keen perceptions on everything I already know about Nick.

She drones on about every second of their time together at the party and caps it off with, "I think there might have been a spark."

I trip on a piece of overlapping gym mat and try to compose myself. "A spark?" Until now, I hadn't considered this feeling might be mutual, but she's serious, her face aglow in dreamy contemplation.

"Yeah, sometimes you just *feel* it. Those seconds when eye contact is more than eye contact."

I might be having a heart attack. There's a sharp pain behind my ribs and what a way to go—studying May's features in a whole new light under the gym fluorescents. The dainty slope of her nose, the freckle on her left cheek, and her jet-black hair so silky it might sparkle. Are these the qualities that trigger sparks?

Has my loss left me sparkless?

I thought Nick and I were the same—equally sparkless, so how can he suddenly spark with someone else?

"I'm going to text him." May digs her nails into my shoulder and jumps. Sarah's mom scowls from the viewing area because her daughter's being ignored. I don't tell May. "Eeeeee, I'm so nervous. Which is crazy, right? We're too old to be nervous! So, explain to me again why nothing's ever happened with you guys?"

It's so insulting to hear it phrased that way because the truth is, everything happened with us. Everything but sparks, I guess. Before I leave, she leans into my shoulder and quietly asks, "You're sure he's not super fucked up or anything?"

What can I say to that? "Ninety-nine percent."

Her eyes light up. "One percent is super hot!"

I can't get out of there fast enough. I run through the sliding doors, and once I'm outside, it all hits me. This is all my fault. My magnificent creation. I invited Nick to that party. I gave May the green light. It's like she orchestrated the whole thing by exploiting my weaknesses, and then I served him up on a silver platter. To May. Who does that?

Once I'm in my car, I just sit there. The details for the motel booking fill my phone screen. There's no point in pretending this trip is still happening. It was never going to happen. Nick always knew I'd find a reason not to go. Maybe this whole disaster was me creating one.

It doesn't matter. He was right. I click on the link and cancel the reservation.

Nick

I'm super fucked up. Something's off with Fiona. I know it. She's shutting me out, and I don't know why. It's like I'm walking through a funhouse with mirrored walls where everything feels like it's tilted sideways.

I'm ass-deep in interlock pavers, and it's only ten in the morning. Gravel. That's what my future driveway will be. That's it.

But I can hardly blame Mrs. Sullivan for having to be here.

When I drove through her yard last winter, the ground was too cold to start landscaping repairs, so Dad promised her it would happen in the summer. He went all out, too, not just replacing the lawn and hedges I tore through but interlocking her driveway. My mistake is costing him thousands.

There's no question it's the right thing to do. Even the

judge thought it was admirable. What a wonderful human my dad is, right? But here's what gets me: he's not doing it for me or because he cares about Mrs. Sullivan. He's doing it for the publicity. What a model parent. What an honorable company. If only he put that much effort into fixing our family, but there wasn't any financial benefit to that, so why bother?

And this mistake isn't even his to own. It's mine.

I offered to work on her yard myself, but Dad robbed me of that by swooping in and making it about his company, so now I have to live with him holding it over my head. *Look at what a screwup you are. Do you know how much you're costing me? Do you even appreciate what I've done for you?*

And I do. Of course I do. But a small part of me wishes the judge would have thrown me in jail. Dad even pulled some strings and had my record expunged, and being indebted to him is a whole other life sentence.

The curtain from the front window is drawn back. Mrs. Sullivan gives me a wave from inside, and I wave back. I'll never forget the look on her face the night of the accident. It morphed from terror to disappointment, and I don't know if I'll ever forgive myself for putting it there. At least she gets interlock. So, even though I might look like the weakest link on the landscaping crew, I work twice as hard as the rest of them.

I drop a brick along the edge of the driveway when I hear a ding from my pocket. Ray, the foreman, is trying to explain the process to two new guys, so I have a second to steal a glance, hoping it's Fi.

Except, it isn't. I don't recognize the number.

971-542-0071: Is this a good time? 😇 🦝

The next text will probably be a link to a survey or a request for a charitable donation. But they don't usually use emojis.

Me: Depends

971-542-0071: It's May

Fiona's friend

We met at the party

She gave me your number 😊 🦥

I try to remember if there's anything we talked about that would warrant a follow up, but I come up empty. I'm sure there's a reason Fi gave her my number.

Me: Hey

971-542-0071: I feel like we got off on the wrong foot

Can I buy you a coffee this week and try again? 🙏 ☕

Everyone's getting back to work, and I can feel Ray's stare burning into the back of my head. I need to wrap up, whatever this is. I text back:

Sure

971-542-0071: Yay! Great! 🎉🐼🫣🙌☀️🎊

That's the last I think about it until later in the afternoon when Ray drops me off at home, and I flop into bed. May texted me the address of a coffee shop nearby. And it hits me. Is this a date?

Because I can't go on a date. I don't want to go on a date. This is exactly why I don't hang out with people because flirting is inevitable, and if you don't flirt back, you're obviously fucked up. There are no earthly reasons I can conjure to say no to her. Every excuse I can think of disintegrates before I type out the words. If I blame it on work, May will call me out on it because she knows I always have time to hang out with Fiona. Saying I'm sick is the most obvious cop-out, but right now, I am feeling pretty sick about it.

There is no room in my life for this. Alex keeps pressing me for this statement, and all Dad wants to know is that I'm over Mom, which to him would look a lot like going out with girls who aren't Fiona. I'm ninety-nine percent sure it's why I said yes.

Fiona still hasn't texted me back since the party. I want to ask her what the deal with May is, but the wrong words always come out. It's like I'm surrounded by a trip wire, and I can't move without taking the whole damn place down with me. Silence is golden for a reason.

Honestly?

I could have said no.

Honestly?

I choked.

Honestly?

I'm going to enjoy telling Dad I have a date.

Even though it isn't one.

Fiona

When my phone buzzes from the coffee table at dinner, I'm hoping it will be Jaden texting me about work. It's Wednesday, and I'm sitting on the sofa with a sad looking sandwich, and the volume on the TV turned up as loud as it'll go to make the room feel a little less empty.

May's name is on my screen when I pick it up. I hesitate before clicking on her text.

He said yes!! 🎎🃏😵😌😽✈🐦

She didn't waste any time. It reads like an answer to a marriage proposal. Before I can reply, a flurry of other texts follows.

May: What should I wear?
You like know him, know him
What does he like?
Call me so I can fill you in

What details could there be already? I want all of them. Then again, I don't.

Me: In bed
Have a fever
Text you later
May: 😢 😫 💟

It's like a landslide of toxic waste is about to wipe out my two best friends. They're goners. I can't believe she went through with it.

So there it is. Nick and May are about to be—a thing?

Lies can snowball so quickly when people give you a few prompts. When I tell Jaden I'm too sick to come in on Friday, the snowball grows like this:

May: Fi, are you okay?
Jaden said you're on your deathbed
Me: No deathbed
Sick though
Sleeping
May: Do you have mono or something?
Me: Ha! No
Sore throat
May: Strep?

Bingo.

Me: Yeah, you know how I always get that 😕
May: Sounds like someone needs a sick
package!

We've been doing this for years. When one of us is sick, the other drops off a bag of junk. It seems like the only upside to our friendship materializes when I'm contagious.

Me: No, seriously

Don't want you to catch anything

So there it is. I'm home with strep throat.

Dad brings up a CVS bag a few hours later and drops it on my bed. He knows what it is. I pull my headphones down, expecting him to say something, but he doesn't. He seems to recognize this as a whole other level of friend drama that he wants no part of.

I chirp a super happy "Thanks!" and wait for the door to close before dumping the contents. Gummy bears, chips, gossip magazines, cough drops, and ginger ale—a warm hug in the form of junk food. Sweet. I tear open the gummy bears and toss the cough drops in my nightstand drawer. I'll get sick eventually, anyway.

It's already Saturday, and May hasn't texted. She always needs to be in a constant conversation, so if it's not happening with me, it must be happening with someone else.

Nick.

The only thing that goes my way is getting an email from Grace. She canceled tonight's meeting because something came up, and I am beyond relieved.

My phone buzzes on the bed.

Nick: Hey

Can we talk?

What does he want to talk about? May?

I don't reply. I don't have it in me to pretend to be happy, or normal, or anything. I'm just empty.

I wish I could erase them. People. Why hasn't anyone invented a pill for this?

Imaginary Nick says, "They have. It's called drugs."

Or maybe I can.

I can start right here. My room. It's a ten-year-old's room, stuck in the past. There's an actual rainbow on my duvet cover, and dusty gymnastics trophies still line my shelves. Ticket stubs are thumbtacked to the wall from all the concerts May and I have gone to, and there's a photo of Mom with her arm around me at the gym. It was the day I told her I didn't want to compete anymore, and she brushed me off, saying, "You don't know what you want. This is good for you, and at least you'll always have good posture." So I quit on the spot. She wouldn't listen; she didn't hear me, and it was like that a lot over the last few years. We reached a point where our lives ran parallel.

I sigh. May has great posture.

My history is suffocating me. Every piece of my past morphs into cats—tabby cats, fluffy white Persians, alley cats, and a giant Cheshire lording over them all, wearing an enormous grin.

The cats have to go.

I grab a trash bag and purge the memories from my room. Everything from one shelf to the next gets swept into the bag. My grad cap is on the floor in a corner, and I reach for it. I picture Dad sitting alone among a sea of pride-filled parents. I could feel his pain from the stage. Mom's absence hovered over the day like a shadow. Not a day I want to remember, so I toss the cap in the bag.

Mom's narwhal album. Why am I hanging on to this? I toss it too, like it's nothing. And my desk? I've had it since I was a kid. It knows too much. I push it into the hall for Dad to move later.

My room becomes a hollow shell. Like me. There's not a cat in sight.

The bag weighs a million pounds, but I drag it outside and heave it into the bin. The lid thunks closed, and I lean against it. I feel weightless. I float that way for all of five seconds before regret crashes down. All I can think about is that smiling narwhal trapped and alone in the darkness. I can't do it. I can't let it go.

I fling open the lid and plunge my hand into the garbage bag. Something gross and gooey sticks to my arm because I'm fully leaning into this bin, but I don't care. I need to find her album. Finally, my fingers touch a rectangular outline, and ripple across some pages. This is it. With a tug, it comes free, but the force sends me backwards, and I fall onto the driveway. The album skids across the pavement. I scramble to my feet, brushing my scraped palms against my sweatpants and scoop it up. The narwhal grins mischievously, two sequins now missing from its horn.

Above me, an inky sky is scattered with stars. I swear I see one streak across the darkness.

I clutch the album tight. Some things are meant to last forever.

Nick

I agreed to meet May at the coffee shop on Sunday night because there was no way I was letting her come to my house. It felt like a trap from the get-go. Like going to a circus where the ringleader says, "Of course, you can pet the tiger! He's used to people. He wouldn't hurt a fly." Except this is news to the tiger, and the second you step closer, it's thinking about how good you'll taste going down.

And maybe I have tigers on the brain, but neither of our stories about them seem as scary as the tiger that is May.

When I walk in, she's sitting alone at a table for four, and is dressed to the nines. She's wearing a cream blouse dotted with navy stars, fitted black pants, and black heels. Boy, must I look disappointing. I pull off my baseball cap and run my fingers through my hair as if that will do anything. I'm still not sure what this is. One of those girl things where she's here to relay some message from Fiona? Some kind of best friend test to make sure I'm a decent guy? This looks like a job interview, and my white T-shirt and semiclean jeans are making me a little self-conscious.

She stands up, beaming, and extends her hand when she sees me. "Hi."

And yeah, now it feels like an interview, too. "Hi," I say, shaking it.

There are two paper cups on the table, and I glance to the back of the room, half expecting to see Fi. Maybe this was always meant to be some kind of group hang that nobody filled me in on.

May smooths her blouse and gestures to the seat across from her. "I ordered for you. Hope that's okay. It's a caramel chai soy latte. Who doesn't like those, right?"

Me. For one.

I must be wearing that answer on my face because she pipes up, "Trust me, it's amazing. You will never go back to anything else once you try it."

"Yeah. Sure. Thank you," I say as we settle into the chairs.

The smell wafts up. Creamy, spiced baby vomit in a cup. I know I'm supposed to pick it up now, the way she is with hers, take a slug, and tell her how amazing it is, but I just can't do it.

"You should have let me pick you up. It's so blah out. I feel bad you had to bike here."

She picked a tiny café closer to my house, so it wasn't too far. "Nah. I don't mind."

Her fingers tap against her cup, and she keeps glancing at mine. This is becoming a thing. I'm going to have to drink this shit.

So I pick it up, flash her a grin, will my brain cells to shut down the taste department, and take the tiniest sip.

"Mmm, yeah, that's . . . wow. Tastes as good as it smells," I say and put the cup back on the table. "A little hot, just going to let it cool a bit."

She's happy enough to burst. "Eeee, I knew you would like it." She starts throwing her arms all over the place while she talks. "I just have this knack for knowing what people like. I know it sounds crazy, but people are always like 'How did you know I would love that?' People should let me order for them all the time."

"A rare gift." That's all I need to say to spur her on. I scan the walls for a clock. All I can think about is how the hell am I going to get rid of this drink?

When she finally stops talking, I ask, "Is Fi coming?"

She looks confused. "Fiona? No . . . why?"

"Oh. I wasn't sure. I haven't heard from her in a while. I've been trying to—"

She waves her hand in my face and cuts me off. "Yeah, she's got strep. You have no idea what a germ factory it is at the gym. It's like the kids are just constantly sick, you know? I keep telling her to take Echinacea and Vitamin C, but she doesn't listen. Has she not been sick since you've known her?"

"I don't think so, no."

"It's a whole thing. She goes full hermit. She won't even let me through the door. I used to have to text her mom to make sure she was still alive because it's like being sick makes her fingers broken."

"Oh, shit."

"Don't sweat it. She'll resurface."

May's phone rings from her purse—some Ariana Grande song that will now be stuck in my head for the rest of the night. She answers and starts quietly arguing with whoever is on the line. Then she's yelling. When she ends the call, she starts gathering her things and looks at me like she just remembered I'm here.

"This is the worst, but I have to go. Little sisters, you know?"

Thank God for them. "Hey, when duty calls."

"Do you want to come with me? I'm just shuttling her home from the movies. We can talk in the car. Or let me give you a ride somewhere?"

"I'm good, thanks."

"I'm going to kill her. We didn't even get to talk about anything. And you didn't even touch your latte. You had . . . like . . . two sips."

"I'll take it to go," I say, swiping the cup from the table.

May flies out the door, and the second she tears out of the parking lot, I dump the drink in the nearest trash can.

My phone is already buzzing with texts from her before I even leave the place.

That was fun!

You are so nice to talk to! ☕

Let's do it again soon! 🫣🐿️

But the only person I want to hear from is Fiona. She still hasn't answered the last text I sent. It's stressing me out. This doesn't feel right, even if she is sick. This is the first weekend we haven't hung out, and having to wait another week to see her feels like forever. She's never missed a meeting, though. She'll be there. She has to be. I send her a text:

See you next Saturday?

Fiona

My room looks like I robbed an Ikea. I kind of did. It's almost entirely white, peaceful and calm—a clean slate, everything I want to be. It's like I've landed on the moon, and the only imprints made will be mine.

My new desk is the only thing not white because I didn't want it to remind me of the last one. It's an acacia wood slab that I got at the countertop section. Thank you, Pinterest. I'm assembling the metal legs now, and then I'll drop the slab on top.

I bailed on work again last night, partly because I'm still furious at the parents, but mostly because of May. I texted her and Jaden and said I was still feeling tired. Kept it simple.

Which just leaves me to deal with Nick. There's a meeting tonight, but there's no way I'm going, so I told Grace I'm sick. Of course, she believed me, because I've never bailed on a meeting before. Then I told Dad that Grace was away again. And Nick? I still haven't texted him back. I want to, but I don't know what to say.

I'm sitting on the floor with the Ikea instructions open in front of me. I can't figure them out and screw the leg pieces together the wrong way. Two attempts later, they look right.

There's a soft tap at my door. "Knock knock."

Dad always says the words. I expect him to come in like usual, but he doesn't.

"Come in," I call out for the first time ever.

He opens the door and checks out the table legs. "Want a hand putting the top on?"

It's the easiest part, but I feel like he needs a win here. "Sure, yeah."

We each take a side and gently lower the slab on top of the legs. He takes a step back and studies my room. "Looks good, Fi, real good! A little stark."

"It's minimalism, not stark. And clutter's bad for focus."

He puts his hands on his hips. "Okay."

"I didn't spend a lot."

"Didn't ask." He picks up his cordless drill from the floor. "I guess it does have a calmness to it."

I nod. That's because the cats are gone.

"Anyway, I'm heading to Rob's for a few hours to watch the game. That okay?"

I can't believe it. He's going out. "Yeah! Go ... whoever. Rah."

"Won't be too late."

He heads downstairs, his keys jingling in his pocket. The door closes, and the truck pulls out of the driveway. I should feel relieved, but I don't. It's peace all around me, but I feel like an imposter. Loneliness sets in, and I don't want to be sad tonight. There's only one thing to do: throw myself the world's biggest pity party.

In the kitchen, I grab a bag of barbecue chips on the counter and, oh, look at that open bottle of red wine sitting right next to them, as if rays from heaven are shining around it. With the wine in one hand and the chips tucked under my arm, I grab my Legoland Fiona coffee mug from the cupboard.

The box is still on the counter with Mom's camera inside. A few glasses of wine might be the liquid courage I need to look at the pictures. A few glasses more might be enough to forget them. It's a slo-mo hero's walk upstairs—my arms full of wine, chips, mug, camera, and no witnesses.

I kick my bedroom door closed and set everything up on the floor. The wine bottle has a screw cap so I twist it off, and soft glugs fill my mug like a meditation. Next up is music. My Spotify playlists are organized by months, which is basically a sliding scale of my descent into depression through music. I cue up a top-forty playlist instead and turn on my Bluetooth speaker.

The whole point of overhauling my room was to keep the sad out, but tonight, I already feel it. Sadness seeps through the cracks of my door and spreads across the walls. Thick black globs of sad drip from the ceiling like candle wax. The weight on my chest is heavier now.

"You need to relax," imaginary Nick says.

So I chug back hearty gulps of wine—to relax.

And now that I've let a sliver of Nick invade my thoughts, May pushes her way through the cracks with him. Did they go to our chip truck? Is she hanging out at his house? Did she meet his dad? Fucking Brooklyn? Did they swing on our swing? I imagine her replacing me entirely, and I should be happy for them because isn't that what I wanted? For both of them to be happy? Maybe not with each other.

The half-eaten bag of gummy bears sits on my nightstand, and I feel so guilty for hating her. How can I hate her when she was there for me after Mom died? We've been friends forever. Yeah, sometimes she knocks me down a peg for her benefit, but I don't think she means to, and does that cancel out the good parts?

"I don't know how you can be friends with her. Seriously, Fi, she's nuts," imaginary Nick says.

I nod in agreement. I mean, what is the line between a flawed friend and a toxic one?

Maybe I can stay in this room forever. I don't need to go to New York for school in January. What's so great about traveling, anyway? It sounds horrible.

"Traveling's fun, Fiona," imaginary Nick says.

"That's bullshit," I say out loud to myself.

My mouth fills with velvety red wine. I hold it in my cheeks for a minute before swallowing. It's creating a cocoon on top of my cocoon. Thousands of fluffy white cotton balls expand around me, and the world grows fuzzier. I turn up the music.

I'm done with you, Nick. I can do or not do whatever I want. I don't judge you for being anti-social in group.

"Yes, you do," imaginary Nick says.

My phone buzzes against the hardwood, and the timing is so freaky I jump a little.

Nick: Yo

It's seven-thirty. They're well into the meeting. I guess he figured out I'm not going. Seconds later, it buzzes again.

Nick: Fiona!

I know you're there

I know you're reading these

WTF

Answer me!

Are you okay?

The texts are stressing me out, so I click off my phone and slide it across the floor, cupping my wine mug in both hands.

The music stops. My room plunges into quiet. I pick up Mom's camera and play with the aperture wheel on the metal body. It's scratched and dented in places. Is it charged? All I have to do is press the power button. My thumb hovers over it, but I'm hit with a wave of panic, so I put it on the floor and slide my laptop closer.

On Spotify, I search for a my-mom-is-dead playlist. I get a few hits. Deadmau5 comes up, followed by my mom is dumb, but underneath is a dead-mom playlist. Someone's as twisted as I am. I get goosebumps when I see the songs. Some of these have been played in my car before, and the few Bowie tracks make me positive it's Nick's. It's like finding his diary. I didn't know he had this. I shouldn't read into it, but I want to. I don't know what this is.

I don't know what *this* is.

I play it from the top.

More wine glugs into my mug, and I question for a second how many glasses might be in a mug. I'm already tired but don't want to sleep, so I get up.

The house is dark. We have three rooms upstairs, and I head for Mom and Dad's at the end of the hall.

I never come in here. The air is thick and stagnant; it's all kinds of creepy. If one of those ghost hunters ever came over, their ghost-o-meter would go haywire. The bed is made, probably from a week ago since Dad usually sleeps on the couch.

I go into their bathroom and open Mom's makeup drawer. Everything is stacked in neat rows with tubes and pots from Glossier and Maybelline. Nothing fancy. I press a pink lipstick into my lips. The color is too bright, so I open another and apply layer upon layer of pinks, reds, nudes, and plums while singing off-key to some random song blaring from my room, where all the words have become *Nooooboody loooves you, Fiona.*

Before I close the drawer, I spot a frosted glass bottle with French writing—a lotion she bought in Paris on a work trip and secretly ordered ever since. Dad would've flipped if he knew how much it cost. I pump an opalescent dewdrop onto my finger. It's like Mom's entire being is in this tiny orb. I press it into my cheeks.

My eyes are closing, so I drift back to my room and flop into bed.

Sleep comes instantly.

Rain hammers against the roof. I wish I could crack it open and let it inside. Maybe it could wash the sadness off the walls.

"Fiona!"

Imaginary Nick's voice pierces the air.

"Fiona!"

My eyes spring open.

"Fiona! Open the door!"

Not imaginary Nick.

I stumble out of bed and peek through my curtains. The doorbell rings incessantly, but I don't see anyone. Then Nick takes a few steps back and looks up. He's soaked. He sees me and clutches his heart like he's relieved. The relief morphs into looking really pissed.

"Open the door!" he yells.

The room sways when I turn around, and shaking my head doesn't help. I throw on my ratty blue oversized robe and take a breath before flying down the stairs.

I swing open the door, and Nick charges through, bringing in sideways sheets of rain. He scans my living room for evidence that the world is ending. In the driveway, I spot his toppled-over bike. He biked here. In the rain. Which is crazy. I close the door, and he sweeps his rain-soaked hair away from his face.

"You weren't at the meeting!" He sputters, still breathless.

"I know."

He heads for the kitchen, his sneakers squeaking against the floor and grabs a dish towel from the oven door. He rubs it through his hair and wipes his face. "I thought you drove into a car or jumped off a railing or something."

"Well, that would be hard because the railing's at your house." I think it's pretty funny, but he shoots me a look.

That's when he notices my face. He narrows his eyes at my lips.

"Oh, shit." I drag my sleeve across the clown show of lipstick streaked across my mouth.

As if that'll do anything.

"You're drunk," he says, draping the wet towel over a chair.

That's debatable. I'm in the trying-not-to-be-sick phase. There's a whole conversation happening in my head. It goes *Don't be sick, don't be sick, don't be sick, eat something, don't be sick.*

But yeah, I'm still drunk. I brush by him on my way to the kitchen and attack a loaf of bread on the counter, shoving a slice into my mouth and dropping a second in the toaster.

"Where's Bob?"

Chew. Chew. Chew. I hate this. I hate what he's doing. He's playing Mr. Responsible.

"Why aren't you talking to me?"

"I am talking to you."

"You know what I mean. I don't mean now."

Yeah, I know what he means, but why is he putting this on me? "Why aren't you talking to me?"

"What?! I haven't heard a word from you, Fi!" he fires back. "May said you had strep."

It's a dagger to my chest. So they have been texting.

My toast pops. It's burnt. I scrape off the charred bits, letting them fall to the counter like ashes from my torched heart and eat it. Dry.

"What the hell? Was I supposed to come over? May said you like to be alone when you're sick, and you go into this whole hiber—" He stops, and a lightbulb goes off. "You're not even sick. You were never sick!" He throws his hands in the air. "What is wrong with you?"

It's the statement to end all statements, and what can I say to that? It's like the world's biggest insult. "Oh, wow. Well, how much time do you have?"

"You've been lying to everyone!"

"Hey, I never said I had strep. May assumed I had strep. I just didn't disagree."

"What?"

I push past him and go to the living room.

"Why didn't you answer my texts?" His voice is getting louder now.

"What texts?"

"I texted you like a hundred times tonight."

"My phone was off."

"Bullshit."

He lunges for me and grabs my robe, searching for the pockets. We fight over the fabric, but it's an easy victory for him. He pulls out my phone.

"Give it back."

He holds it high above his head, and there's no way I can reach it. He towers above me. He opens my texts because stupid me doesn't password-protect my phone, and all of his messages fill the screen.

"Oh, look at that! There they are!"

He glares at me and thrusts my phone back into my hands. "Okay, what the fuck is going on? Did something happen? Are you okay?"

He's genuinely concerned, and it's sad. I'm sad. "No."

"No, what?"

"To all of the above." He waits for more, but I backpedal. "I'm fine. Forget it."

"Honestly?"

He's standing a foot away, and we stare each other down. Honesty hangs in the space between us, but neither of us wants to reach for it.

"Yeah."

He's thinking it. I can see it in his eyes. We're on the cusp of a whole other conversation. It's like a game of chess, only totally unfair on account of my chess board hanging diagonally in the air.

"So that's it? You obviously don't want to talk to me."

"Why do you keep saying that? I am talking to you."

He paces across my living room and stops, raising a finger. "This is about May."

He actually does it. He moves his queen across the board. It sounds so petty to hear it said out loud.

"No!" I say, as if it's the most ridiculous thing I've ever heard, but it's so transparent even I don't believe it.

"We went out for coffee! She said you didn't give a shit."

My stomach twists. I can't even look at him, so I head back to the kitchen. "No, I'm super happy you guys are connecting. It's so cool that you're talking about what kind of shits I give."

"I thought you would be there. Then, I thought you were setting us up!"

I spin around to face him. "Why would I do that?!"

"What am I supposed to think, Fiona? You gave her my number!"

"Crazy me! I guess I assumed you wouldn't jump at the chance!"

He takes a step back. "What are you talking about?" He's genuinely confused, and my heart breaks a little. "Why did you give her my number?"

"She asked! What was I supposed to do?"

He shakes his head. "Uh, I don't know. Tell me, maybe?

Give me a heads up—"

"But why? You made plans instantly!"

"So I wouldn't be blindsided!" he says, throwing his hands in the air.

I pace back into the living room, and he follows two steps behind. "Whatever. You know, I think it's great! It's really great!" I say.

"Great. I'm glad it's great." We face each other at a stalemate. "So now you're done? You can cut me loose, just like that? If it's so easy for you to get over things, why did you ever go to those meetings in the first place? Why not just hit the restart?"

Every drop of rational thought leaves me. "You come in here throwing your honestly, honesty, bullshit at me, and then you give me some crap about not wanting to bother me—"

"That wasn't bullshit," he interrupts, but I'm so not done.

"I hope you'll be happy together! She's totally crazy, by the way, and you abandoned me at that party like an asshole when I back you up all the time. And you didn't even text me before that. I flat out texted I love you, and you didn't even reply."

It's an incomprehensible disaster of a rant. His eyes are so wide he looks like his head might explode. "What?"

"So don't give me honestly as if honestly is just for me, okay? You're not the fucking honestly police."

"What?"

"Nothing, forget it." I try to walk by him, but he grabs my arm.

"No, and you didn't text *I love you*. You texted *love you* like every other girl on the planet."

I shake my arm free. "Wow! How unoriginal of me."

"It's a throwaway, Fi. Did you mean *I love you*?"

Checkmate. Why is he so good at this? I raged myself into a corner. I shake my head and don't stop like a bobblehead stuck in a crosswind. I'm way too tipsy for this conversation. This isn't happening. No, I don't love you. No, no, no.

"Did you mean *I love you*?"

"No!" I shout as if it's a ludicrous idea. "It's just, you could have texted it back is all."

He runs his hands through his hair. "Wow. Tell me we're not dissecting my shitty texting skills right now. I hate texting."

"No, you don't. You don't hate texting."

"Oh, you got me, I love it. I love texting."

"I'm just saying you could have texted it back."

He stops and flutters his eyes for a flabbergasted second, cocks his head to the side and pulls out his phone. Two seconds later my phone dings in my robe pocket. I pull it out to see *Love you* on my screen. It's cold—cardboard and meaningless.

"Are we good?"

"Great. Thanks." But I'm not done. One more drunken gem springs free before I can stop myself. "Did you tell her about your mom?"

He steps back, as if he's been slapped, letting the full dysfunction of the question sink in. He's trying to work out why I would ask this. He's Nick. Of course he knows why.

"No." His face softens, and his voice is calm. He puts the fighting gloves down and takes a step toward me. "Fi, what do you want from me?"

His eyes plead with me. He's throwing me a lifeline in the

form of a question, and all I have to do is answer it. Honestly. But I can't. I'd rather drown.

"Nothing. I didn't ask you to come here."

He absorbs the rejection. The smell of burnt toast wafts through the air, and it's all I can think about. Anything but what just happened here.

"You know you weren't the only one who didn't show tonight. That girl Maddie, she OD'd a few days ago."

I close my eyes. *No.*

"I'm not going back anymore. I'm done," he says, and somehow I know I won't, either. This feels like the end.

Headlights flood the driveway. We hold a look like our entire relationship depends on these next thirty seconds of privacy, but neither of us utters a word. Dad's truck door slams. The front door opens, and he comes in carrying a paper bag of groceries. The tension washes over him like a tsunami. "Nick?" He shifts his gaze between us. Thankfully, he doesn't say anything about the state of my face.

"Sir."

"Everything okay?"

I have to give him something.

"Girl from group died." It's the perfect answer. He'll want nothing to do with that.

"Sorry to hear." He lowers his head and goes into the kitchen to unpack.

Nick crosses the room to the stairs where I'm standing, and I move one step up, so I'm taller than him. He narrows his eyes at me like I'm the devil in disguise. "Wow. Bravo. That was amazing. Maybe you should be the writer because you always know exactly what to say." It's a bitter whisper.

I lean in and whisper back. "I learned from the best!"

He steps away and draws his mouth into a tight line.

"Nick, you staying the night?" Dad calls out.

"No, sir, I was just on my way out."

"You sure? It's coming down pretty hard out there."

"I'm sure." He opens the door to the downpour and doesn't look back.

In my head, I'm screaming—*stop! Don't leave! I'm sorry.* But the relief I feel when the door closes wins.

I find Dad in the kitchen and hug him. He assumes it's about death. How can I explain it's about life?

Nick

I get the text when I'm in my room after I peel off my ten-thousand-pound water-soaked hoodie. All that extra weight made the bike ride home extra fun.

Fiona: please don't hate me

She must have sent it the second I left. And my heart melts with the sting of a fiery burn in the way only Fiona can make it.

I launch my phone across my room. It feels good to throw something, so I grab the open bag of Cheetos on my nightstand and throw those, too. And why stop there? I launch a can of soda, and now my room is a goddamn Pollock masterpiece of Cheetos and Coke splatter. When I'm out of things to throw, I fall into bed. How did this happen?

Grace says I'm a disrupter. If that's true, Fiona's a hurricane. I mean, what the hell, Fi? What was that? I don't even know.

The icing on the cake is an email from Grace with the details for Maddie's funeral next week. Great. I guess not being an asshole looks a whole lot like going, even though I barely knew this girl. But honestly, I'm kind of messed-up about Maddie. All I can see is her standing in front of me, asking to hang out, and me ignoring her. What is wrong with me? Grace told the group she took something tainted at a party as if it was an unrelated issue.

Everything is related.

Maddie reached out to me. One time. I should've listened.

I have no idea what people wear to funerals. Mom didn't have one. I'm not wearing a suit. I mean, forget it. A navy sweater is the most I'll compromise. I throw it on over a dress shirt, pairing it with some gray pants. It'll have to do.

Sitting through a church service is not my thing, so I skip that part and show up for the procession to the gravesite. Our group is hanging back behind Maddie's family and her school friends. It's an impressive turnout. Grace waves when she sees me. Fiona's there, too, deep in conversation with one of the other guys. There's a hint of red woven between her dark strands. It suits her to a T. When she glances up at me, I look away.

I'm still kind of pissed. I mean, I don't know what she wants from me. I tried to be real with her at her house and she kicked me out, so what do I do with that?

The rest of the funeral is massively uncomfortable. Part of me wants to go up to Grace and say, "See? What did I tell you," but it would be a dick move, even for me.

"What's it all about, Nick?" Mom always used to say. I think she regretted kicking out Alex and Max, especially when it became clear that Dad's We-need-to-live-our-lives speech meant live them separately. The unhappier she became, the more she said it. Always staring off somewhere—out the window, into the refrigerator, into the black hole of the kitchen drain. *What's it all about?* If we were on a game show, I'd guess family would be in the top three answers, but there I was, sitting a foot away from her, so that couldn't be it.

A priest gives the service over an open grave, and Maddie's parents are crying. Birds chirp from a tree nearby. It's really nice outside—a great day for birds.

Fiona's staring at me. I can see her in the corner of my eye. I don't want to look at her, but I can't help myself. I cave.

A soft breeze blows a few stray strands of hair across her face. She's pastoral. The lace of her blouse grazes her collarbone, and the sun highlights her like a painting. She's the only one here wearing white. A guy from group is behind her with his hand on her shoulder, and all I can think is it should be me. I should be that guy, but I'm over here and don't know why. So, we hold this stare that somehow says everything yet not enough.

Someone starts to cry beside me, and I shift my eyes back to the ground.

I'm pretty sure Mom wanted her ashes spread under a Keith Urban concert stage, but that was never going to happen. I don't think Keith Urban's people would let it for one, and two, there weren't any ashes to spread.

There were teeth. Alex told me this while eating a bowl of cereal at the kitchen table. I'm not sure what happened to them. Does a country fly back a box of teeth and hand them over to the family, or are they held in an insurance adjuster's vault for evidence? I don't know, and I never asked.

Dad found out first. He was working in Portland. When headlines about an airline crash popped up on the newsfeeds, his foreman showed him and said, "Wasn't Liz headed to South America?"

I wish I could have seen his reaction. Alex said it sounded like he'd been crying when he called her, but I don't believe it. I think she added that for my benefit or imagined it for hers. They found out on a Friday and spent the next day and a half together trying to get information from the airline. They didn't tell me until Sunday when they knew for sure she was gone.

It's so weird to think about. I spent that whole weekend partying, and Mom was dead. I should have been crying, or . . . I don't know. I don't know what I should have been doing, but it was definitely not having the time of my life with people I didn't care about. And I felt so justified, too, like what did you all expect for leaving me home alone for this long?

I knew something was wrong the second Alex and Dad pulled into the driveway in the same car. When I was little, Nana told me about a Magpie landing outside her kitchen window the day her sister died. She said it was telling her the news. It sounded ridiculous at the time, but now I get it. Alex opened the car door for Max and scooped him up in her arms. He was hugging a plush white polar bear. The sight of it all was telling me the news. Alex looked up to my bedroom window, and I knew.

She knocked on my door a few minutes later and asked me to come downstairs.

Max was watching TV in the living room. Alex sat at the table, and Dad put on a pot of coffee even though it was four in the afternoon.

"Nick, there was an accident," he said, matter-of-factly while counting the scoops of grounds. "There was a plane crash."

They looked tired, like two people who had already spent a weekend processing this. I leaned against the wall and listened.

Everything was a total blur, and at the time, I assumed this was news to all of us. I think Alex came over and hugged me. Then, they started talking about funeral arrangements and using words like "recovery options," and I was still two days behind asking, "How do you know for sure?"

I joined Max on the sofa in the living room while Alex vented to Dad about safety measures and airline responsibility. Their voices sounded like a distant fog. Cartoons were on the TV, but I don't think he was watching them.

"Hey," Max said, not looking away from the screen.

"Hey."

"Sorry about your mom." He said it so casually, because he didn't really know her. Alex was stubborn and only came by on holidays or birthdays.

It was a knockout punch, and the moment that made it real. How crazy is it that the first expression of empathy came from an eight-year-old? My hands were shaking. I collected myself as best as I could and went back upstairs.

"Nick," Alex called out after me.

That's when the googling started. I guess I was looking for proof that this was a mistake and they were wrong. It was a terrible idea. Of course, there was footage of the wreckage—a burned-out shell of a plane, and I watched it and rewatched, scrubbing through the frames, one at a time, searching for some kind of proof she was in there.

It was the teeth. It all came down to the teeth.

So there was no funeral. Mom's friends didn't understand, but we aren't religious and with no body to bury and no ashes to spread, we agreed her funeral was a one-woman show in the Amazon. Then, my friends slowly faded into the mist with her. It wasn't their fault, they tried, but suddenly I was living on Mars, just fighting to breathe, while it was life as usual for the rest of them.

Alex and I chose the South Falls in Silver Falls State Park as the place where we would remember her. We used to go there all the time, minus Dad because he was always busy. Mom would sit on the wet rocks overlooking the falls, and we'd run around behind her, throwing stones over the edge. Then, we'd roast hot dogs over a firepit and feed birds out of our hands.

We didn't have any ashes to scatter so Alex and I burned some of her things—one of her shirts, her slippers, and a photograph. We took those ashes to the park with Max and tossed them into the falls. We didn't tell Dad. We wanted the moment to be ours. It was far from traditional, but it was us.

I'm kind of glad it worked out that way because looking at Maddie's casket hovering above this hole is unimaginably brutal. I bail before they lower it.

Funerals are bullshit.

The house is quiet when I get home, and all I can think about are the people who used to fill it. The funeral messed with my head, and maybe I can sleep off this sadness. I go to my room and tear off my sweater, but I'm too wired to sleep, so I sit at my desk in front of my laptop. Max's minifigure is beside it, watching, like it's asking something of me, and I don't know what.

A blank page is on the screen with Victim's Statement Nick Bennet on the top. The cursor blinks at the end of the words.

I don't feel like a victim. If I wanted to write a victim's statement, I would have done it when I was eight or ten. Or every year after, when things got worse. Now, I feel pain and sadness, but that's been around a long time, too.

My fingers rest lightly on the keys. I type:

Dear South American Airlines,

Funerals are bullshit. I mean, I should be thanking you for crashing a plane in the middle of the Amazon.

I stare at this for a second, and then delete it.

Dear South American Airlines,

Jane Goodall had a chimpanzee named Frodo. She didn't even work in South America. What earthly reason could you have for selling a Jane Goodall South American Tour?

I delete this. I write:

Dear South American Airlines,

You know, you really fucked me. You stole her happy ending because if she was alive, there was a solid chance she would have left him. You know what that bucket list was? A countdown, and every time she crossed off another number, she was that much stronger, that much closer to making it. And I really wanted her to make it. So where does that leave me? I guess I have to pick up the baton. I still have a shot, right? Maybe I can be the one who makes it, but how can I do that, South American Airlines, when the baton lies in ruin somewhere in the middle of the Amazon? What am I supposed to run with?

I delete this. I write:

Dear South American Airlines,

I am not a victim, but I am alone.

I delete this. Max's minifigure is judging me. I know it.

The cursor blinks on the screen. I write:

Dear Mom,

I didn't fuck up the house.

Nick

Now that May's looped me into her circle of text friends, I can't get out. She's what I imagine a debt collector's like, and it's enough to make me never want to go into debt.

She texts me all the time. In the morning, in the afternoon, at midnight, and it's a little cruel because they constantly get my hopes up, thinking *maybe it's Fiona*, but it never is. I could have said something to her at the funeral, but I want her to be the one to reach out, especially after what went down at her house.

A reminder on my calendar pops up for Monterey this weekend. I click it off. We'll be okay by then. We have to be.

I'm trying to seem functional, so I text May back, but it's hard to be jazzed about all the stuff she keeps talking about. I mean, she sent me a picture of two kinds of shoes and asked me which ones were cuter. Why? Why would anyone ever ask me this? And worse, I answered her! I replied:

The blue ones

It's like she's trying to rein me back into this world of normal, and I don't even mind. It could be working.

So, when she asks me what I'm doing today, I tell her about my driving test this afternoon to ward off any let's-hang-out requests. But then she responds with a dozen animated emojis and insists on picking me up. I don't argue because I'm hoping her incessant chatter will take my mind off my nerves that have been building since last night.

This day has been looming on my calendar for a while now. I purposely arranged for the test to happen before the Monterey trip. I never told Fi because she'd make it a big deal, and I didn't want the extra pressure. But to May, I'm a blank slate, and there's something so easy about being around someone who knows nothing about you.

The second I spot her black Acura rolling down my driveway, I swipe my hoodie from my desk chair and race down the stairs because I do not want her coming into this house. When I swing open the door, she's standing in front of it, her fist raised, ready to knock.

"Oh. Hey," She steps back, surprised by my timing. She cranes her neck, trying to glimpse inside, but I quickly shut the door behind me.

"Hey. Is it cool if we head out? This is kind of a big deal. I don't want to be late, you know?"

"Yeah, of course. You can give me the tour some other time!" She waves it off, and we head back to her car.

Not. Likely.

And just when I think this couldn't have worked out any better, I spot Dad's truck turning into the driveway. We're almost at her car, so in my head, we can make it out of here without any interaction.

Then May sees the truck. "Is that your . . . gardener?"

It's a pretty accurate description of Dad. "Uh . . . no. That's my dad."

"Right!" She swirls a finger in the general direction of our lawn like a wizard's wand. "The landscaping thing. I forgot."

My hand is already on the passenger door handle, but it's still locked. Dad's door opens, and I shoot May a pained stare wondering if she's ever going to unlock these fucking doors, but she just smiles. "Aren't you going to say hi?"

No, I wasn't, but now I guess I have to. The smile I give her is so plastic it hurts. Fiona would call me on it. May seems oblivious.

She comes around the car to my side, beaming in my dad's direction. Dad walks over and transforms into Mr. Charming.

"Who do we have here?" he asks.

"Dad, this is my friend May. May, Dad."

May shrugs her shoulders, excited. She slides her yellow clutch under her arm and steps forward, her hand outstretched. "Nice to meet you, Mr. Bennet." She tucks a lock of her long black hair behind her ear, revealing a gold hoop earring. Her outfit could be straight out of a magazine with her navy puffy, short-sleeved blouse and jeans that look like they're spun from gold.

Dad can't hide his thrilled expression. It's like he just won the lottery, or I won the lottery. May definitely looks like the kind of expensive prize some people pray for.

"And it's lovely to meet you." He shakes her hand, beaming right back at her. "This is great. It's good to see you spending time with new people, Nick."

May basks in the compliment and doesn't notice it's a dig toward Fi. "May's Fiona's best friend, Dad, so . . . "

Now, it's his turn to put on a plastic smile. "How nice," he says to May. "I only meant that it's nice to see you expanding your circle. Different people can help get you on the right track."

I hate him so much right now.

May nods in total agreement. "So true, you're only as good as the people you're surrounded by."

"That's it exactly!" Dad points at her like this girl knows her stuff, and May throws her head back, bashful, as if he's just too much.

And this is some kind of hellish nightmare that needs to end.

"We really need to go," I say to May.

"Right! Well, it was so nice meeting you." She waves good-bye and finally unlocks the car doors on her way back to the driver's side.

"Where are you headed?" Dad calls out.

I glare at May, hoping to signal her so she won't say anything, but it's too late. "Nick's driving test! Wish him luck," she chirps.

My back is to him, but I can feel his eyes searing into me. I open the passenger door, and he moves next to it before I get in. "Already that time, huh."

I can't bring myself to meet his eyes, so I focus on his

shoulder instead. "Five months flies by." The truth is, five months was up two months ago, but he didn't even notice.

"You put in all the paperwork and everything?"

"Yup."

"Okay. I might be out later, but text me and let me know how it goes." He taps the car door frame twice.

It sets my blood on fire. He can't even pretend to want to take me out or wait for me to get back. *Fuck you* is what I want to say, but when I catch his eye for a fleeting second, I decide he's not worth my rage. "Will do."

May starts the car as I duck inside. Dad waves as she guns it out of the driveway.

She didn't notice the exchange. To her, I'm just a hapless guy who sucks at driving, not a guy who had his license suspended.

So, today is kind of huge for me. I've finally paid my dues. It's scary when someone holds out a ticket for a second chance because all you can think about are the million ways you could blow it.

Being in a car with May is like being trapped in a pinball machine. She bounces from one subject to the next so fast, and I'm just trying to keep the ball out of the gutter. She starts by quizzing me over the most basic driver's ed stuff. Then she cranks the music when Billie Eilish comes on the radio, giving a whole new meaning to car dancing. She grills me about my social media accounts, refusing to believe I have none, and gives me a lecture about why California is the only place I should consider going to school.

When we get to the DMV, my head is throbbing. Before I go in, May grabs the drawstrings on my hoodie and stares deep into my eyes. "You've got this Bennet. Right?"

"Right."

"Let me hear you say it."

I say it with zero percent of her enthusiasm. "I got this."

"Damn straight!" She brushes off my sweatshirt as if it's covered in crumbs or something, even though I'm pretty sure it's perfectly clean. Then she turns me around and pushes me forward, and it's all just so wrong.

When I come out thirty minutes later, May's sitting on the curb, furiously texting. She finishes doing whatever she's doing before jumping to her feet and waiting with wide, expectant eyes. "So?"

I hold up the temporary license they gave me, folded into a tiny square. "Uh, yeah, I got it."

May jumps into my chest and wraps her arms around my neck, screaming. Her force sends me backward, and I kind of just pat her on her back because I don't know what to do. It feels like we've leveled up in the video game of friendship, and nobody gave me the memo. She steps away from me and slides her orange bra strap back over her shoulder. I just want to get the hell out of here before someone realizes they made a terrible mistake and tries to take the license back.

"You did it! This is amazing. We need to celebrate. What should we do? Do you want to come to my place, and we can have drinks?"

That feels like exactly the wrong way to celebrate this. "No, it's cool. It's not a big deal."

"Are you kidding! This is huge. At least let me buy you a triple chocolate frappé at Starbucks."

She seems hellbent on this idea. I don't have the heart to tell her I'm not into drinking twelve pounds of liquid sugar, but at this point, the only way out of this funhouse is through.

So, I say, "Sure."

"You're driving, though!" She tosses me the keys, and I instinctively catch them.

"No, really, I'm not insured . . ."

"I trust you, Nick. You're not going to wreck my car."

You shouldn't trust me, I want to say. *I mess up everything.* But May's already headed for the passenger door and rattles it wildly—my cue to unlock them. She beams at me, while I fumble with the key fob because it's been so long, I barely remember how to unlock the doors.

It's hard not to feel like Fiona in this equation. It's like I'm living her life. I mean, are we the same person? May's enthusiasm isn't exactly contagious, but it's nice to hang out with someone who sees nothing but sunshine and rainbows around every corner, someone who lifts the anchor once in a while. Still, she's no Fiona—she'll never be. Fiona's like finding magic in this world.

It's May standing next to her car, but I see Fiona staring at me through chestnut strands of windswept hair. Fiona, dropping her keys twenty times before she gets the doors open. Fiona, glaring at me for whatever smart-ass comment I lob her way. Fiona, laughing and then freaking out because her tears are burning her eyes, and she thinks she's dying from eye cancer. So maybe Fiona and I are both anchors, but the bottom of the sea sure is beautiful. It's fucking Atlantis. And I want to text her right now and say *I miss you. I'm sorry.* But May shouts, "Come on, Bennet, let's go! My feet are killing me!"

It's the blue shoes.

We go to the Starbucks downtown. The one Roger drove his car into. Fi and I never come out this way. The quaint parts of towns are always the most congested. It doesn't help that today was the farmers market, and all the organic produce hunters have flooded the coffee shop for their twelve pumps of whatever.

May seems disappointed when I don't mimic her ridiculous order. Hearing her rhyme it out in all its sugary glory to the cashier was enough to make the words iced espresso leap from my lips.

She calls me boring. We can barely hear each other over the roar of small talk, so we take our drinks outside and walk down the sidewalk, still littered with stray lettuce leaves and stomped-on flower stems.

Her venti chocolate frappé is so massive, she needs to hold it with both hands. "Would it be crazy to turn this day into a dinner thing?" she asks as if the idea just came to her.

"I think my dad might want to do something. Just, you know, family."

"Oh, true. Well, what about this weekend? You can come over for dinner. Meet my parents."

Meet my parents? I don't know what she thinks this is turning into, but it needs to end like now. "Actually, I'm going to Monterey this weekend."

She stops in her tracks. "Monterey?"

"With Fi."

She steps away from me as if some giant puzzle is coming together in her head. "Fi said she canceled Monterey."

This is news to me, and it blows to be hearing it from May. Then I wonder what other things she's told May, but I'm not about to get in a contest over who knows what about Fiona. And it doesn't even matter. She can cancel all she wants. It doesn't mean it's not happening. It doesn't mean a damn thing.

"Well, it's happening." I say, tossing my empty cup into a recycling bin.

She gets this funny look on her face like she's figured out the secret to the universe. "Wow. You're in love with her."

If it's possible to feel slapped by a string of words, it just happened. And I don't know what to say, so I just stand there with a surprised look on my face, which seems to be all the confirmation she needs. She dumps her drink in the trash, still half full, as if it soured.

"Why the hell are you out here with me, then?" she asks, throwing her arms open wide.

It doesn't seem like the right time to remind her that she's the one who's been texting me and who insisted on picking me up today. And this is just perfect—yet another person who wants to kill me. They can't all be wrong. I must be some kind of giant asshole.

"You spent the entire night at the party flirting with me!" she says.

"I wasn't flirting with you!" I fire back.

I mean, so what? I followed her around the yard, we had a few laughs in the living room. She touched me a few times. I may have gotten her a drink.

And it hits me like a ton of bricks.

Finally, I see it through Fi's eyes, through May's eyes, and it doesn't look good. At all. But what can I say? I used to go out—a lot. I talked to everybody. At parties, my hands have slid across endless chains of shoulders and waists. None of it ever meant anything. Old habits took over so quickly, and I didn't think.

I didn't think.

"Are you going to tell her?" May snaps me from my daze. There's something mildly threatening in her tone.

Arguing with May is not a road I want to go down, so I shove my hands deep into my hoodie pocket and say, "Can you please keep your assumption to yourself?"

"Assumption? That's how you're going to play this? You can't bullshit a bullshitter. I'm not going to keep this a secret. She's my best friend."

"Is she? Because I don't think you've been 'best friends' for a long time."

That really pisses her off. Her mouth drops open, and she's got that enraged girl fire behind her eyes like she's about to shred my asshole into a million pieces. She doesn't yell, though. She gives me that condescending superiority shit instead.

"We've been best friends since sixth grade. So what? You've had a few heart-to-hearts with her, and you think you know her better than I do?"

She's talking to me like I'm the world's biggest idiot. "Yeah. I do. She's not the same person you used to know. People change."

"People *don't* change. Not really. That's why you're so scared, isn't it? That you're still the same guy you always were. You know, she lost her students because of you."

She's baiting me. And as much as I try to resist, she's got me hook, line, and sinker. "What?"

My obvious descent into insecurity refuels her. "Fi thinks it's because of the counseling, but it's a small locker room." Her intensity rises with each step she takes closer. "I heard the parents gossiping. It's *you*. One of their stupid kids went to some house party you had and got really messed up. They dumped her because she hangs out with you."

So. Many. Parties. "But you're out with me right now!"

"They can't fire me! I'm a state champion. So, now you're going to what, Nick? Morph into some romantic hero? Show up on your white horse and marry her?"

This is more than anger. She's ready to bury me right here on the sidewalk, and for some stupid reason, I keep answering her. "Yeah, maybe I will." Obviously, I'm just serving her words straight back to her, but it's such a misfire. She's the worst person to be saying this completely insane shit to.

May lets out a guttural guffaw. "You're going to *marry her*? You haven't even—You can't even—" She raises her hands in front of her, stopping herself. "Okayyy. You're delusional, dude. I'm outta here. Good luck with that."

She storms off toward the parking lot, and I can't help but wonder how many visits to the farmers market end this way.

Thankfully I don't have a car because I would Roger the shit out of it right now.

And damnit, May is wrong.

She's wrong about Fiona, and she's wrong about me. I know Fi more than she ever will, and I know who May is, too. She won't tell Fi a single word about this conversation because it's embarrassing. There's no glory in it for her. She's banking on me keeping my mouth shut, hoping I'll just disappear, so they can slide back into their shitty hierarchy of friendship. Which means she doesn't know me at all.

Because Monterey is happening. People do change. May is wrong about all of it.

She has to be.

Fiona

My phone buzzes from my nightstand. In a sleepy haze, I flop my hand against the table until I find it. It's six A.M.

Dad: Fi?

Me: Is the house on fire?

Because it's freaking six!

Dad: No. Nick's in the kitchen.

I read the words and reread them. They soak in, shattering any lingering veil of sleep.

Is he joking?

My phone buzzes in my hand.

Dad: He has a bag. Says it's for your trip.

Should I send him up?

The trip? We haven't spoken in weeks—since the night I went completely nuts in my living room. Why would he be here now?

Me: No! I'll be right down

Every second I sit here thinking about this is more time for Dad to grill him, so I scramble out of bed and search my room for some kind of miracle that might make me look pulled together. And yeah, there's nothing, so I throw on my robe, cinch it tight around my waist, and race downstairs, hoping this isn't real.

It's real.

Nick and Dad are sitting at the kitchen table like this is a regular thing. Nick shovels spoonfuls of my Lucky Charms into his mouth and Dad's face is covered by the morning newspaper.

"Hey," Nick says through a mouthful of cereal.

"Hey."

"You said six, remember?" he says, holding up his phone like nothing ever happened.

"I did?"

Two months ago, before our friendship fell apart.

"Uh-huh."

There's an entire conversation that we should be having, but it's impossible thanks to Dad just sitting here. Dad flicks the paper back and eyes me over his glasses.

"Right. Let me grab a shower."

Nick pushes his chair back. "You'll take forever. Shower later."

"No, I can't . . . I can't drive like this." Half asleep, basically. "I'll be quick."

He carries his bowl to the sink and washes it. "Where's your stuff? I'll pack up the car." He glances back at me and reads the caught-in-the-headlights expression I'm wearing.

"You don't have any stuff."

I shake my head.

"You shower. I'll pack."

I look from him to Dad. "Yeah. Okay." I back out of the kitchen and head upstairs, knowing Nick will follow. Instead of turning toward the bathroom, I go into my room and close the door behind him.

"Whoa! What the shit happened to your room?" He takes it in as he spins around. "I like it!" He shakes off his disorientation and moves to my closet, sliding open the panel. Then he pulls my backpack from the floor like he owns the place.

"What are you doing?"

He unzips it and drops it on my bed. "I'm packing," he says like it's obvious. He brushes past me and pulls open my top drawer. "After arriving on time, I might add, for a trip that's been planned forever." He finally notices the drawer is full of my underwear and jolts back. Then he fully commits and scoops out a handful.

"Nick. Stop. I'm not going anywhere with you."

He holds his hands out in front of him, fist full of my underwear, like Chris Pratt trying to get a handle on his velociraptors. "Yes. Yes you are."

"Are you out of your mind?" I whisper-yell. "And why are you doing this at six in the morning? You know I can't have morning conversations."

"Fi. We have to do this."

"*We* don't have to do anything." It's tough talking to him with a pair of my yellow duck print boy shorts in his hands. They were a gift from May. I knew they'd find a way to haunt me. "Can you put those down?"

He heads for the backpack and drops them inside. "You won't do this without me."

"Yes, I will."

"Oh, really? When?"

"Soon. Like today." I close my eyes because I don't know what I'm talking about—morning conversations. "It doesn't matter. I don't *need* you to go with me to Monterey."

He's already back at my dresser, a little more nervous about which drawer to open next. "Nick!"

His shoulders sag, and he turns to face me. "I know you don't *need* me. I want to go with you, okay? I messed up. Huge. Even though I feel like you should own maybe five percent of this—" He stops short when he catches the death stare I'm sending. "Or not. That's fine." He rakes his fingers through his beachy waves. "Look, I don't know how things got so carried away."

My mind is reeling. "What does that mean?" When I hear carried away, I imagine him and May plowing through the pages of the Kama Sutra in his bedroom.

"It doesn't mean anything." He shrugs, searching for a way out of this. "It means . . . I don't know what it means. I got confused."

"And now you're not?"

"No. I'm still pretty confused. As a general rule." He flashes me a smile, and in that heartbeat of a second, I know I'm going with him. "But I'm not confused about this," he goes on. "This trip was meant to be, and it's happening, and—" He straightens, drawing his lips tight. "Fuck it. I miss you. I miss hanging out with you. And what's it all about, right? Nothing is more important to me than this—than going with you to Monterey, so please?" His eyes meet mine. "Please."

The sight of him this way, flustered and determined, the need in his voice, I mean, as much as I want to murder him, I want more of this. More of Nick. I missed him too, but I'm not about to say it. Instead, I say, "What time is it?"

He wakes up his phone. "Six-thirty."

"Give me ten minutes." He goes to open another drawer, and I stop him. "Maybe not that one, 'K? Just closet stuff."

He squints at me, a mischievous smile spreading across his lips, and he steps back, raising both hands. "What's in the drawer, Fi?"

"I mean it!"

His head lilts to the side. "Come on. You know I'm going in there."

"Oh my god. Stop."

At least he pretends to behave and crosses the room to my closet. When I'm at the door, he calls out, "I missed you too, Nick," in a high-pitched voice.

"I missed you too, Nick." I mimic back in the same funny voice he used.

"Still counts. I'm taking it," he calls after me.

When I get back to my room, Nick's not there. I peek out the window and see him and Dad talking as they load up the car. Dad puts a hand on Nick's shoulder. It looks serious. Maybe he's threatening him within an inch of his life. I throw on a pair of shorts and a T-shirt.

Nick calls from downstairs. "Fi! Let's go."

I grab the narwhal album from my nightstand. Then, I rush into Mom's bathroom, open the drawer, and drop her face cream in my bag.

Downstairs, Dad hands me a sweater. "Drive safe. Text me when you get in."

"Are you sure this is okay? I forgot to . . . I just . . . "

He pulls me into a hug. "I put some cash in your backpack and my credit card for emergencies."

"Thanks, Dad."

He turns to Nick. "Be careful."

"Yes, sir."

And we're off. The warm scent of freshly brewed coffee fills the car. Dad filled two travel mugs for us, and Nick is holding his. My hair is still wet and soaking through the back of my T-shirt.

Neither of us says a word.

The only thing distracting me is the immediate urge to take inventory. I'm cataloging everything I wanted to bring and am sure he forgot. Nick eyes me. He knows what I'm doing. "It's all there, Fi."

"My glasses."

"In the bag, both pairs. Allergy meds, Advil, sunglasses, contacts, your I-won't-touch-hotel-floor socks, and . . . "

Ugh, he did go into my sock drawer.

He reaches into the back and pulls out a small stuffed moose.

"Minou?" I say, secretly thrilled he brought her, the one keepsake I couldn't part with, but I downplay the whole thing. "You didn't have to bring Minou."

"Whaat?" He covers Minou's ears in mock horror. "How can you say that? She's devastated."

He fiddles with her coat, and for the first time, this trip feels real to me. My mind races through the last half-hour. "Hey, what did my dad say to you in the driveway?"

"You mean other than 'Be careful, Nick,'" he says in my dad's voice.

"Yeah."

He hesitates and watches the cars whip by out the passenger window. "Nothing."

The way he shifts away from me makes me think there was more to it.

"So, where are we at?" I emphasize the *we*, and he knows what I mean. I mean *us*.

He takes a drink of coffee, letting the question settle. "On Fourth Avenue headed for the highway."

Classic Nick. And I missed that, too. Just like that, we seem okay. Or as okay as we can be.

Then I remember. My mouth falls open, and I gasp. "I canceled the reservation!"

Nick blinks at me in mock horror. "What? You canceled?" Then, his face transforms into a smile. "I know. I rebooked it."

The freeway entrance sign blazes past us. "Which way am I going?"

"Did that, too," he says, waving his phone. "All routed out. Head for the I-5 South, and we'll be on that for a while."

I take the ramp onto the highway.

"And when we stop, we can switch up," he says.

"Switch up?"

From his wallet, he slides out a plastic card, his license. He smiles, beyond pleased with himself.

"What? You got it?"

"Yup."

"When?"

"Last week. May took me."

Her name lands like an anvil between us. I keep my eyes on the road and pretend I didn't hear it. Be cool. I can be cool.

"I was going to fail, too. By my third mistake, it was game over, and the lady was about to write something on the paper, so I broke out the Mom story."

My eyes widen. "Noooo, you didn't?"

"Oh yeah, the whole damn thing. She was full-on crying when we pulled into the DMV."

"Was it the real version?"

He pauses. "It was."

"Wow. Heavy. Wait. Was she the first person you've told?"

"Yeah! It felt pretty good, too, kind of like therapy, but she couldn't get out of the car fast enough, and how could she fail me after that? It was a total pity pass."

"That's insane but not a great endorsement of your driving skills."

He shoots me a look. "I can drive."

"Uh-huh."

"Minou has complete faith in my driving abilities, don't you, Minou?" He holds up Minou and forces her head to nod.

"What made you finally do it?"

"This trip. You. What kind of asshole would I be letting you drive the whole way?"

And then I remember exactly what I forgot to bring. I blink at Nick in a panic. "I forgot her camera."

He meets my eyes with all the calmness in the world. "I didn't."

It's a long drive to Monterey. Neither of us addresses the elephant in the car. We listen to music, we sing, and we stop for drinks at a place with a giant pink frosted donut on a pole reaching for the sky.

It's ten when we finally pull in. I text Dad, letting him know we made it. The motel is a long two-story white stucco building, and across the street are blinking storefronts of the massage and tattoo parlor variety. It's a little shady. A few homeless people are on the sidewalk.

We share the same weary expression. "You booked it for more than an hour, right?" I ask, and Nick breaks into a smile.

"I think an hour's plenty. Do you want to go somewhere else?"

Yes. Yes, I do want to go somewhere else. "Like where?"

"I don't know."

I pick up my phone and type "Monterey hotels" into google then click it off. "It's fine. We're tired. Let's just sleep."

"Okay, so we'll sleep."

Nick parks. It's the unsafest spot in the lot, not even remotely near the entrance. We take out our backpacks, and I follow him through the revolving doors into the lobby. An older woman at the front desk smiles sweetly, asks us where we're from, and gives us two keys to a king room—a downright luxury compared to the double we squeeze into at his house.

It takes all of five minutes for our stuff to cover the furniture. The place is okay. It's a little like a dentist's office if you stuck a bed in the middle of the waiting room. There's a beige loveseat, a flat-screen TV, and local magazines spread across a metal coffee table—not as cool as it looked online.

I slip on my I-won't-touch-hotel-floor socks and pajamas, and wash my face in the glass bowl that really does look like the pictures. Nick's already in bed when I come out of the bathroom. He took the side closest to the entrance—the serial killer side—and I didn't even have to ask. The room is so dark I trip over both of our shoes, trying to make it to the bed.

Do we need to talk about what happened? Our fight is kind of a blur, but I can't stop thinking about how hurt he looked that night when I said I didn't ask him to come over.

His face is lit up from the glow of his phone. He keeps glancing at me as I do my crazy hotel routine of kicking away the gross duvet and shining my phone light around the edges, searching for signs of bedbugs. I finally settle under the sheets.

"Nick?"

He doesn't look away from his screen. "Mmm?"

"Why did you come?"

He lowers his phone and is quiet for a minute. "Because . . . it's important."

"I thought after that night . . . "

"I would what . . . never talk to you again?"

"Something like that."

The light from his phone dims, but I can see a hint of his bright blue eyes through the darkness. "What is this? Midnight confessions?"

I glance at the clock. "More like eleven P.M. confessions."

He sighs. "What can I say? There was a huge Fiona-shaped hole in my life without you."

"Honestly?" This will get him.

He puts his phone on the nightstand and lays back. "It was what it was. Yeah, I was pissed, and I don't understand why you didn't text me, but I'm not a child, Fi. I'm not going to like, unfriend you or whatever."

"I'm sorry," I say. "Everything just snowballed insanely fast . . ."

His eyes meet mine. "I'm sorry, too."

Fiona

Slivers of light shine through the edges of the blackout curtains. Nick's still fast asleep, even though doors outside have been slamming for at least an hour. A toilet flushes from the room beside us, and our air conditioner kicks on with the force of a jet taking off. I was awake most of the night because of the noise, but Nick can sleep like the dead wherever he is.

Today is the first anniversary of Mom's death. When I told Grace I was thinking about this trip in the spring, she worried my expectations were too high. I'm not sure what I'm looking for. Closure? Something life changing? So, yeah, I guess they're pretty high.

I quietly scoot down the bed with my phone in hand, and sneak outside to the corridor. The view is even more spectacular in the morning light. The parking lot concrete really glistens under the rays of the sun. There aren't any messages from Dad, so I start to text him but stop. Today warrants a call.

"Hello." He sounds chipper.

"Hey!"

"Who's this?"

"The sea king holding your daughter ransom. Send ten thousand bucks, or you'll never see her again."

"Pro tip, sea king, I'd pay at least fifteen."

I nestle into one of the filthy white plastic chairs outside our door. "Noted."

"So what magic is in the water in Monterey that makes you get up this early?"

"The noisy air conditioner."

"Ah. I'll pick one up today for your room."

"Ha, ha."

He falls quiet, and I'm not sure if I should say anything about Mom because he hasn't. "Nice place?" he finally asks.

"The parking lot looks pretty special."

"Well, be careful."

"I will."

"How's Nick?"

"Still sleeping. Glad he came, though. Nice to have company."

I smack my phone against my forehead. If I could rewind and swallow my words, I would. I've entirely abandoned Dad today. It's not like we made plans, but the guilt of leaving him is hitting me hard.

"Are you okay?" I ask.

"You kidding me? Got some of the guys coming over to watch the game tonight. Red Sox and the Dodgers, going to be a good one."

I want to believe him. "That's great. Sounds like fun."

There's a pause on the line.

"Try to have a good time. It'll be over before you know it."

Does he mean this day or the weekend?

"I was just heading out to the store," he adds. "Gotta get some things for the game."

"Oh, okay, I'll let you go. Love you."

"Love you too. Send me some pictures of the beach."

"I will. Bye, Dad."

My heart sinks when I hang up. It wasn't enough of a conversation, but I didn't want to push him.

When I go back inside, Nick is pouring water into the coffee machine.

"Coffee?" he asks, stifling a yawn.

He doesn't mention my call, but he must have heard me. These walls are paper thin. "Yes. Just not this coffee."

Nick eyes me, confused.

"Hotel coffee machines are full of gross bacteria."

"Fi, *hotels* are full of gross bacteria. Especially this kind. This room is probably covered in jizz."

"Coffee pot included. You're literally about to drink jizz."

Nick smiles. He shakes his head and puts the cup down. "Hey, Siri, where's Starbucks," he says in his radio voice. Nick studies the map. "Ten blocks?! Fuck it, I'm taking my chances. You in?"

"Yeah. Fine. I'm sure it's fine."

"It's totally fine," he says, pressing the brew button.

"Why are you up so early, anyway?"

He raises his arms in a stretch, and his T-shirt rises a little, showing the slightest glimpse of his skin. It's nothing I haven't seen before, but being alone in a motel room makes it feel a million times different.

"Funny you should ask. I woke up, you were gone, and I had a slight panic attack that you drove me all the way down here so you could ditch me in Monterey."

"Mmm, that would be an expensive Uber home, for sure."

"Then, I heard you outside."

I nod.

"How's Bob?"

I'm glad he left out the Zombie part. "Good question. Acting like it's any other day."

"That's just how he is. You know he's thinking about it."

"Yeah."

Nick fixes my coffee the way I like it—two sugars, a dash of cream—and hands it to me.

It's times like this I wish Dad could see how wrong he is about Nick. Today, Nick is the rock, and I'm the TNT.

"So, what's the plan?" he asks.

Other than going to The Narwhal, I don't really have a plan. "Wanna go to Carmel?"

"That's my favorite thing to do in Monterey." He raises his paper coffee cup, and I knock mine against it.

Carmel is only a ten-minute drive, but it feels like a different world. The quaint cottages, with their gently sloping rooftops and curved doors, could be torn from the pages of *The Hobbit.*

A warm breeze from the ocean sweeps through the streets, and a light fog clings to the morning air as we stroll down Ocean Avenue.

We're surrounded by couples, an army of twos, with their hands intertwined. If there's any place meant for handholding, maybe not in the world, but on the West Coast, it's here. It doesn't bother me that we're not one of them. Who needs a hand when he packed Minou?

Nick and I take turns pointing out all the cool things we see. The stonework leading to alcoves, the scrolling wrought iron on the doors, the thatched roofs. A million details line the streets.

We duck into a shop called The White Rabbit, and it's like stepping into *Alice in Wonderland.* The place is brimming with Cheshire cats and red queens. Nick buys a small backwards clock for Max. We take a few selfies, and I text them to Dad.

I drag Nick into every pastry shop, and we eat our weight in carbs. We walk until we're at the cliffs overlooking the sea, and we're so high up it feels like we're at the edge of the world. We spend the rest of the day drunk off ocean views. Part of me wants to forget about The Narwhal and stay here all night, but as the sun dips lower, Nick drags me back to the car.

Tonight is finally happening after months of imagining this day. I'm nervous and don't know why. I turn off the shower and wrap myself in a Caribbean blue towel.

Mom's face cream is on the bathroom counter. I want to take a part of her with me tonight, so I pump it twice into my palm, but nothing comes out. I press the pump again, but there's still nothing, so I shake the bottle, and all that comes out is air. My chest tightens. This isn't happening, not tonight. My fingers travel up and down the sides, but the cylinder is seamless, there's nothing to unscrew or cut open, and whacking it against the counter doesn't help. Bottles are never empty, there has to be something inside.

Nick knocks on the door. "Everything okay?"

I fling it open. "It's not working. This isn't working."

He eyes me wrapped in the towel, then glances at the bottle. When you're mad with grief, it's easy to recognize the madness in others.

"You need to open this!" I thrust the bottle toward him.

He takes the bottle and struggles with the cap the way I did.

"I tried that already." I reach for it, but he holds it away from me.

"Give me a second!"

He bangs the frosted tube against the desk, repeating what I've already done.

"Forget it, give it back. I'll do it."

"Chill. You just gave it to me."

"Don't tell me to chill. You don't understand."

"I do understand."

I sit on the edge of the bed and bury my face in my hands.

Nick wields the bottle like a weapon, pacing the room for something—anything. Then, he drops it on the floor, picks up the wooden desk chair and smashes it over and over again.

The bottle shatters.

Pieces of glass scatter everywhere—they may as well be my heart. He calmly lowers the chair, kneels down and collects them, carefully scooping out the rest of the cream clinging to the edges. Then he kneels in front of me and gently dabs it onto my nose, chin, forehead, and cheeks. He annoints me with cream.

How has a year passed? She disappears more and more each day.

He places the rest of the pieces on the bedside table.

"I think you broke my mom's bottle."

"Looks that way, yeah."

I'm a little relieved it's gone. Maybe it was meant to happen here.

My fingers are cold against my cheeks as I press the cream into my skin, inhaling the fresh, marine-like scent one last time. "I know, I'm crazy." My words are barely a whisper.

Nick fiddles with a notepad on the desk. He faces me. "You're not crazy. I get it. I mean, I can't ever watch 'The Lord of The Rings' again."

The Jane Goodall book on his desk. The name of her chimpanzee. His mom's trip. "Frodo," I say quietly.

"It'll get ugly," he says, heading for the bathroom. "Give me ten minutes."

The shower turns on. I get up and root through the bag he packed for me. Everything's a revelation. There are clothes here I've never worn before. My fingers brush against something satiny at the bottom, and I pull out an emerald camisole. It shimmers in the light like a jewel. The thin straps are worn and a little fuzzy, and there's a small dark stain along the hem. It's been hanging in the back of my closet forever. It could work with my dark blue jeans.

When Nick comes out of the bathroom, he's holding a towel around his waist, and he freezes at the sight of me. The camisole dips in a v, showing off more skin than I ever have. It's a far cry from my usual T-shirt, sweatshirt look. I'm leaning over the desk, putting on lip gloss in the mirror, and suddenly feel self-conscious like I'm more naked than he is.

"What? Is this stupid?" I ask, tucking the gloss in my bag.

"No," he stutters. "It's perfect."

Things haven't been this awkward since the night of our fight.

"Thanks. You packed it."

"Yeah, but it's all you, Fi."

The part of me that watches love stories in movies knows this should be a moment, but I'm on edge, thinking about what tonight will bring. A huge part of me wants to bail on the entire evening. "Maybe we should just stay in."

Nick grabs his jeans and a black tee. He smiles. "We're going."

"But . . . "

He disappears into the bathroom. "I already ordered an Uber."

When he comes out a minute later, I pretend to be asleep on the bed. He grabs my hand and pulls me up. He freezes at the door, and I crash into him. "The album. Are we bringing it?"

I blink, panic filling my eyes. I was thinking about burying it there. Nick suggested burning it, but now I'm not sure about either. I feel like I've let go of enough for one day.

"Forget the album. Let's just do this," he says, reading my mind.

Outside, a salty breeze from the ocean rustles my hair. Our Uber pulls up and Carly, our driver, doesn't even need The Narwhal's address. She knows it well.

As we settle into the back seat, Nick pulls a small white box from his pocket and holds it out to me.

I eye him, confused. "What's this?"

"Open it," he says like it's obvious.

On top of the box is a small sticker with scalloped edges and a white rabbit in the middle. He must have bought it when he got the clock for Max. I wriggle the lid free. Nestled on a bed of pale blue tissue paper is a necklace, a tile of Alice with the Cheshire cat, and the words, "We're all quite mad here." Beside the tile is a miniature compass, and it all hangs on a silver chain.

A Cheshire cat. It's like he was in my room all those times I imagined him. This is some next-level kind of connection, and I can't tell him, either. I don't want to give him the satisfaction of knowing I talk to him when he's not around.

He downplays the whole thing. "I know you don't ever wear this stuff. You don't have to wear it. It just spoke to me."

"I love it," I say.

"Yeah?"

"Yeah. You have no idea how perfect this is."

He gives me a curious look.

I hand him the necklace while I turn slightly. He dangles the charm in front of me, his fingers lightly brushing against my neck as he carefully fastens the clasp. It seems to take forever yet doesn't last nearly long enough.

We're quiet for the rest of the drive. I trace my fingers over the tile and watch the streetlights go by in a blur out the window. Carly turns up a narrow dirt road leading to a hill. A blue glow pulses from the top, and as we climb higher, a building rises from the horizon like a vision in the Sahara.

The Narwhal.

Fiona

The Narwhal reveals itself from a sea of towering redwoods, like a secret between the trees.

We get out of the car, and Carly peels off, leaving us in a cloud of dust. Nick watches it fade from view and turns to face the bar. "So, this is it, huh?"

A few pickup trucks line the mostly empty lot. Christmas lights are still strung around the weathered porch, and the outline of a crooked narwhal flashes above the entrance in blue neon. The horn is burnt out. Unlike the picture from Google, this narwhal has arms that are moving, pointing to the entrance with every flash of light. This must be a new addition.

I pull out my phone and take a picture. "It's a little creepy, right?"

Nick glances around. The wind rustles through the trees and the faint sounds of laughter filter through the air from inside. "Nooo," he says, but then a smile breaks. "It's definitely a vibe. It's like we've been dropped into a dream sequence."

"Like this is one of those old saloons where someone walks in, and all the cowboys pull their guns out?"

"Yeah. Or a drug house in the middle of a deal, and they pull their guns out."

I face him. "You're so contemporary."

"It's like we've been beamed down, so there, I'm also futuristic." He takes a step forward and when I don't move, he reaches for my hand and leads me to the entrance. "We'll just stay for a drink."

"They're not going to serve us."

Nick tilts his head to the side. "Ninety-nine percent sure no one will care."

He keeps hold of my hand as we go in, tapping the back of it with his thumb. He's just as nervous as I am.

A sorry-looking group of locals sit at the bar and some obvious tourists are seated in booths.

When the host notices us, she abandons her animated conversation at a table nearby and walks over. Her hair is a wild heap of strawberry curls, and a blue gingham shirt is tied around her waist. "Evening. How y'all doing?" she asks with a southern drawl. "Here for dinner?"

"Drinks, but we don't know, maybe?" Nick turns back to me, and I give the smallest shake of my head. "Drinks," he says.

"No problem, if you change your mind, just holler. You can take a seat over there, and I'll be right with you." She points to a booth along the side of the room.

A big screen TV hangs above the bar playing the baseball game Dad must be watching at home. Some guy's on a stool with his ass crack on full display and a mug of foamy beer in front of him. Turns out, The Narwhal isn't even a charming dive. It's a complete dump. I imagined some oasis filled with secrets about Mom. Reality is so disappointing.

We slide into the booth. "This place is a shit hole," I say, leaning over the table.

He leans forward to meet me. "It's a giant shit hole."

The host returns to take our order.

"I'll have a frozen margarita, please."

She eyes us both for a long minute as if she knows she could call us out, but she doesn't.

Nick flips over the laminated drink menu. "You know what, make that two."

I poke his leg with my foot under the table when she leaves. "You hate tequila."

He scans the room. "If there was ever a place to drink shitty tequila, I think this is it."

"So? What do you think the deal was? Her album is full of pictures of this place."

"Maybe she was high?"

The host drops off our drinks. I take a giant sip and make a face. It's sickly sweet.

"Easy, tiger," Nick says.

"Excuse me," I call out after her. She turns around, and I give her a nervous smile. "Do you know if the owner's around?"

She eyes me, warily, like I'm about to jump up and serve her legal papers. "You're looking at her."

"Oh. Hi." I glance at Nick, and he gives me an encouraging nod. "My mom was here twenty years ago and photographed the bar. I know it's a long shot, but any chance that rings a bell?"

Her eyes soften. "I guess you can't ask her?"

I shake my head, and somehow she understands.

"A lot of people come in here and take pictures. It's kitschy that way. I wish I could help, but . . . "

I sink back into the red vinyl. What was I thinking, wanting to come here? "Thanks, anyway."

Another customer waves for her attention, and she leaves.

I fiddle with my straw. "This was a total waste."

"Fi . . . "

"Why do you think it meant so much to her?"

"I don't know. Maybe she was with someone." He picks at the thick rim of salt on the edge of his glass. "I kind of like the place. It's got character. And the floor—" He gestures to the hardwood. "That has to be original."

I nudge my head toward the guy on the bar stool. "Happy ending him."

"Who? Ass crack?"

"Yeah."

Nick draws in a mouthful of slush from his drink. He points to the glass. "You know, I feel like I'm on vacation with this." He steals a glance at ass crack and refocuses. "It's his birthday. He thinks his wife hates him, so he doesn't want to go home, but she's spent the whole day making a cake. It's on the table right now, with candles lit, and she's waiting for him to walk through the door so she can tell him how much she loves him."

I nod. "That's sweet. You made him kind of endearing."

"Meh. Not my best."

And I have a brilliant idea. He can do Mom. He should do Mom. "Second time's the charm."

"Second time?" He takes his mouth off the straw and smiles, eyeing me curiously. He leans back against the booth, and his smile fades. He knows what I want.

"No," he says.

"Come on."

"No. No way. I am not touching that one."

"You do it all the time!"

"No! It's not the same as doing a stranger."

"You're not raising her from the dead." He shakes his head and downs more of his drink, but he's thinking about it. He's caving. "Pleeease. You have to give me something. Don't leave me with this place being just a shit hole."

"Fiiiiiine. Okay."

I could hug him. He takes in my beaming face and says, "Don't look at me."

"Right. Sure."

Nick wipes the salt from the corner of his mouth, licking it from his thumb. His fingers drum against the table as he focuses on a spot in the middle and blanks out. I'm watching him, even though he told me not to. Finally, he meets my eyes. "Are you sure you want me to do this?"

"Yes!"

He rests his palms on the table and draws in a breath. "It was raining. Coming down in sheets so hard she couldn't see. She had to pull over for the night. Wound up in an empty motel with nothing to do. Across the street were these lights.

A flickering narwhal. It seemed like a sign. It was a sign. So, she took her camera, ran over, and the rain stopped as if she crossed into another dimension. There were newlyweds inside. They eloped and were celebrating with strangers. She wanted to take pictures, but they stopped her. No one could know, they said. So she made them a deal. She'd take pictures of everything around them. The lights they danced under, the photos on the wall that watched over them, the stools they sat on when their arms were interlocked in a toast. The next morning, she couldn't find their number, so she rushed back here, but the place was empty, as if none of it ever happened. So she kept the photos to remind her of what it is to live and love . . . "

My eyes flood with tears. I look up and blink them away.

He notices and stops. "Fi. I'm sorry. I'll shut up."

All I can do is stare at him. There are no words for what he's given me.

I get up. "I'm going to the bathroom."

He nods, his eyes heavy with regret.

Everything's a blur as I hurry across the bar. I don't know if it's because of Nick or the tequila.

The bathroom door closes, and I lean against it. I close my eyes. I thought he'd come up with something short and sweet. I didn't expect his words to hit me so hard. My face is flushed with heat, so I go to the sink, rinse my hands under the cool water, and press my chilled fingers to my cheeks. *Breathe, Fiona.*

When I come out, Nick is scrolling on his phone, his glass empty in front of him. What's left of mine is a radioactive green now that the slush has melted.

The room smells of dishwasher tabs and stale bar food—artificial. The owner's photos of her Airstream adventures cover the walls with images of happy faces, cookouts and driftwood. I follow a trail of them to the back where a glowing jukebox sits in the corner. I'm scanning the titles when the warm scent of sandalwood hits me—the soap at the motel. Nick is behind me. My senses are in overdrive. I don't want to move and ruin this closeness, so I sway back ever so subtly until my shoulders press against his chest, and he doesn't step away.

"Do you think she used this?" I ask.

"Of course she did. Who wouldn't?" he says softly.

The jukebox titles are a mix of classic oldies and nineties hits, and I wonder what Mom would have picked when coins clink in the machine.

Nick leans over me and punches two buttons. The familiar thuds of "Stand By Me" fill the air.

"You think she played this?" I glance over my shoulder at him.

"No. But at some point, the memory has to be yours."

Everyone is staring. The guys at the bar scowl at us because the music is interrupting the game on TV.

"Who cares about them?" Nick says, turning me away from the bar.

"Let's just go." The pressure on my chest is building. "Stand by Me" is not on my side in this battle.

Nick takes my hand as I try to pass him and pulls me back. "Dance with me."

"What? Are you drunk?"

"I'm not even remotely drunk. Dance with me."

"Here?"

"Here."

We're surrounded by empty tables. This place isn't exactly set up for dancing. He steps closer and slides a hand around my waist, taking my hand in his. I'm embarrassed by the spectacle before realizing it's not the prevailing feeling. This closeness, this contact. My other hand slides up his arm to his shoulder, and he pulls me closer. I rest my head on his chest, and he rests his chin on my head. We sway together that way.

"I don't think people dance like this anymore," I say.

"I wouldn't know."

Nick strokes the small of my back with his thumb.

"Get a room!" Ass crack yells.

"We have one, thanks," Nick calls out, pulling away from me. He flashes me a smile, his eyes, waves of blue. "You ready?"

"Yeah."

He goes back to our booth to pay the bill. "Fi." He waves me over. "Check this out."

As he steps to the side, I notice a framed photo hanging on the wall just above the booth behind us. We didn't see it earlier because people were sitting there. I inch closer. It's blurry, but I think it's them—Mom and Dad.

I look at Nick. "Do you think?"

"Solid chance." He glances around, then plucks the photo from the wall, and tucks it into my bag. He grabs my hand, and we hurry toward the exit. I'm expecting someone to stop us, but nobody does.

The faint thuds of "Stand by Me" follow us outside. We stand side by side on the hilltop, shrouded in a gauzy blue haze. My mind is adrift in a sea of stars, stuck somewhere between past and present, reality and fiction. I'm so lost in my thoughts, I don't even notice the Uber approaching.

I only know it's here because Nick squeezes my hand.

I look down.

He never let it go.

Fiona

When we get back to our room, Nick belly flops onto the bed.

"Do you want to use the bathroom first?" I ask, dropping my tote on the chair.

"No," he mumbles into the sheets.

I swipe my pj's from my bag and head in to change. It feels like heaven, peeling off my outside clothes and slipping into comfort. I wash up and click off the light.

"Nick?" I whisper, taking soft steps across the floor.

He doesn't answer. He's passed out with his sneakers still on. I drop my clothes on the desk and slide the picture from my tote.

The room is dark, and I don't want to wake him, so I turn on the flashlight from my phone. It's a blurry photo, but definitely them. Mom is laughing, and Dad looks, well, like he usually does—unimpressed. A flower is tucked behind his ear. I can't tell what kind. I place the photo on the desk and rub my eyes. What am I looking at? Dad could tell me, but I don't want to text him. I want to see the look on his face when I show him this.

Nick's feet dangle off the edge of the bed. I gently slide his sneakers off, and he curls his legs closer to his chest. I drape a throw blanket from the loveseat over him, then crawl under the sheets and try to sleep.

A slamming door from our neighbors wakes me the next morning. The clock on the nightstand blinks six-thirty. Nick's arm is draped around Minou. He's in a white T-shirt and gray plaid pajama bottoms. He must have woken up last night. When he's sleeping, I don't have to worry about what my face gives away, so I take this gift of a minute to study him—his full lips, the expanse of freckles lightly scattered across his cheeks like distant stars in the Milky Way, the way his sun-kissed sandy hair flops gently over his eyes. It's getting long, and I can't help myself. I reach for a lock on his forehead and gently sweep it away. It flops back down. He lets out a soft moan and hugs Minou tighter.

He doesn't budge when I slide out of bed. I shrug into a clean white T-shirt and shorts, and take a makeup wipe to my face.

There's a notepad on the desk, so I scrawl, "At the beach," on the paper, with a heart drawn beside it. I hesitate. Since the love-you text, hearts on notes might hit differently. But whatever, I've always drawn hearts on notes. Hearts on notes is normal Fiona behavior, so I tear off the page, neatly fold it and drop it on the bed beside him. I grab my bag from the floor and slip out of the room.

A pathway from the motel takes me to the highway, and it's so early it's nearly empty. The beach is across the street. The wind is brisk this morning, and sand whips around my face. It's low tide. Two women hunt for newly exposed shells along the shore. Five dolphins swim by in five minutes. It's beautiful.

We used to go to the beach close to home all the time. Mom and I would spend hours collecting shells while Dad relaxed on the sand. I would search for the whelks, her favorite, and she would scoop up the scallop shells because they were mine. Once our hands were full, we'd reveal them to each other like treasure and choose a favorite to take home. She called the loud rush of the waves free therapy and even had three crisp waves tattooed on her ankle. Dad would laugh and say he thought he was the free therapy. We haven't been to one since she died. I take a picture and text it to Dad.

Far to my left, the beach ends at a red-and-white barrier. Beyond it is a rocky cliff. It would make a nice picture. I feel antsy now that a few more people are milling about, so I head toward it for privacy. The waves lap against the shore, and pools of white foam form around my ankles, the water warmer than the air.

I walk until I reach the barrier. The area is peppered with signs: Rocks are Slippery When Wet. Dangerous Currents. Do Not Enter. They warn me to turn around, but I want to carry on, like a broken robot who can go nowhere but forward. Mom would love this view, wild and free.

So I climb over the barrier.

Nick

I wake up in an empty bed. I sit up and call Fi's name, but she doesn't answer. That's when I spot the note on the covers. It's neatly folded across the middle on motel stationery; it's so Fiona to fold it as if this is some forties movie, and the words need protecting.

At the beach. There's a heart drawn beside it.

I drop it next to me and flop back into the pillows. It's as good a sign as any to go back to bed, but my mind's racing. Last night was kind of intense. It all comes back to me in fragments. Fiona's hazel eyes welling with tears, sliding my hand around her waist, that song. I close my eyes, reliving it all, then open them just as quick.

Yeah. I need to get out of this room. Shake it off. Snap back to reality. What was I thinking? This weekend is about her. Not about me. Not about us. I hope I didn't make things worse.

I get dressed and grab my sunglasses. Fiona's stuff is all over the place and clearly won't fit into the five-inch safe they provide, so I just leave everything and get the hell out.

I'm not sure where to go or what to do with myself. It's instinct to text Fi, so I do.

You okay?

I watch the screen for a second. If she's at the beach, she won't hear her phone buzzing over the waves. She probably wants to be alone, so I head for the lobby. The revolving doors are already in motion when I get there. There's a small complimentary coffee station inside, so I pour myself a cup. All that's left is sweetener and powdered creamer—hard pass. I put a lid over the black, tarry sludge and use my imagination as I take a sip.

The lobby is ten degrees cooler than comfortable. The kid behind the reception desk doesn't look much older than me. He's wearing two sweaters and surfing on his phone. The rest of the room is empty. It's freshly renovated, painted in beachy blue hues with light wood accents, but none of it can mask how old the place is. It smells old. Old and painted over.

Sunlight spills through a set of glass doors at the far end. A sign on the wall says Pool in black letters with an arrow beneath pointing to the doors. I head for them.

The pool reno didn't go as far as the rest of the place. It's a concrete rectangle with a worn blue diving board and globe lights strung around a grungy white fence. It could almost be chill except for the noise from the highway across the street. If you stand on the diving board, you might be able to see the ocean.

There's a kid by himself in the water. He looks around ten, a little older than Max, and he's floating on his back, staring up at the sky with swimming goggles covering his eyes.

I roll up my jeans and sit at the edge, dipping my legs into the subzero water. The disturbance makes the kid flip upright. He watches me for a second and swims to the opposite end, picking up a handful of batons. He throws them into the water, waits for them to sink, and dives after them, resurfacing with a few.

"You gonna swim?" he asks.

There's nobody else here. He's talking to me. "No."

"How come?"

"Cause it's cold."

"Not once you get used to it," he says, jumping up and down in the shallow end.

I smile. "Don't you have parents?"

"Yeah."

"Where are they?"

"Why? Are you a kidnapper?"

I shake my sunglasses free from my T-shirt pocket and slide them on. "Do I look like a kidnapper?"

"Hard to say," he says. "Anyway, they're getting ready."

I don't ask for what.

He pushes himself back from the edge and resumes floating on his back. He's staring up at the sky so intently that I look up to see what's so interesting.

A brilliant sun blazes above us.

And this feels so familiar. I was ten when Alex had Max. She was seventeen. When Max was six months old, Mom took us to Florida for a week to stay at Nana's timeshare in

Boca. I think Nana offered it up for my benefit. She knew how much Mom and Dad were arguing about Alex, so she gave us her extra week and told Mom not to bring Dad. Not that he would have gone anyway. Spending a week in a one-bedroom condo with all of us? Yeah, I don't think so.

So, it was just the three of us, well, the four of us, I guess. The place was crawling with more old people than I'd ever seen in my life. It was like a grandparents' convention had convened at the hotel.

Mom was all about Alex and the baby, but when they stayed in the room, we had some time to ourselves. We had races in the pool because she wasn't a big ocean person, and every afternoon, we walked to the marina, where she would excitedly point at the fish swimming in the water between the boats.

The rest of the time, I occupied myself. Max cried a lot, and Alex and Mom were usually fighting, but I didn't care. I built sandcastles with moats that stretched down to the ocean. I saw a snake and even got stung by a jellyfish. I'm glad I have that scar. It's like the universe didn't want me to forget what I have, not what I'm missing. It wasn't perfect, but to me, it was the greatest vacation of my life.

The kid's parents step out of the lobby. They're dressed up in country club attire even though it's midmorning.

"Adrian!" his mom yells. "I said, ten minutes!"

Adrian straightens from his floating position and treads water, facing her. "How long has it been?"

She shakes her head, exasperated. "I don't know. Way longer than that."

"Oh. Okay."

"Let's go! Come on!"

Adrian's dad is typing on his phone and hasn't looked up once. His mom's phone rings, and she answers, walking back into the lobby, with his dad trailing behind. It's all so disingenuous, it's worse than if they were arguing.

Adrian dives under the water again for the hell of it and surfaces with the rest of his rainbow-colored batons. He swims over to me and drops them on the pool deck in a puddle. "Here, you can use these," he says, breathless, as if he's trusting me with something of great importance.

"Cool," I say, nodding.

He hoists himself out of the water, leaving giant wet footsteps in his wake as he heads for the door. He pulls the swimming goggles over his head and sweeps his sopping hair away from his face.

"Hey," I call out. He turns back to me. "You having a good trip?"

He smiles wide. "Yeah! It's the best!" And he disappears through the lobby doors like a mirage.

Like me.

I pick up a bright blue baton from the wet pile beside me, and let it roll across my palm, throwing the others back into the water. They slowly sink to the bottom. Adrian will find them later. I'm sure no one else is crazy enough to go in this pool. I get up, slide my shoes onto my wet feet, and head for the gate at the side to make my way to the beach.

Because that's where Fiona is, and I don't care if she wants to be alone. I can't be anymore. The bright blue baton feels like magic in my hand. I slide it in my pocket.

One is enough.

It's something I can run with.

Fiona

Climbing over the barrier doesn't seem very dangerous. The sky is peppered with clouds, and the waves roll in gentle lulls. I kick off my sandals, leaving them in the sand, and push my bag behind me. The expanse of earth soon narrows, and up ahead, giant boulders jut out from the sea.

I take a careful step forward. The stone is hot beneath my feet, and seawater sloshes in the gap between it and the path. Lightly, I step from one stone to the next until the rock surface narrows, and I'm balancing more than stepping between them, but I'm good at this. I know how to balance. I look back. The barrier is barely visible, so I stop.

It's a beautiful view. Tiny sailboats dot the horizon, and a lone seagull hovers in the breeze. A sweeping cliff is to my left, and I feel so small out here, my presence a speck in this landscape.

I slip my hand inside my bag for Mom's camera. When I imagine her holding it, she's on a bent knee, a strand of auburn hair tucked behind her ear, and her face scrunched up like it always was when she looked through the viewfinder. It's the only picture that matters.

Whatever is on here will only be a reminder of her death—not her life with us.

A wave crashes against the rocks. Water splashes my legs, and I waver. The ocean only takes a second to change its mind, and the waves are crashing harder now.

"Fiona!" My name rings out in the distance.

I turn and see Nick jogging down the shoreline.

Another wave breaks, spreading water over the rocks, and it trickles down the cracks before rolling out to sea. My shorts are soaked and a saltwater mist seeps through my lips.

"FIONA!"

Be still.

Nick scrambles over the barrier and runs until the ground ends. His eyes follow the trail of boulders. He does the math—tall, uncoordinated boy plus slippery rocks equals certain death. His chest heaves with panic, and he extends an unreachable hand. He spots the camera in my hand.

"So do it," he yells.

I look out to the ocean. The tide is coming in. The waves multiply in the distance, each one larger than the last, and so much water pools around my feet that I slip for a second. Before I can find my balance, I'm pummeled again, and turn to shield my body from the impact.

Panic sets in.

"Do it!" Nick yells, more urgently now.

The sun breaks through the clouds. It's so bright, I raise my arm to shield my eyes. The water calms, and I take in the vast expanse of cerulean blue. The golden rays of sunlight shimmer across the surface, making the water glitter like diamonds.

It's perfect.

With a sweeping throw, I let it go. The camera sails through the air and disappears into the waves—barely a blip on the radar of the universe. It's gone in a heartbeat, like her. Hope surges through me. For what, I'm not sure.

"Fiona." Nick's tone is low and stressed.

But it's okay. It's an easy pivot on my toes to face him. I glide from one stone to the next without missing a beat. *See? I've got this,* I want to say. This will be the easiest part of my day, but a rogue wave crashes and my foot slips. The rock slices along my calf, but I don't fall because Nick's hand grips my arm. He catches me.

He helps me onto the path and pulls me into him. I wrap my arms around his waist, and he rests his head on mine, and we stand that way for what feels like forever as the waves crash and spray all around us.

When he pulls away, he crouches down and wipes at the blood on my leg. "We need to put something on this." He squints up at me, the sun bright in his eyes.

"Doesn't really hurt."

He stands and draws in a breath, holding back his words. He wipes his hands on his jeans. "Then maybe we can call an ambulance for me because I think I'm having a heart attack." He stumbles back, clutching his chest.

"Sorry." I wince, grateful he didn't go there.

He grips my shoulders and searches my eyes. "Are you okay?"

"Yeah," I say with a slight nod.

"What can I do?"

I reach for his hand on my shoulder. "You're doing it. And maybe get me some nachos."

He slings an arm around me, and we head back down the shore. "That, I can do."

We spend the rest of the day on the beach, my leg wrapped in a bandage. A sea lion waddles over and plays in the sand nearby. Nick asks me to take a picture of him with it, so I take at least a dozen on my phone when a couple strolls by and asks if we want one together. It's way more awkward than it should be. Nick hands over his phone, runs back and slides an arm around my waist. He flashes the peace sign. The sea lion slaps its fin against the sand in front of us and we laugh.

He texts me the pictures. There are two. The second is the good one. We're smiling, the sun is setting behind us, our faces are sunburned and windswept, and the sea lion's fin is raised in a perfect wave.

In the first photo, the one the woman said she had to retake, my mouth is open mid-laugh because I thought we were about to be attacked. Nick doesn't even notice because he's looking at me, his lips curled in an easy smile. The picture's a little blurry, but it's my favorite.

Soon, a silver glow from the moon replaces the sun. Nick is lying on the warm sand with his eyes closed while I sit next to him. It would be so easy to sleep here, listening to the waves rolling gently to the shore.

A loud whoosh escapes from the ocean, and a whale breaches the water right in front of us.

"Nick," I gasp, my hand instinctively landing on his stomach.

He places his hand on mine and bolts upright.

The whale expels a fountain of water and slips back into the inky sea.

"No way!" he says.

We share a surprised look, then glance around for other witnesses so this might seem more real, but the beach is empty. It was just for us.

He looks at me, eyes wide. "Did that really just happen?"

It sums up how I feel about most of this summer. "Yeah. I think it means we won at Monterey."

He lets out a soft laugh. "The elusive Monterey bingo." His phone buzzes beside him. Alex's name is on the display, but he clicks it off without answering.

"It's late. We should go inside," I say. "And I'm hungry."

Nick shakes the sand from his hands. "There's a few places on the strip. You want to go somewhere?"

I get up and make a face. "Can you just bring something back to the room? Grab a slice or something."

"Help me up," he says, holding out a hand. I grab it, and he lets out an exaggerated groan as he stands. "Cheese?"

"Pleeeaaaase. You have a room key?"

He pulls it out and waves it around.

With our shoes in our hands, we leave the beach behind.

By the time he comes back with a couple of slices, I'm already packing. The TV's on, and he sits cross-legged on the bed with a maps app open, studying the route home between bites. He's trying to figure out if it would take too long to drive the coastal route back and see all the sights he keeps discovering on Google. Alex's texts are still buzzing through asking him to call her about the lawsuit, but he ignores them.

Since I've packed all my things, I start to pack his, too. He watches me fold one of his shirts and tuck it into his backpack.

"Thanks," he says with a warm smile.

The flip side of my heart.

Tears prickle in my eyes and I quickly turn, blinking them away.

It's this picture of us.

It's over too soon.

Fiona

The next morning, Nick checks us out. I toss my backpack in the car and wait for him in the parking lot. Across the street, the red lights of a tattoo parlor, the Tatomb, blink on and off above the shabby entrance. It's been on my mind since the night we pulled in.

Nick comes out, folds the receipt into a square, and tucks it in his back pocket. "You ready?"

"Almost."

He follows my gaze across the street. "Then let's hit the road."

"Just give me a minute." I leave him behind, heading for the sidewalk.

"Where are you going? We're already leaving way late. I don't want to do a night drive," he calls out after me. He slams the trunk of my car and catches up, sweeping his hair away from his face. He's been grouchy all morning, and I get it. Too much sun and sand, and he has to work tomorrow.

"I just want to check it out."

But I don't. I've been slowly talking myself into this all weekend, and it's now or never.

The door jingles when I push it open. It's empty inside and smells faintly of bleach and incense. There's a chair deep in the room with a beaded curtain separating it from the entrance and a ton of designs taped across the walls. Hearts, birds, symbols, all the usual suspects are on display.

A petite woman steps out from the back, dressed in ripped jeans and a t-shirt. "You legal?" she asks, giving us the once-over.

"Yeah," I say.

"IDs."

Nick side-eyes her. "We don't need ID just to be in here."

But I'm already placing my license on the counter. She examines it.

"You getting or looking?" she asks.

"Getting," I say.

Nick's mouth falls open. "Wait . . . are you serious? You're doing this?"

The way he says it makes me think twice, but I back out of everything, so I stubbornly commit. "I am."

The woman opens Instagram on her phone and holds it out to me. "That's some of my work."

Nick leans over my shoulder as I scroll through the art on her account. It's kind of intimidating. There are a ton of giant tattoos. The account name is MikiArt. "You did all this?"

"Studied under the best." She beams. "You know what you want?"

I'm panicking because I don't. Something small, ideally, but I don't want to copy Mom. My mind jumps to yesterday. The beach. "I think so."

Nick says, "Let me guess, my name in a heart on your ass?"

Miki gives him an amused smile. Nick's charms are irresistible to everyone.

"Because that's what I'm getting." He flashes her an extra charming smile back.

She leads me through the beaded curtain, and I catch Nick studying the drawings on the wall.

"So I guess I have to get one, or else I'm a chicken shit, right?" he calls out. "What should I get? Some random band logo on my shoulder? An anchor? This is sweet." He flicks a sailor's anchor with a vine crawling over it.

"You don't have to get anything."

He gasps. "You're not getting the word *breathe*, are you?"

"You're the creative one. I'm sure whatever you come up with will put mine to shame."

"No pressure there."

It's the most painful thirty minutes of my life, and I didn't even choose anything complicated. I went with a small outline of a scallop shell. Something to remind me of our days at the beach. When it's done, I feel a rush of exhilaration, then remember this is permanent. What did I do?

Miki checks over her work and says the redness will fade in a day. I sling my bag over my shoulder and leave through the curtains.

"So? Are you in?" she asks Nick.

"Yeah. Yeah, I'm down," he says with a grin.

He shoos me out the door, sending me to a sandwich shop down the road so I won't peek.

When Nick comes out, he's pulling on his hoodie.

"Hey!" I yell from the parking lot, waving a paper bag.

He flashes me a wave and froggers his way across the street. We jump in the car, and I pull out of the lot.

Nick rips the paper bag and reaches inside. "So? What'd you get?"

He means the tattoo. "Hummus wraps with stuff."

He smiles at my answer but plays along, unraveling the wax paper and biting into the wrap. "So good."

He holds the bitten wrap out to me, and I lean over, taking a bite. Gobs of hummus fall on the center console, and I sweep it up with my finger. "Oh my god. Yum."

"Right?"

"I would come back here for this alone."

The wrap is demolished before we get onto the highway. I watch Monterey grow smaller in the rearview, and a silence settles over us. Everything feels different, and now we're going back to a place where everything is the same. It's like the tape is rewinding with every mile.

"Did you get what you needed?" Nick finally asks.

And I'm not really sure. "I think so."

He puts on some music, and we fall into our routine of singing until we can't stand the sound of music anymore.

We left too late to take the scenic route back and stop at

a Starbucks outside of San Francisco. I park around the back and toss Nick the keys so we can switch up. After we get our drinks, we lean against the hood. Nick with his iced espresso and me with my iced tea.

"So." Nick studies me, a smirk on his face. "You're killing me. Spill about the tat."

"What'd you get?" I ask, tugging at the hem of his shirt.

"Nuh-uh." He steps back. "You first."

"Guess."

"Ohhh, what is this—who knows who better?"

"Well, I obviously know you better, and I pay more attention to things."

"Okay, then you guess first."

I pace in front of him. The thing with Nick is, as much as I know him, he can be so abstract. I have no idea what he'd settle on for a tattoo. "Fiona."

"Wow. Nailed it."

He's joking, but my eyes widen, feigning excitement. "Seriously?"

"No!" He says in mock disgust.

"Mom?"

He laughs. "No."

"Pi, or Pissis or whatever." The mountain he's talked about visiting near the crash site.

He tilts his head to the side. "I'm impressed, you remember. Thought about it, but decided not to go there."

"Good call. Bullshit?"

"I'm not in prison!"

I squint in concentration. "Bear." His mom used to call him that.

"Ouch. That hurt." He clutches his chest and staggers back. "No, but maybe you do know too much about me." He gives me sad eyes, and I feel guilty for mentioning it.

I tuck a strand of hair behind my ears. "If I keep guessing, this will just get sadder."

"Good point."

He turns around, his back facing me.

"Where is it?"

"Left shoulder."

I pounce on him, tugging at his neckline, but he makes a strangling sound, so I lift his shirt from the back, and my hands travel up his body until I see it. The word *echo* in lowercase black script. Nick's always had a thing with echoes. He's told me how he, Alex, and his mom used to yell into the void at the falls. It should have been an easy guess.

He spins around to see my reaction. "So?"

"It's perfect. So poignant and devastating."

He raises his arms in victory. "That's what I was going for."

"I like how the line continues after the O, like it's still going somewhere."

"Me too." He snaps his fingers. "Come on. Your turn."

"You didn't guess."

He looks up to the sky, thinking, and then into my eyes. "A narwhal," he says, sounding so sure.

I knew he would say that. "Ha! Nope."

"Camera?"

I shake my head.

"A date? Tube of film? Balance beam?" He drums his fingers against his cup. "Face cream. Can I see? Where is it?"

"Left hip." My fingers point down to it like an arrow. He

puts his cup on the car and steps closer. I step back, suddenly insecure. After everything we've been through, I shouldn't be, but the tattoo feels private, like it's just for me. "Just forget it. You don't need to see."

"Come on!" He steps closer again, eyeing me curiously. "No fair. I showed you mine."

"Are you sexually harassing me right now?"

"Yes. Yes, I am. Now show it!"

My nervousness heightens. I lift my shirt a bit, and he closes the gap between us, glancing around the parking lot as if we're about to do something verboten. He gently tugs at the waist of my shorts.

"Fi," he says, softly, his head falling to the side as he studies it. I step away, waiting for him to say more. "It's amazing." He thinks for a minute. "Did you choose it for the symbolism?"

Symbolism? Please tell me this doesn't mean something weird like I'm in a cult. "What do you mean?"

"Scallop shells are associated with pilgrimage, rebirth, Venus, you know . . ."

"Oh." I squint at him. "How do you *know* all this stuff?"

He slides a hand down his face. "Don't judge me. I went down a rabbit hole once."

"A shell rabbit hole?"

"It was for a paper on Botticelli for art! Did they not teach things at your school?"

"Yeah, but it was so long ago. Like ninth-grade material."

We laugh.

"Well, now I want to say that I did a deep dive into shell lore, but, no. I've just always loved them."

"Huh," he says, threading the strings together in his mind.

A hint of a smile plays on his lips. "I love that I know this about you. Did I see a hint of color?" I nod. A glimmer of pink lines the scalloped edges. "Let me see it one more time," he pleads.

"You get three seconds, tops." I lift the corner of my shirt again, and he folds down the edge of my shorts.

He studies the shell, then his eyes connect with mine. He's standing so close. "You made the memory your own," he says quietly, brushing his thumb low across my hip.

I shiver. And it sucks that my body betrayed me this way without my brain's permission. I step back, but he caught it, and I die a thousand awkward deaths.

A car pulls into the spot beside us.

Nick wipes his palms against his jeans. He looks as surprised as I feel. "I'm sorry."

"Noitsokay," I say rapid fire, heading around the back to the passenger side.

"Zombie Bob's going to kill you," he says, once we're in the car, as if nothing happened. "And probably me."

"No. We are taking this to the grave."

"Deal."

We're acting normal, but that's all it is—acting. Imaginary Nick says, "Why did you shiver when I touched you?"

Real Nick says nothing. Real Nick watches the world go by while he selects a song I will inevitably read into. Real Nick plays something by Frank Ocean. It's unreadable. He drums his fingers against the steering wheel. He flicks his feelings to off, and I wish it were that easy for me.

Nick

When Fi pulls into my yard, an older black Lincoln is idling in the driveway. I think the world can agree that nothing good comes from a random car idling in your driveway at night. She cuts the engine. "Are you expecting . . . "

"Nope." I push open my door and head for the Lincoln. Classical music blares from inside. I knock on the tinted window, and it rolls down a few inches, revealing an older man with white hair sticking up like he'd been sleeping. "Can I help you?" I ask.

"So sorry about the noise," he stutters, turning the music down. Papers are scattered all over his car, and he waves a hand over them still getting his bearings. He plucks a sticky note from the dash that I'm pretty sure has my name on it. He peers over his glasses at me through the crack in the window. "Are you Nicholas Bennet?"

In the movies, someone always answers with, "Who wants to know?" And I toy with it, I do, but I have a sinking feeling, and I don't want to drag this out, so I keep it simple. "Yeah."

He fumbles around for a briefcase on the passenger side floor and opens his door. Fiona's coming toward us with my backpack slung across her shoulder.

The guy steps out and shakes my hand. "Clyde Owens, attorney at law. I have some business to discuss with you, Mr. Bennet."

His brown suit is wrinkled and saggy like he fished it out of the trash. A lump of panic rises in my throat because my first thought is that the court realized they made a huge mistake and wants to revoke my license or put me in jail.

"What business?"

Clyde looks at Fiona. "It's a private matter. Regarding your lawsuit."

Alex's lawsuit. I almost wish it were the jail thing. "Sorry, Clyde, you've got the wrong Bennet. I don't have a lawsuit." Clyde follows me up the stairs to the door. "Isn't it a little late for you to be here?"

"Well, yes, but I drove down from Portland and didn't want to make another trip tomorrow."

I'm guessing Clyde is not big-time as far as lawyering goes. I bet he lives in that Lincoln—classic Alex. She probably found him on a grocery store bulletin board.

"Is there someplace we can speak privately?" he asks.

Fiona comes up beside us as I unlock the door. "I'll put your bag inside and take off."

Which is crazy. "What? No." I reach for her arm and turn back to Clyde. "Look, whatever you have to say to me, you can say in front of her. Take a seat in the kitchen. We'll be right there."

Clyde scrutinizes the house as if he's expecting a killer dog to jump out at him. Then there's a long, drawn-out screech of the chair legs against the kitchen floor. Fucking Clyde.

Fiona moves my hand from her arm. "It's okay, really. I should go."

She takes baby steps back toward the door, trying to tip-toe her way out. It feels wrong, her leaving this way after our weekend. "I want you to stay."

She winces, eyeing the back of Clyde's head. "But this is private."

"Are you kidding me? Please stay." I don't know what this guy's going to say, but I don't want to hear it alone. Fiona shifts her weight and glances back at her car, still unsure. "You know I'm just going to text you all of this, anyway."

She finally caves. "Okay. Okay. Fine."

We go to the kitchen, and papers cover the table. Clyde watches Fiona pass behind me.

"She's staying."

He nods, pushing up his thick black-rimmed glasses. "Have a seat, Nicholas."

Fiona sits at the far end of the table. As removed, yet present, as she can be.

"First of all, Mr. Bennet, I'm sorry for your loss."

I don't know why I'm so nervous all of a sudden. It's like I'm being held together by silly string. I don't want to be listening to any of this. "Yeah, thanks."

"You're aware there was a civil suit against South American Airlines initiated by your sister, Alexandra . . . "

"If this is about the statement, I haven't done it, and I'm not doing it, so you can tell Alex it's not happening."

"The airline wants to settle, Mr. Bennet."

That's when my hearing goes mute, and my heart starts to beat out of my chest. "I don't understand."

He slides a stack of papers my way, marked with little flags where I'm supposed to sign beside. "I've already been to see your sister, and she's on board with the settlement, but your signature is also required."

The words in front of me are a blur of black ink. *Elizabeth Bennet Settlement* stands out. There's a two with a lot of zeros after it. "But . . . how? I thought this kind of thing took years."

"Lawsuits are bad business for airlines. As I explained to Alexandra, if you hold out for a trial, I believe you'll win considerably more, but she seemed keen to settle. The settlement will be split equally between you and your sister."

The pen feels like venom between my fingers. I drop it and push the papers away. "I don't want it."

"Mr. Bennet—"

"I don't want it. Send it back. Donate it. I don't care."

"It's two million dollars," he says slowly, as if impressing the importance upon me.

It's laughable. I can't figure out if it's an insult or an over-payment. And I can't be in here a second more, so I shove away from the table and head for the door. Behind me, Fiona says, "Can you give him a day? Do you have a card?"

A few minutes later, the porch door screeches open, and Clyde pauses beside me on the stairs. I expect him to argue with me, but he only rests a hand on my shoulder and then leaves.

Inside, I hear Fiona sweeping the papers together. She

comes out with a sleeve of chocolate chip cookies and sits next to me, wearing my black Seattle hoodie. She takes a bite from a cookie, and the sound of her drawn out crunching fills the air. Her silence is killing me.

"Can you say something?" I finally cave like she knew I would. She looks at me, midbite and a chocolate chip falls, sticking to her chin. She wipes it away and licks her fingers. "What would you do if someone came out of nowhere and said, 'Take all this money.'"

She shrugs. "I don't know. All my private lessons bailed on me, and I'm pretty broke right now."

"You wouldn't take it. You tossed her camera into the ocean. There could have been an epic million-dollar photo on it."

She faces the driveway, her eyes growing wide. "Damn! Didn't think of that."

"You wouldn't want it," I say.

"It's not the same."

"It is."

Fiona mulls it over. "The camera was a leftover from the accident and something that should have disappeared with her. Burn the bucket list if you want to get rid of something. That's closer."

But in my head, it's infinitely easier to decline a million dollars than burn the bucket list. I just can't. "How can I ever get away from all this if I'm reminded every time I buy a fucking sandwich."

She picks a stray grass clipping from the cookie. "Yeah, but . . ."

I give her a look as if to say, see.

"It's a lot of money." The moon is a bright crescent above us. Her gaze shifts from it to me. "You haven't wrapped your head around it, but it's all perspective, right? Look at what you do with the happy endings."

"The happy endings are a lie, I tell myself. They're a bullshit coping strategy."

"People lie to themselves all the time," she says.

"You think I should take it."

"I think you should look at it as an opportunity, not an anchor. It buys you time. You can get out of here. You can travel. You can finish her bucket list."

"Yeah, I've already watched 'E.T.'"

"If you don't want to deal with it, put it in a different account. But don't let the grief make the decision."

I lean my head against the porch railing. "I can't believe you waited so patiently to say all that."

"Patience is a virtue?"

I laugh. "Is it?"

My phone rings. Alex's picture comes up on the screen. I've already missed about a hundred calls from her, so I answer it. "Hey."

She's talking a million miles a minute. Fiona leans in and touches my leg.

"I'm going," she whispers.

"Hang on a second," I say to Alex, covering the phone with my hand. I get up and follow Fi to her car. "Stay. You should stay. It's late."

She turns back to me. "It's always something . . ." she says with the faintest smile.

It takes a minute for me to get it. The endless reasons I find for her to stay. Because it's late, because it's raining, because her dad's not home, because I need her. I will always find a reason. And I have no idea what to say to that.

Because all I can think about is the contract on my table. The words scrolling through my brain in black and white. This unexpected finality. This pressure to respond. And I feel like I'm choking—drowning under paperwork and obligation.

Alex's tinny voice yells my name from the speaker.

"I'm going," she says again, and for the first time, she really does.

Fiona

When I get home, the house is dark, but I hear the shower running upstairs. I quickly dig the picture from my bag and scan the kitchen for a place to stand it upright. I put it front and center on the counter beside Dad's mug.

Then I sit on the couch in the darkness like a spy interrogator and wait. Dad doesn't notice me when he comes down the stairs. He goes into the kitchen, opens the fridge, closes it and moves to the sink.

Silence.

The frame lightly scrapes against the counter.

He moves to the archway between the two rooms, the frame held low in his hand. "When did you get in?"

My folded arms on the couch routine isn't fazing him, so I bolt up. "That's what you're going to ask me right now?"

He heads back into the kitchen.

"Dad! What is that?" I ask, following after him.

"Picture of your mom and me," he says, putting it back on the counter. "Where'd you find it?"

"On the wall of the place you said was a school project!"

"It was part of her school project." He turns on the faucet and fills the coffeepot with water. "They really put this on the wall, huh?"

"Why didn't you tell me?"

He hits the button on the coffee maker and stares at me with squinty eyes like he's not sure he wants to tell me anything.

"Dad!"

"Fiona, I love you, but it's not all about you. Some memories are mine, and that night was one of them. I'm sure you have moments you want to keep just for you." His gaze shifts to the necklace Nick gave me, and I resist the urge to touch it. "But I'm glad you found it. I think your mom would have wanted you to."

"So you wanted me to go there?"

"No." He sighs, taking his travel mug out of the dishwasher. "But I'm proud you decided for yourself. Did not expect this." He lights up, taking in the picture. "What'd you think of the place?"

I lean against the wall at a loss for how to put our night there into words. "It was pretty bad. But also pretty great."

He gives me a knowing smile. "Sounds just like I remember it."

It's only been a week since the trip, but it feels like a lifetime. Nick hasn't texted me since the lawyer visit. Sometimes I feel like I'm too involved in his business. His loss came with this whole other legal element, and as much as I want to be there for him, I don't want to influence him. What if my advice is horrible? I mean, look at me. I'm the last person I would take advice from right now. I thought I'd give him space, a few days to figure things out, hopefully with Alex, but I didn't think it would take this long.

I run down the stairs to find Dad basting a tofurkey with some kind of glaze.

"Smells amazing," I say, slinging my gym bag over my shoulder.

"You know, I've been doing this for two hours now, and I can honestly say, it's not worth it."

We haven't had a formal dinner since Mom died. It never seemed worth the hassle for just the two of us. But he has the night off for the first time in ages, and he's pulling out all the stops. It's a little painful watching him struggle, but I melt knowing he's trying.

"You went hard on the potatoes, huh?"

The colander beside him is filled to the brim. "No such thing. You want mashed or roasted?"

"Half and half?" I suggest, slipping into my shoes.

He gives me an exasperated stare.

I raise my arms in defense. "Or not? I'm good for whatever."

"Half and half actually sounds pretty good," he says.

There isn't a stitch of free space left on the counter. It's a disaster, scattered with most of the fridge contents. He scans through them, picking up a stick of butter. "You working today?"

"Last-minute shift."

He eyes me over his glasses. "But, you'll be home to eat this, right?"

"Wouldn't miss it! Later!" I fly out the door and text Nick on my way to my car.

How'd it go with Alex?

When it doesn't seem like he's going to reply, I leave.

Jaden switched classes to Sunday this week because the gym was booked for a party on Friday. When I pull into the lot, I spot May's car and park as far away from it as possible. My stomach wrenches at the thought of going inside. I don't want to deal with the judgy stares from the parents, or worse, face May because I've been avoiding her. I don't even know why I'm here. I've all but officially quit kinder gym. When Jaden asked if I was coming back after the strep fiasco, I should have said no, but I was too chicken, so here I am.

May spots me as soon as I step inside. She's surrounded by kids and can only wave from across the gym. I wave back, and it feels so normal, it makes me question if this drama between us ever existed, or if it was all in my head.

I'm a spare today, so I don't have a group to teach. My job is to put away pylons and other equipment, making me feel especially useless.

Sarah runs up to me and wraps her small arms around my waist. "Fiona! Can we do walkovers now?" She's giving me those puppy dog eyes again, jumping up and down.

I hold up the pylons. "Can't, kind of busy."

"You don't look busy."

I scan the gym. Her mom is surfing on her phone in the viewing area. I promised her we would do this weeks ago. How can I say no? "Sure! Why not? Let's do it." I toss the pylons. "Show me what you got!"

Sarah tries a walkover and flops hard on her back against the mat. "I can't do it."

"Try again." This time I spot her, helping her spring up from a bridge. "You did it!" I excitedly say, giving her a high five.

"I fall without you, though. How do you balance and get up?"

She means the walkover, but it hits deep. "You're asking the wrong girl."

"But you can do it," Sarah says.

"And so can you! It's practice. That's it. Not a magic trick. And wanting it as badly as I know you do is the most important part."

Sarah tries again. She struggles, but pulls herself up. It makes me so happy, I let out a loud cheer, and then see her mom scowling at me from the viewing area.

"I did it!" she shouts, running around the gym.

It's the best feeling—making a tiny difference for someone. Sarah's mom doesn't get to steal that from me. This gym was such a huge part of my life, but I think I'm ready to leave it behind. It's hard to grow in a place that won't grow with you.

I head toward Jaden, who's waving a bubble gun over an excited group of toddlers.

"Hey."

"Hey, Fiona." He barely notices me.

"So, I quit," I announce.

Now he looks at me. He knits his brows together, still squeezing the trigger of the bubble gun.

"I'm quitting," I repeat, deflating a little because he doesn't fight me. Maybe he even hoped this would happen. "And for the record, it sucks that you didn't stand up for me. Going to counseling is not a bad thing."

His mouth falls open. "What? Who told you that?"

"May said that's why they pulled my lessons."

Jaden's face softens. He lowers the bubble gun. "It was never the counseling Fi, it was the company."

It doesn't register. "What?"

"Your friend, Nick? Had a bit of a history, apparently. I thought you knew. I asked May for the best way to break it to you, and she said to let her handle it."

Of course, he'd confide in May. He's still in love with her. "So, she lied to me?"

"I didn't know."

"But that's . . . " I shake my head, still not understanding. "So stupid. Any history he had was before Nick."

"The parents don't see the difference."

Nick is the reason my students dropped like flies. *Nick* is the reason I'm broke. All at once, I feel sorry for him and angry. All this time, I thought they were judging me for therapy, and this is so much worse. They're judging me for my judgment.

"I'm sorry." Jaden touches my shoulder and lowers his face before mine because I'm staring at the mat in a daze. "Fiona?"

It breaks my trance. "Yeah?" I step back, and see the regret in his eyes. "Thanks for telling me. Good luck with everything, Jaden."

He tries to follow me, but the kids surround him jumping for more bubbles. I can't get out of the gym fast enough. The sliding doors open, and I stumble through, feeling more like they spit me out than let me leave with a shred of self-respect.

I take one last look at the gym. I imagine packing it full of cats and leaving them there. At least I can start over at school in New York and leave my history here.

My phone rings. It's Nick's home number. Weird because he never calls me, especially not from a landline. I answer as I cross the pavement. "You are not going to believe what just happened."

"Fiona?"

The voice on the other end has the same buttery smoothness but older.

"Mr. Bennet, I'm so sorry, I thought you were Nick."

A pause. "So he's not with you?"

My heart stops. All of me stops. Something's wrong. "No . . ."

"Have you spoken to him recently?" His voice is serious and *why is he talking so slowly.* My mind races through the worst possible scenarios.

"What's going on?"

"There was an . . . incident."

That's when May bursts through the sliding doors, hands on her hips. "Did you just quit?" she yells.

I put my hand over the phone and face her. "Yeah." I raise a finger to signal for her to hang on and turn back to my phone.

"What kind of incident?"

There's a deep sigh from the line. "He stole my truck."

Did he just say *stole*? Still, I'm relieved. Stole, I can work with. "What happened?"

"He took off with it about an hour ago. I don't want to get the police involved."

"Yeah, no, you shouldn't do that."

"I thought he would be with you."

I cover the phone again and face May. "Have you heard from Nick?"

May shakes her head.

"Can you give me an hour? I'll call you either way," I say to Mr. Bennet.

"An hour. Okay."

"I'm sure it's just a misundersta—" He hangs up before I finish the sentence.

A strip of pavement separates me from May. It may as well be an ocean.

She finishes typing something on her phone and glances up at me. "Fi? Are we okay?"

A frustrated laugh bubbles inside me because what the hell is okay anymore? "Why did you tell me it was the therapy?"

Her hands fall to her side. "I was trying to protect you."

"By making me feel like I'm crazy?"

"I knew how much Nick meant to you!"

"But then you asked for his number!" I say, exasperated.

May steps forward and stops at the curb. "Because you said he was like an AA sponsor, and I didn't want to damage that support system for you. I didn't think there was anything more between you."

I bury my face in my hands. She bites at her lip and seems so uncertain, and I'm hit with a pang of reconciliation.

"So? Are we okay?" she asks again.

As angry as I was—am. I also kind of miss her. We're like one of those best friend necklaces. Broken, but the pieces still fit. We'll figure this out.

So I just nod. "We will be."

She holds up her phone. "I texted him. I'll let you know if I hear anything."

"Thanks."

"And Fi? I wish you would have told me. I would have never..."

My mind reels. It's such a loaded comment. How do I even begin to unpack that?

I dismiss her with a wave. "I've got to go."

"Text me later," she calls out after me.

I sink into the driver's seat and text Nick.

Hey

Where are you?

Your dad is freaking out

He was so upset after the lawyer's visit last weekend. I guess I underestimated how much. My mind races through all the worst-case scenarios, then drifts to May's "I would have never" comment. I'm pretty sure nothing ever happened between them, but would have never what? What if he texts her first? I get angry all over again. Ten minutes ago, I was feeling oh so confident. Now I'm a neurotic mess sitting in my car thinking about May-isms and "I would have never" when Nick's dad is hovering his finger over 9-1-1, itching to have him arrested.

Where is he? I scramble for my phone and click on my friend finder app. I never use it, but we added each other months ago. His name pops up on my screen, and I press on it, waiting for a blip to appear on the map. I zoom in on the location. Silver State Falls Park. It should have been an easy guess. The waterfall he used to visit with Alex and his mom. But why wouldn't he call me when we made a promise?

That night in his room he locked his finger with mine. *Promise me right now, that you won't pull any Rogers or jump off any railings without texting me first.*

I made light of it, but for him, it was real. It was real, and it meant something, so I made the promise. *I made the promise.* But . . . he never made one back.

Fiona

It's a thirty-minute drive to the park, and his dad's one-hour time limit is dangerously close to expiring. When I pull into the lot, I spot his dad's truck parked on the grass at the far end. He's done a number on it. There's a massive dent over the right rear wheel and a ton of scratches. What did he do? I park next to it and call his dad. It goes to voicemail. "Hi, Mr. Bennet, it's Fiona. Found him! He's okay. You don't need to call the police. We're just going to talk for a bit, so he'll call you later. Bye."

That should buy me some time, but my panic rises because I still don't know what I'll find out here.

The heat at the park is magnified. It's late August heat—a thousand sticky, breezeless degrees.

I head for a trail map, water bottle in hand, and try to figure out the most direct route to the falls, except there isn't *one* waterfall here. There are ten by my count. *Ten?* A dozen routes are plotted out on the board, twisting and turning in bright-colored lines. It's so misleading. It looks like a trip through Candyland when the actual trail is more like a haunted nightmare—dark path, creepy trees, mosquitos, and who knows what else. The upside is that I'm not May, so the odds of me running for my life in my underwear are next to zero. I glance at my phone. Nick still hasn't texted me back. He could be anywhere. I'll have to hike the whole damn thing.

It's two miles to the first falls, if you can call it that. It's barely taller than I am and trickling the smallest stream of water. Clearly, people know this. No one is here. I wish I could say I'm having some profound connection to nature, but really I'm dodging the bugs flying into my face every two seconds. Why couldn't Mrs. Bennet have been a fan of the ocean like Mom?

I hike on to the next one and find droves of families, roasting hot dogs and marshmallows over a firepit. No Nick.

Access to the third is closed, and there's still no sign of him at the next two. The falls are breathtaking, though— the roar of the water enough to temporarily numb my anxiety. I imagine filling tiny boats with my cats and watching them fall over the edge, disappearing into the mist below.

I hike my way from one to the next, and soon, my white sneakers turn dark from the muddy trail. At the viewing area of the South Falls, I stand next to a couple of hikers joined in an embrace. There's still no sign of Nick, and panic washes over me. I should call his dad. I should call my dad.

Then I see him.

He's on the other side of the gap, sitting on the cliff near the edge, a bottle between his legs. His shirt is tied around his head like a bandana, and he's soaked from the mist. He looks so small, so alone. Seeing him this way feels like the ultimate invasion of privacy.

He raises his head and spots me.

"Fioooonnaaaaaa!!!"

It's a battle cry. He's wasted. Nick hoists the bottle in the air. "Haffa drink." He stands and stumbles forward, dangerously close to the precipice, before catching himself and swaying back. He smiles, pleased with himself, as if not falling is a major accomplishment.

I move away from the overlook, searching for a way to get to the other side. He mirrors my movement, stumbling on the rocky ledge with every step.

"Sit down!" I yell across the void. "I'm coming. Just stay." I fully resort to dog signals.

"I'm pouring you a drink," he yells back. He makes a grand gesture of pouring a capful of whatever that is and immediately throws it back. "I'm pouring you another drink!"

This is a nightmare. I search for a path leading to the top of the falls, but there isn't one. There's only a trail about an inch wide, and it looks more like the Rainforest. Branches scrape across my legs and arms as I push overgrown swaths of brush out of my way. There are a million cobwebs—*do they regenerate by the second?* And puddles of mud so huge they might lead to the multiverse.

Up ahead, I spot a bridge, and bridge is a generous term. It's a series of narrow wooden planks with wide gaps in between, fastened by rope with two thick cords as handrails—open concept as far as bridges go. Some would call it rustic. I call it insanity. I hesitate. Balancing on a rock firmly grounded in the ocean is nothing compared to dealing with a swaying, unstable foundation hovering over rapids.

Imaginary Nick says, "What are you talking about? It's a bridge, Fi. It doesn't get any more stable than this. It has actual handrails. What you did at the ocean was insane." Imaginary Nick would even walk to the middle and jump on it to demonstrate.

The bridge sways as I step onto it. *Don't look down*, but I have to. There could be broken boards. It's nauseating watching the water rush under me in a dizzying fury. With light, swift steps, I hurry across, my hands grazing over the ropes. But whatever pride I feel for reaching the other side turns into instant irritation. *Nick.*

A grassy path leads to the waterfall. The ground slopes steeper, and the grass becomes slippery. I carefully edge my way down.

"Fiona!" he calls out, still sounding surprised. Even drunk, he can see I'm struggling with the slope of the trail, and he extends a mud-covered hand to help me down. He notices the mud and wipes his hands on his wet jeans. He's a few feet below me, so I have to sit on a rock and jump the rest of the way. I crash right into him. "Whoa, whoa, whoa." He steadies me with a hand around my waist. "There's a path, right over there." He vaguely gestures to someplace behind me.

"Of course there is," I say, not finding this nearly as amusing as he is. Now, my shorts are wet. He reeks of booze, so

I step away and take in the makeshift camp he's set up. There's a bag of chips and his good headphones, which are soaked and definitely ruined.

"What are you doing here?" he asks, overly happy.

"Looking for you."

"Great!" He stumbles back and picks up the bottle on the ground. "Welcome to Casa Nick. Have a drink."

I drag his backpack over and sit on top of it. "No, I'm good."

"Come on."

He plunks himself next to me and shakes the bottle under my face. I take it, tilting it back against my closed lips. He's too drunk to know the difference. "I've been texting you."

"Yeah?" He pats his pockets and scans the cliffside. "I don't know where my phone is. Holy shit. Where's all my stuff?" He runs his hands through his hair, dislodging the shirt tied around it and paces across the cliff.

"I'm sitting on it! It's literally under my ass."

He eyes the bag like he's not sure it's the right one and finally settles next to me. The falls roar in front of us.

"We were worried about you."

"We? Who's we?"

"Your dad called me."

He laughs, his head falling back, then looks at me again. "You're funny. That's funny."

A small audience on the other side of the falls is watching us.

"Isn't it beautiful here?" he says, oblivious to them.

"It is."

"It smells so clean, right?" he says, drawing in the deepest breath. "I wish I could smell this all the time." Then, as if it dawns on him. "Wait. You hate this. You hate nature."

I nod. "Still true."

"You hiked for me?" He claps a hand against his chest and sways back from his force.

"Mmmhmm."

He reaches for the bottle, and I cringe as he takes another drink. It's already a quarter empty. I have so many questions, but he's a mess, definitely not the right time to ask, so I swallow them.

He hands me the bottle, and I try to distract him. "Yeah, I took the scenic route." He faces the direction I'm pointing, and I spill the rest of the alcohol into the ground beside me. When he turns around, he sees the empty bottle pressed against my lips.

"Did you drink all that?" he asks, surprised.

"Oops."

He takes it from me and slides it away. "No, it's okay. It's all good. Maybe I've got another."

I tug at his pant leg, pulling him back. "Why don't you have some of this." I draw my water bottle from my bag. "Mmmm. Yummy." He's not impressed and pushes it away. The cutesy act isn't working, so I get serious. "Come on, Nick, just a sip. You need water."

He takes the bottle and chugs the water, handing it back to me empty. A ray of lucidity shines through. "How'd you know I was here?"

"I tracked you."

He nods. "You know, Alex has that, too." He rakes a hand through his damp hair. "I signed the papers. So, she got what she wanted. She could be here. I mean, she should be here, right?" He hangs his elbows over his bent knees.

"My dad . . . my dad should be here. I bet he only cares about his truck right now. None of them are here. But you're here, you know?" He blinks away the tears pooling in his eyes. "And you shouldn't be. You lost your job because of me."

"You know?"

May must have told him. He wipes his nose with his wet sleeve. Our eyes meet, but he doesn't say anything.

"It wasn't really because of you. It was because of them. It's their loss."

"But it was still because of me." His voice breaks. "I'm sorry. I shouldn't have dragged you into my bullshit. You should go."

"Hey, I'm not leaving you," I say, nudging his shoulder with mine. "Mostly because I don't know how to get back."

He coughs out a snotty laugh, and his pain melts into me. I want to fix it, take it away, but I can't. I clasp his hand in mine.

"Why aren't they here?" He turns to me, his eyes spilling with tears.

"I don't know."

He looks out to the waterfall, and his shoulders heave with heavy sobs. "I'm sorry. I'm so sorry."

He's not talking to me anymore. I pull him onto my shoulder, partly because he needs someone to hold him, mostly because I don't want him to see that I'm crying, too.

"This is bullshit. This is BULLSHIT," he yells over the roar of the falls. His words echo against the cliffs.

I want to tell him he'll be okay, that his mom loved him, and so do the rest of his family. But I hated it when those things were said to me, so I just hold his hand. I can be here.

He rests his head on my shoulder, and we watch the water fall and the hikers come and go until the sun dips lower and streaks of fiery orange spill across the sky. Someone yells from the other side that it's getting late, and we should leave. And all I can think of are the hundred-and-one ways we'll die in this forest. Before we get up, I spot something shiny and black among the stones. It might be a piece of obsidian, so I tuck it in my bag to keep as a memory.

The walk back takes twice as long and is ten times as miserable. Nick throws up like a dog marking trees. A cool breeze sweeps through the trail and the bugs come out in droves. I struggle to decipher the markers on the map while wrangling a drunk guy on my arm. It's like being out with a toddler, a distractible, exceedingly heavy toddler.

When I get him back to my car, I'm covered in mosquito bites. He tries to give me the keys to his truck, not understanding that I can't drive two cars at the same time. It'll have to stay here for now.

It's seven, and I have a ton of texts from Dad. His big dinner is ready and where the hell am I? I text:

Sorry

Home in 30

Going to Starbucks seemed like a good idea, but Nick won't even look at the coffee or touch the bottles of water. The smell, combined with the wet mud on his clothes, is so strong that he throws the coffee out the window, then opens the door at a red light and throws up again.

"You need to go to a hospital," I say.

His eyes are closed, and his face is caked in dirt. "I'm fine." He mumbles. "Let me sleep."

His head falls against the window. He's passed out.

I don't know what to do with him. Waiting it out in a parking lot crosses my mind, but I need an all-night solution. I have no choice; I have to take him home.

The second I walk through the door I'm hit with the warm scent of roasted potatoes. It's instant nostalgia. Dad's in the kitchen, gliding from one pot on the stove to the next. Nineties rock fills the air, and a glass of red wine is on the counter. He worked so hard to make this dinner, and I'm about to ruin it.

I lean against the archway. "Smells good."

He nearly jumps out of his skin, then turns down the music. "Didn't hear you come in."

"Sorry, I'm so late."

"Actually, you're just in time."

My keys are still clutched in my hand as I try to find the right words for *Nick is wasted in my car.*

Dad can tell something's up. He pulls the dish towel from his shoulder and wipes his hands. "What's going on, Fi?"

"You're going to kill me," I blurt out.

He moves closer. "For what? What happened?"

"There's a small situation. A Nick situation."

"Did he get arrested?"

"No!" Dad's body goes slack with relief. "But he's passed out in my car." Dad goes to the window and sees a comatose Nick in the passenger seat. "I left his door open. For air." I mumble.

Dad sighs and heads outside, still wearing his "Breaking

Bad" apron, with me trailing behind. He takes in the spectacle of Nick splayed out in the car.

"He may have drunk a bit . . ."

He darts his eyes to me. "You think?"

"Just a little. He's a lightweight." I shrug, sheepish. "I didn't know what to do with him."

The old lady across the street is nosily watching us from her porch rocking chair, and Dad waves at her. "You did the right thing." He lugs Nick out of the car, heaves him over his shoulder, and carries him inside.

"Grab the blanket." He points to a plaid throw draped over the recliner. "Lay it over the couch."

It's a scratchy throw, but I don't think now's the time to mention that, so I hurry past and do as instructed seconds before Dad dumps Nick on top of it. He's still out cold. "Get a bowl for the floor."

"His dad's truck is still at Silver State," I say, coming back with a plastic bowl. "I need to call him."

"Why don't you let me do that?" Dad offers, which I am more than happy to do. "But first, I'd like to eat before I get any more irritated."

I place the bowl on the floor under Nick's face. He looks so peaceful even though he's a disaster. I want to touch him, but Dad's right here, and that would be weird.

"So, that's it?" I ask.

"That's it." Dad goes back into the kitchen and pulls some plates from the cupboard. I stand in the archway between the rooms, watching Nick passed out on the couch while Dad hums to the music. The house feels like a cozy YouTube ambiance video sprung to life. Nick shouldn't fit in this picture, but he does.

The plates clatter on the table behind me.

"I'll get the silverware," I say.

We slide into an easy rhythm while his music quietly plays. He even does a slight side shuffle toward me. Mom called it his dancing-bear move. It's a glimmer of light, of life, filtering through, and it catches me so off guard I have to swallow back my tears.

He takes a sip of wine, and his face turns serious. "Hang on. You weren't." He looks from his wine to me.

"With Nick today? No! I would never do that and drive." I scrunch my face up at him. "I'm not stupid."

Dad's gaze returns to Nick on the couch, as does mine. I want to believe he wouldn't either, but I don't know.

I don't know anything for sure.

Nick

Some people sleep on couches really well. I'm not one of them. In a hungover haze, I roll over and fall off, my face smacking against the rim of a plastic bowl so considerately placed next to me. Thankfully, it's empty. I hover over it on my elbows for a second, just in case. The smell of freshly brewed coffee wafts through the air, but it may as well be garbage. It takes a hero's courage to not throw up. Then it dawns on me: this floor isn't mine, it's Fi's, and I have no idea how I got here.

I pat down my pockets for my phone and keys, but they're not there. What did I do? When I peel myself off the floor, I spot them on the table by the door. Flakes of dry mud from my jeans fall with every step I take.

There are like ten billion texts from Dad on my phone. Awesome.

Something sizzles in the kitchen. Zombie Bob is at the stove making an omelette, and I swear he's doing this to torture me.

He pointedly looks from my mud trail to me. "Morning."

"Morning, Sir."

"Breakfast?" he asks, as if having the swamp thing in his kitchen isn't remotely weird.

"Mmm." I hold out my hands and turn my face away from the eggs. "No, thank you, Sir, but I have a bit of a headache . . ."

He gives me an amused look before pointing to a cupboard next to the sink. "Tylenol's on the second shelf."

"Thanks. Is Fi up?"

"What do you think?"

I fill a glass with water and throw back two pills. "You mind if I go up?"

He eyes the walking disaster that I am. "I think I'm okay with that."

On my way to the stairs, I'm feeling all kinds of guilty, like I've let him down, and it throws me because I never feel this way with my dad. Or wow, maybe I've always felt this way with my dad.

"Nick."

I stop.

"I talked to your dad last night."

It takes everything I have not to answer with sarcasm. "Yeah? How'd that go?"

"He was upset. It wasn't a long talk, but I told him where he could find the truck and asked him to give you the benefit of the doubt."

Dad must have loved that. It was nice of Bob to try, but I bet Dad will hold it against me.

"Thank you, Sir." I nod. "For . . . everything." I hope he knows how much I mean it.

"And Nick?"

I look up.

"You can call me Bob."

The word sounds foreign, like speaking alien or something, and I would feel nothing short of ridiculous speaking alien to Fi's dad, but it means a lot. "Thanks . . . Sir."

He turns back to the stove, shaking his head, and slides his omelette onto a plate.

Fiona's door is open a crack, so I knock once and push it open the rest of the way. She's out cold.

It's like walking through a snow globe—blindingly white —feminine but not girly, although her pillowcases have legit ruffles on the edges. Oh, Fiona. She acts like she doesn't know what she wants, but she always does. It's the kind of room that begs for a California sunrise to fill it and for the photo to be posted on Instagram.

A small, square photo is pinned on the wall next to her bed. It's the picture of us with the sea lion in Monterey, with a red heart drawn around it. That was a good day. I try not to read into the heart because Fi draws them on everything.

"You're alive."

I turn at the sound of her sleepy voice and hand her my phone with Dad's messages open on the screen so she can read the one hundred and one ways he's going to kill me. "Not for long. How pissed was your dad?"

She rubs her eyes. "Well, you know he loves a project."

"Right."

After a few seconds of snooping around her desk, I realize handing her my phone was a giant mistake. The texts from May are a few under Dad's, and when I go back to her, she's already scrolling through them. She doesn't let go easily when I try to pull my phone from her hands.

I don't have anything to hide, so I'm not overly bothered by her snooping, but all of May's texts to me are flourished with suggestive emojis. Every sentence is punctuated with hearts, winks, and odd assortments of fruit. I don't think Fi will read into those. She's known her longer than I have, and has to know May is just one of those people.

"Is it cool if I take a shower? Might help my case if I don't look like one of the 'Walking Dead' when I get home."

"Yeah. Towels are in the closet."

She doesn't say anything about the texts, and I don't know if May ever told her what went down between us, but she deserves to hear something from me.

"Hey." Fi looks up at me. "You know, nothing happened, right? Like nada." Her eyes are wide, as if she's surprised I went there. I nod, then leave for the bathroom.

"Nick."

My hand grips the doorway, and I duck back in. She props herself up on her elbows—God, she's beautiful. She's in a white tank top that's not totally opaque, and I mean, it's impossible not to notice. A flake of mud hits the floor, reminding me of how awesome I must look right now.

"Are you okay?"

I'm not sure how to answer that, so I just kind of shrug.

"You know . . . "

"Yeah." She hesitates then says, "What happened to the truck?"

Her words are tinged with judgment, and my eyes flicker with surprise. "I was sideswiped."

"Were you drinking?"

"At the falls."

"Not before?"

It hurts to hear the doubt in her voice, even though I'm the one who put it there. "No," I say as openly as I possibly can. "I'm serious."

"Okay." She nods. "Maybe you should talk to your dad. Tell him—about the falls."

It takes all of two seconds to think about it. "Yeah, I don't think so," I say and leave. I bet she thinks he'll go easier on me, but he doesn't deserve to know. The falls are sacred. I'm not filling him in on the memories he chose to miss out on. I'm not telling him a damn thing.

Surprisingly, the shower didn't wash away this shitty feeling, but at least I'm clean. Fiona's deodorant is some organic spray, and it feels weird spritzing my pits with neroli essence, but it smells like her, so there's that.

Her toothbrush is on the counter. She'll kill me for this, so I turn on the faucet to drown out the buzzing sound. Then I remember I have a clothing problem. My muddy jeans are congealed in a glob on the bathroom floor.

I go back to Fiona's room with a towel wrapped around my waist. She's still in bed, deeply invested in something on her phone. She's fiddling with the necklace I gave her and moves the charm up to her lips. Then she stares at me, like really stares, with the charm still pressed against her mouth. I wait for her to make some kind of joke, but she doesn't. It's hard to tell if she's thinking about me or yesterday.

I swallow. "Do I have any clothes here?" It's not an unusual question.

"Uh maybe. Check the closet."

Fi doesn't have a ton of clothes, and I love that about her. There's a pile of old schoolbooks on the floor, a few pairs of sneakers, nothing of mine. "I'll put the jeans back on."

"No. I don't think you can wear those—ever!" She gets out of bed, steps around me and digs through her closet. I glance at her phone on the bed and see her open Instagram feed. It's not a guy like I thought it might be, but New York streetscape photography. *Our plan.* I'm relieved. She still wants this.

Black Adidas jogging pants fly from the closet and land at my feet. I pick them up.

"These aren't mine."

"So, they'll be capris. Or I can get something from my dad."

"These are great," I say, stretching the waistband. "You got any shirts? Preferably of a boy band? To solidify my humiliation for all eternity."

Fi pops her head out of the closet and studies me like she's trying to figure something out. Then she leaves the room for a minute and returns with a perfectly wrapped gift. The paper is black with sparkly gold dots, and there's even a bow, and not those plastic bows, but a proper bow made from tulle or chiffon or whatever puffy fabric dresses are made of.

"Happy Birthday!" she says in a sing-song voice like it's no big deal.

I'm confused. "My birthday's in November."

"I know."

She has a fully wrapped present for my November birthday in August.

"Open it," she says.

I slide off the bow and tear the paper. Inside is a navy T-shirt with the word bullshit in small white block lettering on the top left corner.

It's all kinds of perfect. "I love it."

She tucks a strand of hair behind her ear. "Yeah?" She's staring at the floor, trying to be cool, and I just want her to look at me so she can see how much this means to me. "It's the most thought anyone has put into a gift for me."

She shoves my shoulder lightly. "It's just a shirt."

"It's not. Turn around," I say with exaggerated modesty.

I'm rewarded with her instant laughter.

"Seriously?"

"Go on!" She faces the wall, and I slide the new shirt over my shoulders. Why do new shirts feel so good? The fabric is always extra soft like they've been spun from some magic wheel. The pants, on the other hand, fit like I went shopping in the kids' department. "Ready."

She turns around. "Hey!" She cheers, smoothing the fabric on my shoulders and judging the fit. She takes in the whole outfit. "It's definitely . . . a look."

"Thank you."

"Yeah, yeah," she waves it off like it's nothing.

Fiona always gets weird when people thank her. She just does things from her heart and never wants any kind of acknowledgment. She pulls her bathrobe from behind her door. "Give me fifteen, and I'll take you home. Did you eat?"

"No."

"Grab an Eggo or something."

"I'm afraid Eggos would be ruined for me forever."

"Toast then. You should eat something," she calls out from the hall. The bathroom door closes behind her.

I wait for it.

"Nick!" she yells. "Did you use my toothbrush?"

"No," I yell back.

"Honestly?"

And I won't do it. I won't lie to her, so I say nothing. I wait for her to open the door, but she doesn't, so I flop into her bed and sink into the soft sheets, still warm from her body. If this were my room, I wouldn't want to leave it, either.

Fiona's only one room away, and I miss her already. Whenever I'm with her, it feels so right, and I know that I want this. I want her. But how can I tell her now, when yesterday was such an epic fuckup?

Fiona

Nick's dad's truck is in the driveway when we pull in. The crater-sized dent seems to punctuate it like an exclamation point. Even Nick's accidents tell a story. It looks worse under the high noon sun than it did yesterday.

I turn off the car, but Nick doesn't move.

"You ready?" I ask.

He stares straight ahead. I'm not sure what to do. Leaving him feels wrong, so I get out of the car.

He turns my way. "What are you doing?"

I duck my head through the open window. "Being supportive?"

"Fi, this is my mess. You should go."

It's the first time he hasn't asked me to stay, but I don't think he means it. "He can't kill you if there's a witness."

He gets out of the car, looking beyond ridiculous in my pants. "Unless he kills both of us, and it's a solid possibility."

"I'm staying."

The walk up the driveway is a quiet one, mostly because of the pain Nick's in. He didn't eat the Eggo. He couldn't be in worse shape for a fight. His shoulders sag, and his face is resigned like he's already gone through the argument in his head a million times, and now he has to go through it in real-time.

He pulls open the screen door, and it lets out a piercing squeak to announce us.

His dad's feet thud against the ceiling where his room is and stop when the door closes. Nick tenses. He drops his backpack on the floor, and I follow him into the kitchen. He pulls a couple of Cokes from the fridge.

His dad comes downstairs. "Fiona." He acknowledges me with a curt nod, not surprised to see me, before turning to Nick. "You think we're not going to have this conversation if she's here."

Nick opens the can. "What conversation?"

"What the hell happened to my truck?"

"I was sideswiped."

"By what? A lamp post? Cost me eighty bucks for an Uber out there. Plus the damages. You know you're paying for it! All of it."

Nick bites his lip and keeps his eyes on the floor. "Yeah, I figured."

"I heard you were drinking."

Nick meets my eyes as if I'm the one who asked the question. "Not while I was driving."

"And I'm supposed to believe that?" His dad pushes past us and moves deeper into the kitchen, sorting through a folder of contracts on the counter.

"Yeah, Dad. You are."

"Convenient, isn't it? Hiding out at your girlfriend's all night and having her dad cover for you."

It's the dragging Dad into it that gets me. "He's telling the truth."

Mr. Bennet scoffs. "And how would you know? You said you didn't know where he was on the phone."

"Because I trust him. And I figured it out, which is kind of like your one job."

Nick darts his head toward me. Mr. Bennet gives me a contemptuous smirk, but I don't care. I'm so sick of the way he treats me, and I can't imagine how Nick feels living with him.

"She has a point," Nick says with a shrug.

"Trust is earned." Mr. Bennet grabs his blazer from the chair. "When is this going to end, Nick?" He softens, a hint of humanity coming through. "What more can I possibly do? Do you think I forced her to stay? I didn't lock her up in the basement!"

"No, you would have to be home to do that."

"She didn't want me to be home! She didn't want anything to do with me."

"Yeah, because you're an asshole!"

Mr. Bennet sighs. "Why am I the asshole? Because I'm trying to live some kind of life? Because I'm not moping around, wrecking cars?"

"Dad, you were cheating on her for years!"

"She knew!"

"Why didn't you just get divorced?"

"She didn't want that, either!"

"You bought her the plane ticket!" Nick yells.

The room goes quiet. If a bush was nearby, I'd slowly back into it. His dad straightens like those were the words he was waiting to hear. "So, I killed her? Is that what this is? You need me to be the one who killed her? I didn't make her take that trip."

"But you bought the ticket," Nick repeats. It's barely a whisper.

His dad shifts his gaze between us. "You two think you're so smart. Yeah? Give it time. One day, you'll be the assholes. Funny how that works. There's accountability. Nobody killed her. She wasn't Mother Teresa. She knew what she was doing." His voice grows louder. "And I'm sick of this! It's time to get your shit together. Move on! Stop this deferring bullshit! Do something with your life. I'm not going to keep enabling this . . . you know what? You're fired!"

"You're firing me?" Nick's eyes are wide in disbelief.

"Yeah, that's right. I thought therapy was helping. I thought you were better."

Nick's eyes flutter in astonishment. Therapy isn't a magic eraser for loss. There is no better, only better than yesterday, but his dad doesn't get it.

He grabs his wallet from the table. "Well, this asshole has an appointment. We'll finish this later."

"Say hi to Brooklyn!"

His dad throws open the screen door, and it bounces off the porch railing before slamming behind him. His truck tears out of the driveway.

Nick buries his face in his hands. "Thanksgiving will be a blast this year."

I look at him. "Don't do that. It's not funny."

"I know!"

"He has a point, you know."

He straightens, narrowing his eyes at me. "What?"

"Did you even think about how wildly irresponsible and dangerous that was?"

"No! Did you when you rock jumped into the middle of the ocean?"

"No! But that was different."

His eyes widen. "How was it different? Oh, right," he says, snapping his fingers, "because your dad didn't find out, so you still get to be 'perfect Fiona.'"

"I didn't break the law."

He tilts his head to the side. "Actually, I'm pretty sure you did. But I didn't!"

"You were wasted! Big difference."

"Not while I was driving." He directs a pointed finger at me, his voice firm. "And you're being such a hypocrite. I was with you the whole weekend for your thing."

He says it like he was held at gunpoint. Like it was another duty to cross off the court-mandated checklist. "Wow. I'm so sorry you had to suffer through that."

He steps toward me and stops when I back away. "Why do you get to have a thing, but when I need one ounce of support, you come at me instead?"

I pretend to check a watch I'm not wearing. "Look at that. Took two minutes for your dad's prophecy to come true."

It takes a second for him to get it. He starts to slow clap.

251

"Wow. Well done. Pretty sure it was assholes—plural."

I roll my eyes. "And my thing was about healing and moving on."

"Oh. So you're grieving better than me?"

"Yours was destruction and chaos."

He squints at me. "Because I was drunk?"

"More than drunk."

"And that's the great qualifier of appropriate healing? You're just pissed because you had to hike for five miles!"

"Ten," I yell. "Ten miles!"

"I spent ten hours in a car with you, driving to Monterey."

"Yeah, ten hours sitting in a car. I hiked for you—in the woods full of serial killers!"

He flutters his eyes as if it's the dumbest thing he's ever heard. "There are no serial killers in the woods, Fiona!"

"That's where they all are! And I thought you wanted to go to Monterey."

My head is spinning. This went from zero to a hundred, and I need to get out of here. I fly out the screen door and run down the stairs.

Nick bursts out behind me. He's shouting. "For you. To be with you." He grabs my arm and swings in front of me. "What are we even arguing about?"

"What happened to the truck? That wasn't a sideswipe."

He takes a step back. "Fine. I went to the gym, okay? I knew you were working and wanted to talk to you, but I couldn't do it. I didn't want to go in there and mess things up for you anymore, so I paced around, and when I finally took off, I hit one of those stupid metal barriers. That's what happened to the truck."

I close my eyes. I know it's true. "Why wouldn't you just tell me that?"

"Because I felt like a loser! And a bad influence, and . . . " He blinks. "And an asshole, I guess."

"What would have happened—" I can barely get out the words. Tears pool in my eyes, and they're burning because only I would have tears that burn. "If I hadn't shown up?"

Nick deflates at the sight. He wipes his eyes.

"When I saw the truck, I didn't know what I'd find." My voice breaks. "And I couldn't find you, and I didn't know what to do." I thought I'd lost him forever. "Ten stupid waterfalls." The tears win. They raise their victory flag. Ugly sobs escape me.

Nick pulls me into his chest. "I'm sorry."

He wraps his arms around me, holding me until his shirt is wet from my tears. When my crying stops, we just hold each other for a while. I raise my face to his.

And he kisses me.

It's careful, his lips, soft and warm, but quickly the kiss becomes a riptide of want. Reality becomes a distant memory. All that matters is this feeling, but then some part of my subconscious kicks in, and I push him away. My mind is racing. I'm so confused. All I can think is *No. Nononono.*

This. Us. We can't be an us. I wipe my eyes and collected Fiona takes over. "It's the grief."

He closes his eyes. "It's not the grief."

"This isn't real."

"Bullshit," he says.

"You think you're feeling things for me, but you're not. I've seen it on TikTok."

I can't fill this void that he has. I don't want to.

"Do you honestly believe that? What about Monterey? Are you telling me you didn't feel something?"

This isn't how it's supposed to be. With him hung over and us fighting in his driveway.

My gaze shifts to the ground. "I felt the tequila."

He steps away from me. "So that's what it takes to be into me?"

"No! That's not what I mean. You're a great guy!"

"Oh my god. Stop." He sweeps his hand through his hair. "I guess that explains the night at my house, too? And what about Starbucks, when I touched you, it was what? The sugar high?"

Of course, he knew. He searches my eyes as if he can pull some kind of feeling from me, but the harder he tries, the more my fortress walls grow. I can be his friend. I can love him like that, but this is too much, so I give him nothing.

"It's fucked up, don't you think?" he says. "Whatever this is. It's mutated into some whole other thing, and I *know* you know that. You have to know that, right? What are we doing, Fi?"

"You just feel obligated to be here for me . . ."

He paces in front of me. "I know how I feel."

Then it comes to me. The real reason he cares so much. "Maybe you just want to protect me—"

He shakes his head as if everything I'm saying is nonsense. "No."

"Because you couldn't protect her."

He stiffens and tilts his head as if a gear has clicked into place inside of him. He slides his hands down his face. "Wow. What the hell?"

He can deny it all he wants, but the idea takes root and multiplies behind his eyes. It tells me I'm right, and it sucks because I didn't want to be. "That's all this is."

For once, I get the checkmate. Maybe now he'll understand that these feelings are about our baggage as much as us.

He leans against my car, folds his arms, and squints toward the maple tree in his yard, where a bird chirps. Then he looks at me. "Fi, this was never about saving you. It was about supporting you—supporting each other. This isn't a fairy tale." He stops and stares at the driveway. When he looks up again, there's a calmness behind his eyes. "All this other bullshit— sounds like it's what you want to believe. Yeah, I have regrets, but this," he waves a hand between us, "has always been about you and me. Not my mother, yours, or anybody else, and I'm real clear on that. I don't feel any obligation, I just care about you. I . . . " His eyes close, and he stops himself from saying the words I know are meant to follow.

But Nick can't love me. I'm hollow inside.

"I'm not projecting. And this needs to stop. I can't do it anymore." He pushes away from my car. "I think we should stop seeing each other—for a while, anyway."

"Yeah," I agree, doubling down on this horrible decision.

I already miss him, and he's right in front of me. I need to get out of here.

In the movies, the girl gets in her car, drives away, and races back a minute later to profess her love. But I don't do any of that.

I get in my car and back out of the driveway. I don't even say goodbye. I commit to my bullshit and leave. At least I can commit to something.

Fiona

The road is a desaturated blur from my tears or the rain. Gray. Gloomy. This is my forever view, isn't it? I want to lock myself in my room and never come out. A million cats are in this car, and their ringleader is hanging around my neck— the necklace.

It feels like an anchor tying me to an impossible dream. I yank it so hard it snaps free, and I throw it across the car. Then I cry harder. I already want to scoop it up and put it on again.

In my mind, I apologize a hundred times, but I don't know what comes after *I'm sorry.*

May's words echo again: *Why is it so hard for you to be happy?*

When I get home, I sit in the car with the wipers on. The windows grow foggy and the intermittent thud of the blades lulls me into a state of numbness. I stare into the void as if waiting for an answer to appear, but when none does, my anger builds, and I rail against the steering wheel, but it's not enough. I turn off the car and storm through the downpour into my haunted house.

It's never felt so empty. Dad's at work. Nick and I are done. I have no job and no friends. I'm achingly alone. Mom's wall of portraits taunt me. They have no right to be here when she isn't. Why couldn't she find enough material to photograph in America? If it's tragedy she was looking for, isn't there enough of it closer to home? I've created an award-winning photographic moment right here, and she's not even here to capture it.

Dad always said it would be Nick, but he was so wrong. I do what I was destined to do.

I explode in my empty house.

I go to the portraits. First, the old man with his wrinkled face surrounded by birds in Central Park. I wrestle it from the wall and drop it on the floor. The sound of shattering glass fuels me. Then, I pull down the jazz singer from New Orleans, whose eyes sparkle like the silver beads on her dress. The picture crashes against the floor. I freeze at the last one because it's five-year-old me. My hair is long and braided, my eyes full and bright. I remember the day she took it at Portland State. It was a shoot for someone else, and I kept running into the frame saying, "Mommy, take a picture," so she did.

I'm a ghost, like the others.

I yank it free and let it smash against the floor.

And this feels too good. I grab some empty boxes from the garage and throw all her books and pictures inside. Then

I go through the drawers and closets until I've emptied Mom from this house. I dump the boxes in the garage, and feel so guilty for trying to erase the biggest part of me, that I fall to my knees in a heaping mess of tears.

The cold concrete seeps into my bones and an emptiness takes over. I shift to my feet and spot a box behind the one I just dropped, so I drag it forward and root through the contents—a flutter board, beach shoes, a ball and glove, and a plastic snorkel mask. Cheap little things we would take to the beach, everything encrusted in sand. Something hard and plastic grazes my finger on the bottom. I wrestle it free. It's a disposable waterproof camera. A snotty half sob, half laugh escapes me. These cameras. I can't get rid of them. I dust the sand away. All the photos have been taken. I can't remember what might be on them, but they're of us.

So this one, I'll keep.

I take it back into the house. The hardwood floor is covered in broken glass, and because I'm responsible, I vacuum it up. My well of sadness slowly refills until I sit next to the vacuum and cry.

I sit that way all night.

Morning comes, the door opens, and Dad walks in. He drops his keys and bag on the table by the door, and it takes a minute for my redecorating job to set in. His eyes move from the bare walls, to the vacuum, to me.

"You've been busy," he says.

"Yeah."

He sits on the floor next to me. We lean against the sofa.

"You okay?" he asks, and I don't know if he's ready for the answer. He's exhausted, and I'm sure the last thing he wants is to have this conversation.

"No, not really." A fresh crop of tears well in my eyes. "I quit the gym. I lost all my private lessons. The parents hate me."

Dad shakes his head. "The parents are idiots."

"You sure about that?"

"Fiona, you are the most amazing human I know."

"But I quit." A sob breaks free. "And I don't even know if I still want to go to New York for school."

"Those are problems that can be solved."

My head falls on his shoulder as I wipe the tears away. Dad and his sayings. I could stop there. I've given him enough, but this time, I press on. "Why do you work nights all the time?"

For a while, we're quiet. I'm not sure if he'll ever open up to me, so I do.

"I think I know the answer to that. It's because you don't want to sleep in your bed without her, and I get it. I do. But that leaves me here with her stuff, and it's everywhere. So I lock myself in my room, and tell myself it's not a part of this house, that it's somewhere else so I can sleep." My voice shakes, and I squeeze my hand, trying to keep the tears at bay. "Or I stay at Nick's because I don't want to be alone when you're working all night and sleeping all day, and you don't want to talk about it." Dad meets my eyes. "And I don't want to talk about it either. I feel like I should be dealing with all this myself, but it's not working out so well. I've been trying so hard to be okay, and I'm not."

A weight unburdens itself from my chest now that I've said the words.

Dad puts an arm around me, pulling me close. "You're not alone. You're never alone. I miss her, too. Something awful. Every time I close my eyes she's there and then—" He wipes at the tears forming in his eyes. "I'm so sorry."

"What if I'm broken?"

"Look at me." He turns my face up to his. "You're not broken. I guess I thought if I acted like I was okay, you would be, too. You always seemed like you were on autopilot. Your grades never slipped." He lets out a sigh. "I had no idea, Fi, but that's a bad excuse because I should have. So maybe we're both a little broken. But you know what we do when something's broken? We fix it."

Fiona

The dust settles. Two weeks later, and after countless tubs of ice cream with Dad, I finally come out of my cocoon. Turns out dumping everything doesn't work because you can't throw away the sad. The sad sticks to you.

It's a lazy Friday afternoon at the end of summer. The sound of crickets chirping fills the air, my favorite part of September. It means I can pull out some Halloween decorations. We always go big on Halloween, but we pretty much skipped it last year. A few hollow metal jack-o-lanterns are scattered around the living room floor, and my poison apple candleholder sits on the coffee table. Decorating this early might seem strange to some, but it's normal strange for us, and it feels good to have these small pieces of normal.

Dad's last official night shift is tonight. I'm trying to make sure his final daytime sleep is a good one, so I'm going up to Portland State. Even though I'm not going to school there, I want to take the campus tour for Mom.

The sun shines bright over the gothic buildings, making the university grounds glow like a lost city. I can picture her and Dad sitting under the towering copper beech tree outside the library. Part of me wants to change my plan and go here, where I could envelop myself in their history with the bonus of being within driving distance of Dad.

I stroll through the grounds. New students mill about, excitedly exploring while a few summer-school veterans push past them with purpose.

Up ahead is the Karl Miller Center, the spot where Mom took my picture thirteen years ago. It's the picture we wanted to recreate during our visit but couldn't because she had to leave.

There's no one around, so I position myself a fair distance from the entrance and hold out my phone to take a selfie with the glass windows behind. It'll have to do.

My tears fall as I study the photo on my way back to the parking lot. The sunlight reflects off the facets of glass like endless beams of light, and a Cheshire cat grins mischievously from the chain around my neck. Of course, I fixed the necklace; a piece of me was missing without it. Mom would approve.

"Fiona?"

I look up. Alex is standing in front of me.

"Hey!" I chirp, quickly wiping my eyes.

She scans the quad. "Is Nick here?"

"No, I'm on my own."

"Oh." And then, as if she's not sure she should ask, "Is everything okay?"

"Yeah," I say, because it's what people say, even when they have a full blotchy cry face.

"I was on my way home. It's just a street over." She hesitates a second. "Do you want to come check out the place? If you have time. No pressure."

"I couldn't. I don't want to intrude."

"Are you kidding? I would love it! I haven't had a chance to show it off to anyone yet."

How could I say no? Some things are easier to roll with. "Sure."

As we walk down the path, she points to the oldest building covered in ivy at the far end of the quad. "That's where I met Casey. I never believed in love at first sight or anything like that, and I still don't know if I do, but something in me knew." She smiles. She's different here, less the antagonistic sister, more human being. She pulls up a backpack slung low over her shoulder. "Do you have to get back in time for counseling?"

"No. I don't go anymore. I think I had my fill of the group thing."

"I didn't know. My brother tells me nothing."

We wait on the sidewalk for a stoplight to change. A swarm of students floods around us, like we're in a pack mob.

"You get used to it," she says.

Around the corner and two streets down is the cutest strip of townhouses. The noise from the busy university hub melts away. Mature trees line the sidewalk, and flowerbeds dot the railings.

"This is us," she says, excitedly, stopping before a townhouse with a robin's egg blue door. A floral hydrangea wreath hangs over it. The one from Nick's house.

I follow her up the walk and inside. "It's still a work in progress, so don't mind the mess. We painted last week."

The walls are sky blue with white trim. White subway tile lines the kitchen and the dining room is full of vintage pieces. "The table is Casey's," she says. "It was her nan's."

She leads me upstairs. Their room has a fresh, airy vibe with a few boxes still scattered around. Then she takes me to Max's room. "We wanted to finish his room first," she says.

It's perfect. She used some of their mom's pieces—a blue shag rug, and a paper lantern. A navy tent with glow in the dark stars is attached to the posts of his bed. Some old action figures are on his shelves—Batman, Star Wars, Superman. I glance back at Alex and clutch my chest.

"I know right? Those used to be Nick's. Now, if only he'd come by to check it out." She straightens some pencil crayons on Max's desk. "How's he doing?"

Now I have to come clean. Part of me worries she won't want to talk to me if she knows the truth. "I don't know, actually. We're taking a break."

"A break?" She pauses. "From what?"

This conversation is quicksand. "Each other?"

"Huh." She picks up on my I-don't-want-to-talk-about-it vibe. "That's too bad. You two really seemed to click."

"Yeah. I think things just got a little too real. Part of me feels like we were only together because of what happened, and maybe it wasn't the greatest reason." I don't know why I'm telling her this.

Alex picks up a pair of Max's pajamas from the floor and puts them in his hamper. "I don't know. Casey went through a lot with her parents like I did, so she gets it. And it's nice to have someone who gets it. Not that you need that." She holds her hands out. "Don't listen to me, but for what it's worth, it didn't seem like that was the only reason you were together."

The front door opens from downstairs, saving me from this conversation. "Hey, Babe, can you give me a hand for a sec?" a woman's voice calls out.

"Coming!" She touches my shoulder. "I'll be right back." She dashes away, leaving me there. "Guess what? We have company." Her voice trails as she runs down the stairs.

Max's room is brimming with details. His bookcase is filled with graphic novels. On his red desk is a notepad with a pen next to it, the same layout as Nick's. It takes everything in me not to text him a picture. It's achingly sweet—a room full of promise and dreams for a boy filled with joy and light.

I put my bag on Max's bed and dig through the zippered pocket inside. My fingers brush against the jagged edges of the black obsidian I swiped from the waterfall. I leave it in Max's bookcase next to a microscope and a book about space. It fits here, this small piece of us.

Alex is coming back up the stairs, so I move away from the bookcase and scoop up my bag.

"Fiona, this is Casey."

Casey bounds past Alex and throws her arms around me in a hug. "It is so nice to meet you! Max talks so much about you and Nick. Where is he? Is he here?" She glances around, excited, and Alex draws a line across her throat, trying to murder this line of questioning. Casey finally gets it. "Oh! Okay then! You could've told me that downstairs." She gives Alex an exaggerated stare, and Alex shrugs it off.

Casey tucks her blonde hair behind her ears—although, with her pixie cut, there isn't much to tuck. She has black glasses and is shorter than Alex. They couldn't seem more opposite. Alex has a nomad vibe, and Casey seems like the grounding force. Maybe we all need an opposite, an anchor. It always felt as if Nick and I were both treading water, but I didn't give us a chance to find out who we are when we finally reached the shore.

"You didn't show her our room, did you?" Casey asks.

"I did."

"Oh, Babe, it's a disaster," she groans. "Come, have a lemonade," she offers, beckoning me out of the room.

"Can I get a rain check? I should hit the road."

"See? Nobody wants to hang out with us," Alex says to Casey.

"No one wants to hang out period," Casey argues. "Us included."

I kind of love them. We make our way back downstairs.

"We'll hold you to it," Alex says, leaning into Casey's shoulder. "You're always welcome to drop by if you're in the neighborhood, Nick or no Nick."

"Thanks, Alex."

"I heard you went to Monterey!" Casey says.

"Oh, yeah! I have a picture on me."

It takes a minute to find, but I pull out the photo I printed of Nick, me, and the sea lion. It's Nick's copy. I meant to give it to him but never did. I hand it to Alex, and she and Casey share a smile.

"Can I keep this?" she asks.

"I guess. Yeah."

"Is it weird of me to ask?" She turns to Casey, who shakes her head. "It's just . . . I don't have any recent pictures of him." She takes the picture to the fireplace and places it on the mantle. "He just looks so happy."

We both do. Tears sting in the corner of my eyes, and I quickly blink them away.

"Can we get the hell out of here?" imaginary Nick says. I picture him beside me, beyond annoyed with Alex. His eyes meet mine, and I feel so grounded when they connect, like we're in our own world.

"I'm trying," I mutter softly to no one.

Alex and Casey eye me curiously.

"To . . . beat the traffic," I add louder. "I really should go."

They both give me a hug goodbye.

Outside, I let my head fall against their front door. Tiny blue petals tumble against my shoulder. Strange, because the wreath is fake. I turn around and trace my fingers along the flowers. Peppered between the faux hydrangea blooms are an endless sea of fresh forget-me-nots.

They turned it into something real.

Nick

I took Grace up on her offer—writing the piece for the psych magazine. I'm writing about love and family, and if anyone asks, I'm telling them she chose the subject. I read somewhere that you should write about the things you avoid, the things that hurt the most. So here we are. I'm two pages in, and I'll probably cut a lot.

My eyes fall to the spot on my bed where Fiona used to sit, and I try to guess what parts she'd call bullshit on and tweak the essay accordingly.

I still have no idea what happened with us. There was a time I could text and ask, but those times feel so far away.

There's only one paragraph left to write, and it's an important one. I need to tie all my thoughts together and make it work, but I can't get there. The cursor blinks on my screen. I type:

So what about love?

I stare at the words.

Brooklyn moved in after three months of dating. Dad told me the same way he always does when trying to connect with me: by knocking on my door and standing in the doorway. He tried to be nice and launched into a big speech about second chances and learning from past mistakes, but I honestly zoned out for most of it. I will always miss Mom, and this just hurt too much.

Brooklyn's redecorating the place. She dug up the flowers out front and taped paint swatches to the walls. She's trying to make it feel like home, and I can't blame her. Who would want to live in a shadow? We don't talk much. I think some part of her feels bad about this.

Sometimes she'll knock on my door and ask if I want a snack like I'm ten. Soon, snacks graduated into cappuccino offers, which I also declined. I thought we might finally be connecting when she dropped a bag of Doritos on my bed. It was a nice gesture, but I wanted to tell her she shouldn't feel bad, that we'll never be close because we're not family, and that's okay. I'm okay. This place stopped feeling like home a long time ago. It's all theirs now, and I'm sure they're counting the days until I move out.

I still think Dad's choices are bullshit, but they're his choices. Grace helped me see that. We email even though I stopped going to group. I have a lifetime of my own choices to make, and so far, my track record hasn't been so hot, either. Besides, who am I to choose happy for anyone? We all hurt, but I don't want to live there. Pain is like a drug. It can erase you if you let it.

Max's minifigure watches me from the corner of my desk. "Why are you always judging me, man?" I pick it up and close my laptop. "It's time for you to go home."

I find Dad painting a yellow square on the kitchen wall from a sample pot. "Good morning," he says, even though it's noon.

"Morning."

A new moving box is on the floor with *kitchen* scrawled across the top in black Sharpie. I don't know where Brooklyn's stuff keeps coming from. It's like it magically multiplies. I fiddle with the flap and peek inside. This one's full of cookbooks.

"Hey, do you think I can borrow the truck?"

Dad lets out a soft laugh as if I'm joking, then lowers the paint brush realizing I'm not.

"I was thinking of going up to Portland to see Alex. I could take the rest of Mom's stuff. Make some room for you."

"Oh." He puts the paintbrush down, considering. "I could go with you."

A small, uncomfortable laugh escapes me. It's a nice way of saying he still doesn't trust me, but it sounds like a nightmare. "I'd rather be on my own, you know? If you're comfortable with that."

"Yeah. Okay. Brooklyn would feel more comfortable with it gone so . . ."

I can't believe how much we use the word *comfortable* now. All the paint in the world won't make this place more comfortable for Brooklyn, but I'm not about to tell him that.

Dad reaches for the keys on the counter and tosses them to me. "At least let me help you load up?"

"I'll take you up on that."

So that's what we do—fill his pickup with the rest of Mom's things. I plug Alex's address into the GPS and make my way to Portland. It's Sunday, so I'm pretty sure they'll be home.

I drive, and I drive, and I drive.

The closer I get to her place, the more nervous I feel. We haven't spoken since I signed the papers, and I don't know what I'm going to say to her.

The place is easy to find. It's nestled in a row of town-houses, but I spot it right away because Mom's wreath hangs from the front door. I cut the engine and sit there for a few minutes when their front door opens. Alex steps out in her bare feet. Max runs past her and screams, "Uncle Nick!" loud enough to hear through my closed windows.

By the time I'm out of the truck, he's already in my arms. "Hey, little dude! I missed you!"

"I missed you, too."

"Look what I found." I fish the minifigure out of my pocket and hold it out to him.

"Batman!!!"

"Yeah, he was kind of keeping me company."

"Did you know this Batman is super rare because he has the blue mask and not the black one? But, Uncle Nick, there's a new Batman, and his eyes glow." Max's eyes are wide as saucers.

"I know. I might have it in the back."

"What?" Max squeals.

Alex is beside us now.

"Yeah! Buried under all this shit somewhere." She whacks my arm. "Stuff, I mean. So let me unload, and I'll find it, okay?"

Max runs, screaming back into the house. "Casey, I found Batman!"

"Hey," I say to Alex.

"Hey, yourself."

"I know I should have called . . . "

She pulls me into a hug. "You don't ever have to call."

I wrap my arms around her and can't stop the tears. I'm pretty sure she can tell I'm crying, so we stand there, hugging forever in front of the open truck door. When I step back, she grabs my face in her hands.

"I am so happy you're here."

"Stop trying to make me cry," I say, wiping my tears away.

Casey comes down the walkway slowly, as if she isn't sure she should interrupt. Alex notices me staring and turns around. "You need a hand with this stuff?" she gently asks.

Alex takes my hand and leads me to her. "Casey, Nick. Nick, Casey."

"Hey," I say, but then she's hugging me, too. I glance at Alex. I guess she's one of those people.

"He's so much taller than he looks in pictures!" she says to Alex as if I'm not standing right in front of her. "How was the drive?"

Honestly, it was long. It was uncomfortable. It was nerve-wracking. It was liberating. It was lonely. I watched the landscape morph into a million colors under the rays of the sun. All to get to a place that felt more like home the second the door opened than mine has in a while, a feeling that found me without even trying.

So, yeah. The drive was okay. I mean, I made it.

"Not bad," I say, lowering the tailgate.

We fill our arms with boxes and head inside.

They give me the tour and talk over each other while Max jumps like crazy around us. It's hard to get a word in edgewise, so I let the tide carry me and go with it. The place is open and airy, even though I swear it's two feet wide outside. It's nice to see Alex using some of Mom's things. I recognize her frames and vases that don't fit with the rest of the décor, but it works all the same. Pieces that make the place feel special. There are photos of all of us in the bookcase, and one of Fiona and me with the sea lion on the mantle. It throws me. Did I text it to Alex? Before I can ask, Max tugs my arm, dying to take me upstairs. He's complaining about Alex and Casey talking too much. They stay behind, figuring out what to make for dinner, while I follow Max upstairs to his room.

He closes the blinds and makes me crawl into bed with him. We lie under the tent canopy and make wishes on the glow-in-the-dark stars. He even has some of my old toys up on his shelf, but here they feel like new treasures, instead of stale and forgotten. My heart swells, knowing he gets to grow up blanketed by all this love.

Max talks so much, his voice goes hoarse, and he runs downstairs for a drink.

There's a notepad on his desk, and he's drawing some kind of comic. *Werebear* is scratched in blue pencil crayon on the top page, and it's really good. On the wall are pictures of Mom and him, Alex and him at Disney, and one of Max and me mid-water fight from last summer. We all seem so happy. I check out his bookshelf and spot a shiny black rock next to a microscope.

It looks like an arrowhead. It looks like the cliff of a waterfall.

Alex watches me turn it over in my palm from the door. "That's cool," she says. "He must have gotten that at school."

I put the rock down. I know exactly where it came from. I look at Alex, and I'm not sure what to say.

"Come, let's go downstairs," she says.

Two steps into the hallway, I stop. "Fiona said the place was amazing."

"You're talking again!" Alex lets out a relieved sigh as she walks down the stairs. "I knew the whole break thing wouldn't last. I wasn't sure if she told you she came by." She turns back, and I'm still standing frozen at the top, staring daggers her way. She closes her eyes. "You didn't know."

I shake my head.

She continues going down. "Nick! Why do you do that? Why couldn't you just ask if Fiona was here?"

"Why didn't you tell me?"

Casey is making some kind of panini in the kitchen while Max watches "Teen Titans" in the living room, a glass of grape Kool-Aid on the coffee table in front of him.

"How did you know?" Alex asks.

"The rock. The picture on your fireplace. What the hell? Are you like best friends now?"

Casey closes the fridge and eyes us. "Do you want me to . . . should I . . . " She points outside the room, hoping to escape.

"No. Don't be ridiculous," Alex tells her, then turns to me. "I didn't tell you because I didn't want to upset you."

"It doesn't upset me." She gives me an oh-please look. "It upsets me that you didn't tell me."

"I didn't think it was a big deal. I ran into her at school a couple weeks ago. She was in the quad, so I invited her over to see the place. She was here maybe twenty minutes."

I don't want to hear it. But at the same time, I do. "Why was she in the quad? Did she change her mind about schools?"

"I don't know. I asked about you, obviously, and she mentioned the break."

I close my eyes. "Ugh."

"Which I had *no* idea about because you never talk to me. And that's why I didn't say anything, but now that we're putting it out there, maybe we should talk about it."

"No. We shouldn't."

I take a seat at the table, and Alex sits in the chair beside me. "You know you can talk to us, right?"

"Us? I've known her for like ten minutes. No offense," I say to Casey.

She waves it off. "None taken."

"You can talk to me."

My sister has good intentions, but relationships aren't light switches. They can't be turned on and off this easily. They're more like those flashlights with the hand cranks on the side where you have to crank the handle forever to get a minute of light. I don't know if Alex gets that. "We've never had that though, have we?"

"But I want us to have that. I love you."

"I love you, too."

"I know I dropped out of the big sister race when I had Max, but I was struggling, Nick. I was trying not to be a shitty mom, so I ended up being a shitty sister. But I want to be here for you now." She's quiet for a minute, which is never a good sign. "I know you blame me for Mom."

The words land like a bomb.

"I don't blame you."

"You don't have to say that. I know you do."

For the first time, I really take in my sister. I have maybe sixty percent of her attention right now. She keeps stealing glances toward the living room where Max is and to Casey by the sink. She has a lot on her plate, and she's still trying. I can come in for forty.

"I think I blamed everyone. You, Dad, Mom, the entire creation of aviation."

She's not buying it. I fiddle with the placemat and she puts her hand on mine, stilling me. "Honestly?"

I look up.

"Remember how we used to say that when we were little?" She searches my eyes for our history.

A history I forgot. Fi and I have been saying it forever, but Alex was always the source.

"Always," I say in barely a whisper. She watches me, waiting for more. "Yeah, I blamed you. After you got pregnant, they started fighting and never stopped. You had the best of them."

"The best of them? You're giving them a lot of credit." She unwraps a mini chocolate from the bowl on the table and pops it in her mouth. "I was seventeen . . ."

"I get it, but at least they were around for you. I was on my own, and I've been on my own for a long time." Alex nods. "But nothing changed after you and Max left, so I blamed Dad. Then I blamed myself for being 'difficult,' and now, I'm finally getting how useless blame is. I mean, at some point it had to be her, too, right?" I lean back in my chair. "We all make choices. It's like Dad, you know? Who can we possibly blame for him? Maybe I'm like that, too."

"You're nothing like that. I see you, Nick. I *see* you."

I blink at her. "Okay. Don't say that. Ever." I smile, and she wipes a tear away. "Look at this place. You all seem really happy."

"We are," Casey pipes up, winking at Alex. "Max, come and eat!" she yells. Max runs into the kitchen. Casey slides a panini onto my plate and goes back to the press, taking another sandwich from it for Max.

"Does this mean maybe you'll start opening up to me?" Alex asks, eyeing me hopefully.

"Baby steps," I say, biting into the gooey sandwich. "This is delicious."

Casey moves behind Alex's chair and hugs her from behind. They watch me eat like I'm a zoo animal.

Max picks up his plate from the counter with one hand and the full plastic cup of grape Kool-Aid with the other. "Moooom," he calls out for help, and before they can reach him, the cup falls, and his drink cascades across the floor. He's on the verge of tears.

"Don't sweat it, Max, it's only juice." Casey grabs a towel and tosses it over the spill while Alex refills his glass and brings it to the table. They're seamless together, and that is not easy to find in this world.

Max sits beside me and takes a giant bite into his piping hot panini before spitting it onto the plate, yelping. "Hot, hot, hot."

I take it all in, thinking about my piece for the magazine. *So what about love?*

Maybe we do exist in a revolving door of emotions. Sadness might not be sustainable, but love is.

This is my happy ending with Alex. It's not full of sweeping apologies over an ocean cliff, or racing through the streets to reunite, and there's no unconditional forgiveness because there's a lot of hand cranking to go before we get there. It's paninis and "Teen Titans" on TV. It's messy like the sandwiches we're scarfing down. And it's not even an ending.

It's a beginning.

Fiona

Dad dips a hash brown into a pool of ketchup on a McDonald's napkin. It's Friday, our weekly lunch date. A month ago, they seemed like a great idea—a chance to talk somewhere other than home, but they followed a weird trajectory, moving from dinner at a fancy restaurant to Applebee's to here—McDonald's. The upside is twenty minutes is exactly the right amount of time for these dates.

He takes a bite of his Egg McMuffin, and dabs at his mouth with a napkin while complaining about the latest sports news. When he notices I've zoned out, he stops.

"You know, we can still do the fancy dinner dates," he says.

My eyes widen in alarm. Those were two hours of pure torture. Nobody wants to do that again. "I know."

"What's going on with the school front? Still excited about New York?"

My plan was always to start in January, but I've been waffling. Spending all this time with Dad makes me sad about the thought of leaving. "Yeah, but I could always reapply out here and stay closer to home."

He squints at me. "Why would you do that?"

"So we can hang out more. You can teach me about whatever that sport is you like."

He grins. "All of them."

"See! Great," I say. "We can go to the pubs. I can hang out with your crew." I'm joking, but not about the staying closer to home part.

"There is something I wanted to run by you." He dusts a few crumbs off his shirt. "We should have done this at a real restaurant. Now we're almost out of food and still have all this conversation."

I slap the table. "Dad, focus. What?"

"I'm thinking about . . . listing the house," he says slowly, like he's still wrapping his head around the words.

"What?!" I sputter out a cough, choking on my iced tea.

"Not in any rush, so don't panic. I was going to wait until you left for school."

It's a lot to process. I'm not sure what to say.

"You think it's a bad idea?" he asks, reaching for his soda.

That's the worst part. I don't. But I also want to wrap our house in my arms and hold it forever. "No," I chirp in my high-pitched lie voice.

Dad side-eyes me.

"You coming to New York?"

He lets out a half laugh. "Have you always been this much of a smart-ass?"

"I think it's finally coming back to me." I smile.

"Glad to hear it."

"So. Why now?"

"A friend of mine said they're hiring down in San Diego, so I put in for a transfer, and I got it for whenever I want it."

I nod, taking it all in. Why do I feel like this isn't the first time someone's life has been upended in a McDonald's?

"I don't want to be in the house when you're gone, and I don't want it to be a reason you stay. I think it's time for a little sunshine," he says, stealing my last fry and popping it into his mouth.

It's like that magic trick where the tablecloth is yanked from the table, but none of the dishes move. That's what he's done. He changed everything and nothing, just like that.

"You're welcome to come. I'll always have a room for you. I just think we're in a bit of a rut here. We're stuck, and maybe I can't move my way out of it, but I need to move, you know. I need to move."

I lean back against the booth. "Dad. I think it's amazing."

And I do. I thought he'd die in that house. That once I left, he'd hide himself away, lost in a labyrinth of Mom's memory.

He points to my hoodie. It's Nick's. "How's Nick doing?"

I guess I was inviting the question by wearing this. "I don't know."

"Why not?"

"We took a break. I told you."

"Long break."

Four weeks, five days to be exact. "I think we were spending too much time together."

"I thought you liked spending time together."

"We did."

He raises an eyebrow. "So what'd he do?"

My instinct shouts *Abort!* Change the topic to sports, to anything else, lie, but he's trying, and so can I. "He kissed me, and I freaked out."

"Huh." His eyes widen at my unexpected honesty, then he crumples his napkin, deep in thought. "But you like him?"

I think we both know it's more than that. "It's not that easy."

"Why not?"

"Because. What if we date, and he realizes he can't stand me? What if he wants to hang out with people I don't like at school? What if I don't want to be with him? What if we never talk again?"

Dad leans in. "Isn't that what's happening now?"

I let my head fall back against the booth. "It was just so easy before. Not that it was ever easy, but—"

"You can't do that, Fi. Life throws a lot of curve balls, but you should always take the shot when you have it." He smiles, pleased with himself.

"Wow. That's a lot of sports metaphors you worked in there." But I hear him, I do. I'll miss this—his corny movie lines and metaphors. These twenty minutes. Soon, we'll be separated, and we didn't have nearly enough of these moments—of this time. My thoughts fall to Nick. "I think I also needed to know I'd be okay without him."

"And are you?"

"Yeah. I am." I let out a breath and place my empty cup on the tray. "Hey, remember the morning of the Monterey trip?" Dad thinks, then nods. "What did you say to Nick by the car? I saw you talking from the window."

He meets my eyes. "I said you better make sure nothing happens to her. She's the brightest light I've got."

Tears spring to my eyes, and I blink them away. "Dad . . ." I squeeze his hand. "I love you."

"I love you, too."

Maybe dives are predestined to become the most important places in my life. It must be in my genes. We fill our tray with empty wrappers and slide out of the booth.

"And he said, 'I'd be blind without her,'" Dad slips it in so casually as he dumps the wrappers into the trash.

It's like the air's been knocked from my lungs. I turn away so he can't read my face. How can Nick's words still sink me when they don't even come from him?

"Ready?" Dad asks.

"Yeah. Let's go." I face him, wearing a breezy smile.

But when he heads for the exit, it fades. I trace the outline of my necklace under Nick's hoodie.

In the truck, news radio plays. A few skeleton trees line the sidewalk. Their fallen leaves twirl across the road like they're still going somewhere. There's not a drop of blue in the October sky or anywhere, the world bathed in a dreary gray.

But inside Dad's truck, I feel warm and safe, like a kid again in the passenger seat. The truck smells like him, of cedar and coffee. The light in front of us turns yellow, and Dad stops even though he could have made it through. I lean my head against the window and look at the CVS beside us. It blends into the endless expanse of the concrete parking lot. On the side, a guy leans against the silvery brick wall.

And my heart stops because the guy is Nick. I straighten in my seat. *Nick.* Now my hands are on the tablecloth. I can be the magician—I can change everything or nothing.

The clicking of the turn signal is deafening. The light, in the other direction, turns yellow. My hand rests on the door handle. Any second, the light will turn green, and Dad will drive away.

I can't decide.

I can't decide.

The light turns green, and the truck rolls forward. Dad makes the turn.

My grip tightens around the handle.

"Dad, stop the truck."

He glances at me, confused.

"Stop the truck!"

He pulls over to the curb, and I fling the door open. "I'll meet you at home."

"Where are you going?" He follows my gaze to the parking lot. "Oh, Nick. Gotta take the shot." He feigns hitting a ball or swinging a hockey stick; I can't really tell. Then he smiles and turns up the song that's started to play. "Call if you need a ride."

"Thanks." I slam the door with a renewed burst of courage. It lasts all of ten seconds until I'm on the other side of the street heading for the store. My path veers horizontal as I talk myself out of this, but it's too late.

Nick spots me from across the parking lot. The tip of his nose is red from the cold. He takes his foot away from the wall and straightens up, burying his hands into the pouch of his hoodie.

I stop in front of him.

"Hey," he says.

"Hey."

He pulls at the string of my hoodie—his hoodie. "Been looking for that."

"Yeah. Sorry, I meant to bring it back. You can take it."

"No, it's cold. Keep it."

We nod in awkward silence. He cut his hair. It's a little darker without the highlights from the sun. A sandy brown wave flops against his forehead, and he pushes it away when he notices me staring. Everything about him is a little cleaner, a little crisper.

"How's it going?" I ask.

"Not bad. You?"

"Not bad."

More silence.

"How's Zombie Bob?"

"Good. He's selling the house."

His eyes widen. "What?!"

"Moving to Diego, apparently."

"No shit."

"Yeah."

He shakes his head like he can't believe it. "Wow. Zombie no more, huh? And you?"

"And me . . . " I flick my eyes up to him, feeling insecure about my not-so-epic changes. "Quit the gym. Been working at a store downtown."

"Yeah, I heard."

He knows. May told me she texts him once in a blue moon from California, and I'm okay with it. Did he ask about me, or did she tell him?

"You look different," he says.

"You mean awful?" I make an exaggerated gesture to my sweats.

"No," he says quietly. "I guess you're staying here? For school?"

"New York, actually." I kick at the pebbles on the pavement. "Thought I'd check out a different coastline." He nods a few times but doesn't say anything. "Are you still going there?"

"Yeah, set for January—the lit program."

I smile. I'm just so happy for him.

"What?" He gives me a wary stare as if I might make fun of him, like the night on the porch swing.

He'll thrive in New York. I can picture him running newspapers or blogs, interviewing politicians, or writing a bestseller. I can see his whole future, and it's so bright.

"What?!"

I'll tell him, I will. Just not right now. "Nothing. Sorry. It's amazing, that's all."

He sweeps a hand through his hair. "Yeah, because what the world needs is another English degree."

"What the world needs is you."

It's the awkward silence to end all awkward silences. His eyes sear into mine, and I glance away. A rusted red classic Mustang isn't far behind him. His mom's bucket list. "Number ten on her list."

He looks over his shoulder and to me again, beaming. "It was the only one I could really rally behind. You want to check it out?"

"Yeah!" I say with as much enthusiasm as I can muster, but my heart is breaking.

This distance.

He opens the driver's side door, and I duck my head inside.

"See the trim? It's all original, except I had it modded for a USB outlet."

"So cool." I spot a floral tote on the floor of the passenger side and flinch a little. I pretend not to notice, but Nick caught it. Of course, he did. He doesn't miss a thing—unlike me, who stupidly assumed he was here alone. I mean, he was standing in a parking lot. Waiting. For someone. How did I miss that?

"So, I'm going up to Monterey this weekend," he says casually as if it's some random place and not *our* place.

"Oh yeah?"

"Yeah. I bought a place."

"In Monterey?"

He fights a proud smile. "It's not for me. I'm going to rent it out."

My chest wrenches. Here he is with convertibles and places, and I feel about as mature as a twelve-year-old after my Happy Meal. "You're a landlord?"

"Yeah, Alex gave me the hard sell on real estate, so I did it to shut her up. It's a pretty cool place. Small, but you can see the ocean—at least a sliver of it." He rocks back on his feet, a hint of nerves peeking through.

"Sounds better than a parking lot."

His eyes flick up to mine. "It was a nice parking lot."

Every second of that weekend comes flooding back to me. The necklace, the side glances, the warmth of his arm next to mine, him kneeling on the floor in front of me and not running away. Being alone. With him.

A car pulls into the lot, and the crack seals. It's like we're strangers again, which feels so wrong after everything we've been through.

"So, I was thinking about asking you if you felt like going. Swing by the ol' Narwhal . . . but I didn't know what you were up to these days. I still haven't taken the coastal route down. It'd be nice to see."

"It would be."

"Right? There's this place called Elephant Rock north of San Francisco, and it's got rocks shaped like—"

"Elephants," I say.

"Yes! It's really cool. At least, I think it's cool."

He keeps talking about highway routes and landmarks, and I can't take it anymore.

I won't let us drown under a second more of this aimless conversation. It's backwards and wrong. He *knows* me. We can't just stand here and talk about—highways.

"Nick, I love you." He's midsentence when I say it, and it comes out way more platonic than I intended.

He doesn't miss a beat. "I love you too, Fi."

He's not getting it.

"No," I shake my head. My hands are shaking. "No, no, no. That's not what I meant." I force myself to meet his eyes. "I don't mean *love you* love you, I mean, I'm in love with you."

He straightens and sways a little as if the words are a force. He does his thing where he's thinking and looking at nothing, his eyes fixed on a point somewhere on the concrete between us. I said it. I had to say it for me. The weight lifts from my chest.

"Have you ever happy ending'd us?"

His eyes meet mine. "Yeah." His voice is barely a whisper.
"What did it look like?" This feels like goodbye, and I want this token to hang on to. A keepsake of what might have been.

He swallows, refocusing. I know his expressions by heart. I can almost see the words filling behind his clear blue eyes—like the sky and sea—endless.

"Well . . . there's us on a beach watching the sunset and the sea lions." His words are slow and deliberate. "There's us dancing in a shitty dive bar in the middle of nowhere or driving home in your car every week, listening to music. It's watching you swipe a bottle of chili sauce from a Chipotle. It's smashing open tubes of your face cream, listening to you breathe at night, smelling you on my clothes, and I guess now I can add the time you finally, *finally* fess up in a CVS parking lot." His eyes lock on mine. "It's hard, impossible really, to settle on one because every time I'm with you is happiness to me."

He steps closer and slides his hands around my waist. "Now, can I kiss you?"

His words are barely a whisper, his eyes, wide pools of blue. I lose myself in them, and answer with a kiss—softly pressing my lips to his then pulling away just as quick.

He blinks slowly, his lips still parted, then closes the gap between us, his mouth colliding with mine. His hands reach under my hoodie, finding my skin. I grasp his neck, my fingers tangling in his hair. We stagger back, colliding against the rough brick wall: our breath, a misty fog escaping between kisses. Nick pulls my hips into him and makes me forget where I am in only the way he can.

"Wait," I step away from him.

"Mmm . . ."

"The bag in your car . . ."

He eyes me curiously and opens his mouth to speak, but before he gets a word out, a voice calls out from around the corner.

"Sorry we took so long, they made me wait."

We turn our heads. Alex stops in her tracks, a shopping bag dangling from her hand. "But . . . I guess that's a good thing," she says, taking in our entangled state. Max runs out from behind her, holding a Ring Pop.

"Hi, Fiona," he chirps as if nothing remarkable is happening.

"Hi, Max."

Nick presses his forehead against mine.

"Hey, Fiona." Alex grins from ear to ear. "Still keeping things casual?"

"Please stop talking," Nick says.

"Okay." She swings the bag around in a circle. "So what are we supposed to do?"

"Get in the car."

Alex rolls her eyes at him. "Come on, let's wait inside," she says to Max.

"Can you open my Ring Pop, Mom?" he asks, shaking the wrapper.

"Yeah, sweetie, inside. Am I sitting in the front or the back?" she calls out again.

"Just . . . whatever," Nick says without turning away from me.

He waits for the sound of the car door closing, his arms still around my waist.

I search his eyes. "I thought . . ."

"I know what you thought. It was always you, Fi."

I kiss him again, and we lose ourselves until the horn blasts. Nick turns back, a crimson flush on his cheeks, and Max giggles hysterically from the back seat. This is far from the romantic streetscapes of Monterey. It's messy, it's a dive . . . but it's entirely perfect.

"Do you want to go for a drive?" he asks.

And I'm not even ninety-nine percent sure. I'm one hundred percent positive.

"Yeah. You owe me at least six months' worth."

He breaks into a smile as he takes my hand and leads me to the passenger side, opening the door in one graceful swoop and stealing a kiss before I duck inside.

The car smells like grape candy. Nick climbs in, and the Mustang comes to life with a guttural roar. Max laps at the Ring Pop jewel on his finger and kicks his feet against the seat. He raises his fist and shouts, "I'm Batman!"

Nick smiles. He reaches for my hand and pulls out of the lot.

Ahead of us is an open road and a cool gray sky. The sun breaks through the clouds on the horizon, the landscape, a canvas filling with color right before my eyes. In a minute, we'll leave the gray behind and drive straight into a world of technicolor.

And I can't think of a better picture than this.

Acknowledgments

My heartfelt thanks to you, dear reader, for picking up this book and going along for the ride with Nick and Fiona. I hope you've grown to love them as much as I do. I'm forever grateful for your support. Bookish people are the best people.

Endless gratitude to Jodi Keller for caring so deeply about this story and these characters. Your sharp editorial insights and thoughtful questions pushed me to dig deep to make this story shine. Jodi, working with you has been a joy and a dream.

To Christa Heschke and Daniele Hunter, taking on a story about grief during Covid was a bold move! Thank you so much for believing in this book and championing *Blue* until the end.

To Susan Szecsi and the entire team at Marble Press, I am so grateful for your support.

Also, thank you to Lisa Carlson and Janet Wagner, for the care taken with the copy edit and for saving me from drowning in em-dashes and spotty punctuation.

To the international editors, publishers, and your teams, I'm overwhelmed by your support and beautiful words about this story, Cristian Martín at Planeta Spain, Luzie Bischoff at DTV, and everyone at Globo Brazil, Hachette Romans, and Mondadori.

Thank you so much to the international co-agents, Sandra Biel, Annelie Geissler, Catherine Lapautre, and Elena Bengalia. I am so grateful for your advocacy and counsel.

Meghan Marshall—we met as writers critiquing each other's words, and soon critiquing words became critiquing lives. You lift me up, challenge me, cheer me on, and make me laugh. Thank you for poring over the earliest draft of this book. I am so grateful for your friendship, sharp eye for story, and your character, Ian, for teaching me how to properly eat cupcakes.

Tracey Tong Simpson—we bonded over Brontë novels in the sixth grade (such a flex), wrote letters for six years, and then both became writers. Now, I get to spill my deepest, darkest secrets to . . . a journalist? Thank you for being my Jiminy Cricket, my biggest supporter, and my best friend.

To the absolutely brilliant Jackie Johnson, I am eternally grateful for your friendship and sage counsel, never gatekeeping and always giving it to me straight. There's no one else I'd rather ride this roller coaster with.

My mom, Lilly, I think you've read this book almost as much as I have. There is no thank you big enough to encompass all you've done for me—for staying up late reading every detail, giving me unbiased notes, your endless cheerleading, and legendary pep talks.

My dad, Jim, thank you for constantly pushing me off the ledge, being my very own Yoda, supplying me with everything a writer could ever want and then telling me to "go write." I'm so lucky to have grown up watching you both take risks and fearlessly pursue your passions.

A million thank yous to Jonathan Wright for listening to every story problem and always having a dozen solutions at the ready.

Thank you to the hugely talented Ali Rowan and Eliza Luckey for being thoughtful, supportive critique partners.

And to my incredible son, Cole, I am in awe of your boundless creativity and your love of story. Your ideas are epic and dazzling—way better than mine. I can't wait to see how your adventures unfold.

About the Author

Jennifer E. Archer is an author and screenwriter based in Toronto. Her screenplay *Into the Deep Blue* won the Academy Nicholl Fellowship in Screenwriting and the hearts of many.

When she's not writing, she can be found hiding behind a book, re-watching "Pride and Prejudice," or trying to find peace in nature—really trying. *Into the Deep Blue* is her first novel.

Visit her online at jenniferarcherauthor.com or on Instagram @jennwrites.